M000158376

# LAW AND JUSTICE

## JUSTICE SERIES - BOOK 2

## DONALD L. ROBERTSON

CM Publishing

# COPYRIGHT

**Law and Justice**

Copyright © 2018 Donald L. Robertson
CM Publishing

Books@DonaldLRobertson.com

Cover Design by Elizabeth Mackey

Editing by Melissa Gray & Beverley Scherberger

ISBN Print: 978-0-9909139-9-3

# 1

Clay, his right leg hooked around the saddle horn, relaxed his young body in the saddle. As the stage-coach rumbled past, he lifted his hand in salute to the stage driver, Whip Bingham. Whip's thick wrists and big hands handled the reins of the six horses like he was driving a surrey, not the big, red Abbott and Downing Concord coach.

The early morning sky had brightened and the heat was starting to build. Clay swung his long leg over the saddle and stepped down from Blue's back. The stage had disappeared behind a thick patch of oaks that covered the hill country west of Austin. He patted the horse's neck and untied his canteen. He and Blue had been traveling several hours. Traveling early to beat the broiling sun made good sense during the scorching days of a Texas summer.

He removed his sweat-rimmed black hat and poured water into the crown, then held it for Blue to drink. The horse shoved his black muzzle into the hat, making short work of the water. Clay slid the hat to the back of his head, the remaining liquid running over his thick black hair and allowed the leather cord to slide under his chin.

"Won't be long, boy, and you'll be in a nice, cool barn in Austin." He checked the cinch and swung back onto the horse. He started to tilt the canteen to his mouth when the short bark of handguns ripped away the quiet of the Texas hill country, followed by a single blast of a shotgun, then three more quick shots.

Clay looped the canteen over the saddle horn and kicked Blue in the flanks. The roan leaped forward, carrying the big man toward the sound. Alternating the reins in his hands, Clay slipped the rawhide loops off the hammers of the .44 American Smith & Wessons riding in his holsters. His hat flew off his head, but the cord held it to him.

Blue rounded the bend, bringing the stage in sight. It was surrounded by six men on horseback and one lying on the ground, all wearing masks. Clay yanked the sawed-off Roper repeating shotgun from its scabbard and eared back the hammer. He could see the stagecoach shotgun rider was also on the ground, and Whip was holding his shoulder. The passengers had not yet stepped down from the stagecoach.

Clay dropped the reins. Guiding Blue with his knees, he brought the shotgun to his shoulder and fired the first load of buckshot. It was too far to kill any of them, but it would at least take their attention from the innocent people on the stage. He yanked back the hammer, and the repeating mechanism rotated another shell from the magazine and drove it into the chamber. As soon as he had the hammer full-back he pulled the trigger again. Now he was closer, and this load hit two of the bandits, confirmed by their yelps of pain.

The bandits, at first stunned at the sight of a rider barreling down on them, recovered quickly and began returning fire. Clay heard several rounds snap near his head as they sailed by. He yanked the hammer back for the third time, centered the muzzle on the nearest man, and pulled the trigger. The bandit lurched in the saddle, bent over, but managed to hang on.

At the third blast from the Roper 12-gauge, the bandits wheeled in unison and raced away from the stage, dust and rocks flying. They were followed by two shots from the stagecoach. A departing bandit dropped his reins and grabbed his shoulder. Clay took aim at one of the men's broad back with the shotgun, but he couldn't bring himself to pull the trigger. He'd never shot a man in the back and wasn't starting now. He slid Blue to a halt by the stagecoach and, leaping down, ran to the fellow who had been riding shotgun, now lying facedown in the hot Texas dirt. Clay gently rolled him over. There was a big, bloody hole over the man's heart.

"He's dead, Son," Whip said, from atop the stage. "Name's Cleatus Wells. Fine feller. He got one of 'em, but the blond-headed guy killed him—shot him twice."

"It just looks like one big hole," Clay said, standing and reloading the Roper, while staying alert in case the bandits returned.

Whip shook his head. "He put both of them shots smack in the same place. Never seen such shooting. One of them other fellers put one in me. Lucky for me, he weren't near the shot Blondie was." Whip raised his voice: "You folks climb on out of the stage. It's safe now."

The first man out carried a small black bag. He climbed up on the box with Whip. "I'm a doctor. Let me look at that arm."

"You a doctor?" Whip said. "Why, you don't look old enough to be no doctor."

The young man colored but continued. "I am a doctor, Mr. Bingham. Now let me look at that arm." He grabbed Whip's shirt, put thumbs into the hole in the shirt and ripped it open."

"Dad-blame it. That's a brand-new shirt. It cost me eighty-six cents, and now you've gone and ruined it fer me, I could've sewed up the hole."

Clay moved quickly to the dead bandit. He knelt down and yanked the kerchief from the man's face. He was older than Clay, still young, but wasn't familiar. He called up to Whip, "You know this guy?"

Whip looked at the dead man for a moment, spit, and wiped his mouth with his sleeve. "I don't know him. Seen him around San Antone with several other young fellers once or twice."

Clay stood and strode over to help the passengers from the stage. The first to the door was a pretty blonde girl of about twelve years. "Howdy, ma'am. Mind if I help you down?"

"That would be nice, Mister. What's your name?"

Clay smiled. "Why, it's Clay, Clay Barlow, and what's yours?" He grasped her under both arms and swung her to the ground.

The girl, her blue eyes sparkling, smiled back. "I'm Dorenda Davis, but everyone calls me Dee."

"Nice to meet you, Dee," Clay said. Turning back to help Dorenda's mother from the coach, he saw her slip a big Colt back into her valise.

"Thank you," Mrs. Davis said. "My name is Nancy Davis. You must excuse Dee. She has never known the meaning of 'seen and not heard.'"

"Mother, I'm twelve years old. I'm not a child." She walked to the front of the stage and stared up at the doctor and Whip.

The doctor took a bottle and a clean cloth out of his bag. He poured some of the liquid over the cloth and, with forceps holding the cloth to keep it sterile, again reached for Whip's arm. "Mr. Bingham, the bullet went through the fleshy part of your arm, but I've got to clean the hole out. You don't want it to get infected. This is going to hurt."

Whip looked at the forceps and his arm, then turned his bearded face to the doctor. "Well, get on with it youngster. I've got to get this stage on into Austin, and stop callin' me Mr. Bingham. Whip's the name—use it."

The doctor grasped Whip's arm and thrust the forceps through the jagged hole, rotating back and forth as he pushed it through the wound. The muscles in Whip's jaws stood out like rope, but he didn't make a sound.

"You'll not be driving this stage anywhere today," the doctor said, removing the forceps from the bullet hole. "You need to rest your arm for at least six weeks, and then only light work."

Clay continued the lookout as Mrs. Davis spoke.

"Mr. Barlow, thank you for driving off the bandits. For a few moments, I was sure we would be robbed, if not worse, but it does sound like we may be stuck here for a while."

"Ma'am, you didn't do so bad yourself. Reckon you hit one of them."

"Yes, I believe I did. I'll have no scoundrel threatening my family if I can help it. But it would have made no difference if you hadn't come along. There were too many of them, and they definitely had the drop on us."

With his left hand, Clay reached back and grasped his hat by the front brim and settled it firmly on his head. "Just glad I could help. Are you the folks that ranch west of Comfort?"

"We do. My husband is Niles Davis, and we own the Rocking D. I'm Nancy Davis. You've met Dee."

She pushed an escaped strand of graying blonde hair back under her bonnet. "Clay, I occasionally visit my sister in D'Hanis. I knew your mother before she married. In fact, I met you when you were no more than three or four. You've grown to be quite a man."

Behind them, the drummer had climbed out of the stage and stretched. "Hadn't we better be getting out of here? Those bandits could be coming back anytime."

"They ain't comin' back," Whip yelled down from the driver's box. "There's been too much commotion. We'll take a few minutes more and then load up. Clay, if you'd put poor ole Cleatus and that piece of trash in the rear boot, I'd be much obliged. Reckon I'll just stay up here, what with this arm."

"Be glad to, Whip." Clay touched his hat. "Pardon, ma'am," he said, and walked to the back of the stage. He opened the boot and went to Cleatus's body, scooped him up in his big arms, and laid him gently inside, placing the man's hat over his face. He then went back for the outlaw, rolled him in, and refastened the boot. Picking up Blue's reins, he tied them to the back of the stage. Grabbing the small bag filled with shotgun shells from the saddle horn, he returned to the front.

As the doctor carefully climbed down from the driver's seat, Clay said, "Heard the doc say you'll not be driving these horses for a while. I could help, if you've a mind."

Whip tried to move his injured arm. Instant pain reflected in his eyes, though his features never changed. He leaned over the opposite side of the stage and spit a long stream of tobacco juice, then looked at Clay's big hands and wrists jutting out from his shirt sleeves. "Boy, it looks like you done growed into a man that could handle these rowdies. Swing on up here and you can give her a try."

Clay swung the Roper to the front boot, tossed the bag of shells up on the seat, and turned back to Nancy Davis. "Ma'am, we probably should be on our way. I've got to be getting on into Austin, and I'm sure you folks are tired of riding. It's no more than twelve or fifteen more miles."

"Yes, I think we are all ready for this trip to be over." She paused for a moment. "Clay, I was so sorry to hear about your folks. They were the kind of people that helped build this country. I want you to know, you did the right thing. Don't lose any sleep over those men. They deserved everything they got." She then turned to the coach door and, with Clay's help, stepped up and into the stage.

"Thanks, ma'am. So you know, I'm fine with what I did."

He turned back to Dee. "Are you ready to jump back on board?"

She held her arms up to Clay and gave him a big smile, her

face framed in her blue bonnet and blonde hair. "If you'll help me."

Clay laughed, and swung her back on board the coach. "See you in a couple of hours." He closed the door and climbed up into the driver's box.

# 2

The stagecoach, wrapped in a cloud of dust, jerked to a rocking halt in front of Austin's City Hotel. Clay leaned past Whip and wrapped the reins around the brake lever. He rubbed his forearms. "Whip, you don't have to worry about me coming after your job. I think I'll stick to punching cows."

Whip chuckled and spit a stream of tobacco juice, causing the station agent to jump back and give him a dirty look. "Well, boy, I reckon if you ever want a job it's yours. You handled these ornery hard-heads like you been doing it forever.

"Okay, folks, this be Austin, the end of the road for this here run. Check with the agent if you're goin' on."

Clay climbed down from the driver's box, checked on Blue, then walked around to the other side. The station agent had opened the door and was helping Mrs. Davis from the stage.

Dorenda stepped to the door. "I want Clay to help me."

Nancy Davis turned to her daughter. "Dee, don't be so fresh. This is Mr. Barlow."

"Ma, he ain't much older than me, and I like him." She

flashed her pretty blue eyes at Clay. "Would you help me down, Mr. Barlow?"

Clay laughed, and said, "I'd be honored, young lady. Here you go." He grasped Dee under her arms and swung her down.

When she reached the ground, she stomped her little foot. "I'm not so young. I'm almost thirteen!"

Her mother shook her head, while trying to hide a smile. "You've just turned twelve. Now tell Mr. Barlow thank you."

Dee turned her brightest smile on Clay. "Thank you, Mr. Barlow." She picked up her small bag, which the agent had tossed down, turned with a swish, and marched into the City Hotel.

"Thank you, again, for arriving when you did," Nancy Davis said. "I'm just sorry that Mr. Wells was killed and Mr. Bingham shot. I do hope they catch the men that did this."

A large man with a badge on his vest, stepped up to Mrs. Davis and touched the brim of his hat.

"Ma'am, I'm Deputy Sheriff J. W. Biles. We'll catch the men that did this and make sure they're brought to justice."

Mrs. Davis extended her hand to the deputy. "Thank you, Deputy. I'm sure you will. Now, if you will excuse me, I must see to my daughter." She turned back to Clay. "Thank you, again."

"Ma'am," Clay said.

With the agent carrying her bag, she followed her daughter into the City Hotel.

"Deputy," Whip said, struggling to climb down. "This here young feller came along at the right time. You may know of him, Clay Barlow."

The deputy's eyebrows rose at the mention of Clay's name. "You kill those men over Del Rio way?"

"Those weren't men, they were killers. I brought some of them in. I only shot those that forced my hand."

"Seems several forced your hand."

Clay said nothing, holding the deputy's gaze.

"I want no gunplay in my town."

"Deputy, I just came into town to see my grandfather. I'm not looking for trouble. In fact I've never looked for trouble—it found me."

The deputy gave a curt nod and turned back to Whip. "Where's Cleatus?"

Whip removed his hat and dusted off his pants, then turned his gaze to the deputy. "He's in the boot, shot by that blond-headed robber. We all might be dead if Clay hadn't come along, and I'll tell you, Deputy, you've no call to be treatin' the boy like that."

"You mind your own business, Whip." The deputy turned back to Clay. "You'll come with me now to my office. I need a statement of what happened."

*What's eating this fella?* "Deputy, I'll be more than happy to stop by your office and tell you what I saw. But first, there's some things I need to do. I'll be by when I can." Clay walked over to Blue, untied him, and swung into the saddle.

"Whip, does Mr. Platt still have the livery over on Pecan?"

"He shore does, Son, just east of San Jacinto. By the way, if those rangers ain't in their office, you might find 'em over at the Iron Front Saloon, on up Congress here. Matter of fact, you just might find me there later today."

"Thanks, Whip." Clay reined Blue around and headed south to Pecan, leaving the deputy to take care of Cleatus and the bandit.

*Austin's growing fast*, he thought. It had been four, no, five years since he had been to the city with his folks. He'd thought it big and noisy then, but now muleskinners shouted at each other as they passed in the streets. Everyone hustled about, seemingly on urgent missions, rushing from one meeting to another. He'd be glad when he put the town behind him.

Clay stopped Blue at Platt's Livery, taking the horse directly to the watering trough set up outside the barn's big entry doors. Blue thrust his nose into the long trough, as Clay swung down.

"Dry, isn't it, boy?"

The horse raised his head from the trough and shook it, throwing water over Clay. He laughed, took his hat off, and thrust his head deep into the trough, feeling the cool water momentarily wash away the heat as he held it there. After a long moment, he pulled his head out and shook it.

Frank Platt walked out at about the same moment, stopped, put his hands on his hips, and chuckled. "Reckon one of you needs a stable, just hard for me to figger which it is."

Blue thrust his nose back into the trough and drank noisily.

Clay grinned at Platt, showing even white teeth. "It's Blue here that needs some good care. He's had a rough day." He pushed his wet hair back with his right hand and slapped his hat down on his head. "I'd also be obliged if he could get some oats. He's earned a good meal."

"I can shore take care of his needs. I'll give him a good rubdown, and some oats. Then I'll loose him out into the corral where he'll have room to roll. You want I should take care of your gear?"

Clay pulled the Roper from its scabbard, along with his bag of shells. "Yes sir, that'd be fine. I'll be here for a few days."

Platt nodded, taking Blue's reins. "Feed and stable will run you fifty cents a day. I know it's a little high, but there's a lot of folks in town needin' stable space. You can settle up when you leave."

"That'll be fine." Clay rubbed Blue's neck. "See you later, boy," he said, then turned and headed down the boardwalk toward the courthouse, his Roper slung over his shoulder. Spurs chimed in rhythm as his boots struck the wooden walk. Occasionally he would step out into the street to let a lady pass, tipping his hat.

It felt good to be walking, stretching out his long legs. Unlike most cowboys, Clay enjoyed being on his feet. He had grown up running through the hill country with his Tonkawa friend Running Wolf, and he could still run for hours.

Sweat was trickling out from around his hatband when he arrived at the courthouse. The intense heat would last into the early evening. He stopped at the steps of the courthouse, removed his hat, and wiped the sweat from his forehead with his sleeve. A man was descending the steps toward him.

"Pardon me," Clay said. "Could you tell me where the Rangers' office is located?"

The man stopped, glanced at Clay, and pointed down Cedar Street. "Sure, just continue down that side. The entrance is the last door on the end."

Clay nodded and walked west toward the end of the courthouse. He came to the door, removed his hat, and beat the trail dust from his pants. After putting his hat back on, he opened the door and walked in. The conversation stopped as soon as his wide shoulders filled the door. Four men turned toward him, each of them dropping their gun hand to their side.

"Help you?" asked the older man behind the desk. He looked more suited to sitting a saddle than a desk chair. He had the long-distance squint from years of searching into the hillside shadows for the hidden gunman or Indian. His eyes were the gray of the weathered boards that made up the walls.

"I'm looking for either Major Jones, or Jake Coleman," Clay said.

He heard a spit of tobacco hit the inside of a brass spittoon from the next room.

"Dang, boy, I was beginning to wonder if you'd ever show up," Jake Coleman said, his voice preceding him as he came striding from the other room.

The man's long, brown hair, which reached down to his shoulders, as well as his goatee were now streaked with gray. His thick mustache showed a hint of the aging tone near the corners where it drooped down to join the neatly trimmed chin hair. Wrinkles were gathering like Texas arroyos at the corners of his brown eyes. But his erect stride and wide shoulders belied the creeping effect of age.

He walked up to Clay and thrust out his right hand, his left gripping the boy's thick shoulder. "It ain't been that long, but it looks like you growed half a foot. You're bigger, but you could almost be a dead ringer for your pap."

Clay took Jake's hand in his big grip. "Howdy, Jake. As I got older, Ma always said I looked more like Pa's brother than his son."

Jake nodded. "Well, your ma was shore right. Glad to see you, boy." Jake turned to the man sitting behind the desk. "This here is Clay Barlow."

The men around the room recognized the name, and the older man, about Jake's age, stood up and walked from behind the desk, his hand extended. "Clay," Jake said, "this here is Sergeant Ben Larson."

"Sorry to hear about your folks. Captain Coleman and Major Jones speak highly of you."

"Thanks, Sergeant," Clay said. "Jake looked after me for a while. Kept me from ending up in an army stockade."

Jake nodded. "Those were some bad times. I'm glad they're behind you."

Before the remainder of the rangers could be introduced, the youngest, leaning against the clapboard wall, piped up. "So this is the Del Rio Kid?"

Clay slowly turned his head toward the young ranger and speared the man with his cold gray eyes. "The name is Clay Barlow. You can call me Clay, or Barlow, but I don't answer to that name, and I'd be much obliged if it wasn't used. I have no idea how it got started. It certainly wasn't from anyone that knows me."

"Well, I'd think after killing ten outlaws, you'd be proud—"

"No, you're wrong, Ransom," Jake snapped. "You don't think.

This boy didn't kill ten men. Now git over to the stable and make sure the stalls are clean."

"I ain't meant—"

"Git over to the stables, now!"

Ransom gave Clay a long, hard look. After a brief pause, he sauntered out the door, bumping Clay as he passed. Clay turned to watch him as the boy made his way out the door, then turned back to Jake. "I don't need protection, Jake. I can skin my own cats."

"Reckon you can, Clay. But we don't need anything cranking up here in the Rangers' office. Ransom ain't a bad man. He's just young and feisty. Needs a little edge worn off. His name is Ransom Priest.

"Now this tall drink of water in the white hat is Slim Lemons, and this other feller is Nance King. Everybody just calls him Nancy."

Nancy grinned and spoke up. "My ma figgered it would make me tough, so when Pa named me Nance, Ma just rightly started calling me Nancy. It stuck. I finally got tired of fighting, so everybody just calls me Nancy—my friends anyway."

Clay couldn't keep the grin off his face. He stuck out his hand and said, "Glad to meet you, Nancy."

Jake gave a decisive nod. "Now, I reckon you're here to sign up."

"Jake, In Del Rio, Major Jones said there might be a spot for me in the Rangers. I still haven't made a decision, but I've narrowed my choices between joining up or going to law school."

"I won't kid you, Clay, we could use you."

"I wanted to talk to my grandfather before I made a final decision. He and my folks were set on me reading for the law. I've got to tell him what's going on and get his opinion. I owe him that."

Jake looked at Clay for a moment. "He's a good man. Though he wasn't much pleased when your pa took after enforcing the law instead of practicing it, he won't steer you wrong."

Clay stood the shotgun against the wall and removed his hat. He yanked his red-and-black checkered bandanna off and proceeded to wipe the sweat from his hatband. Then he wiped his wide forehead and the back of his thick neck before putting his hat on the back of his head. "I'm certain sure you're right. As soon as I've talked to him, I'll make a decision. I've waited too long. I'm ready to move on."

"Get straightened out with the senator, and if you decide to join us, get on back here. We've work that needs to be done. Me and the boys are heading down to Laredo. Seems there's been a lot of cattle finding their way into Mexico that belong in Texas. If possible, I'd like you to ride with us, if you get this straightened out today. We'll be leaving in the morning."

"I'll try, Jake. No promises."

Jake turned and launched a stream of tobacco juice into the nearest spittoon, took a tobacco-stained handkerchief from his vest pocket, and wiped his mouth. "Understand, you do what you must. If we've already headed out, Sergeant Larson or Major Jones will be here. Either one can get you signed up and give you an assignment. By the way, keep your eyes open. Cain Nestler's in town. He's as mean as ever, and never misses a chance to smear you. Claims you pistol-whipped him when he was drunk and aims to get even."

"Thanks, Jake. I'll keep a look-out."

"You do that. He's big friends with one of the sheriff's deputies, so walk easy."

Clay nodded to the other men. "I've got to be going, Jake. If I don't make it back in time, I'll see you when I can." He shook hands with Jake, turned and reached for the door.

"You take care, boy."

Clay stepped out of the office, back into the late afternoon heat. The sun was sliding down from its zenith, allowing the day the promise of cooler air in the night. He started back up the street to Congress, hoping he would catch his grandfather still in his office. His grandmother had died many years earlier, and the senator tended to spend most of his day either there or at the capital.

Clay had turned up Congress and was passing one of the many saloons. It had been a long day and even though his body was young, he was getting tired. He had stepped into the street to let a family pass, leaving them the boardwalk, and was stepping back up on the boardwalk, when a rough hand grabbed him by the shoulder and spun him around.

Coordination, reflexes, and training kicked in. He jerked the Roper from off his shoulder and eared the hammer back as he spun around to face the assailant. The muzzle ended up six inches from Cain Nestler's big belly. The man held his hands up and stepped back.

"Seems every time I run into you, kid, you've got a gun on me. One of these days I'll catch you without those guns and teach you a lesson in manners."

"I'd be more careful, were I you," Clay stated, coolly eyeing the muleskinner. "You could end up with dirt in your face." He looked into the big mule skinner's watery eyes, and saw nothing but hate.

The man was dirty and smelled worse than the animals he abused. His plaid shirt was caked with sweat stains and spilled beer. He was big and sloppy. He had a following of similarly dressed gentlemen with him.

Clay looked around. A crowd was gathering. Slightly behind the throng, and leaning against the saloon's exterior wall, was a young man, well put together and dressed like a cowboy. He had a different look to him, without the deep brown of the working cowboy, but he carried himself with a confident air. "Howdy, Mister. Name's Clay Barlow. You mind taking this shotgun and keeping the rest of these rummies off me? If you need more than one shot, just pull back the hammer and it'll load another shell. I'd be much obliged."

The man smiled. "It would be a true pleasure, bucko." He took the shotgun and swung it to cover Nestler's cronies. "You boy's be standing nice and easy."

Hands came up, and the men backed away.

Clay turned back to the big man. "You sure you want to do this? It appears you've been drinking, just like before when you shot off your mouth. I don't want to be accused of beating down a drunk."

Nestler smiled and flexed his big hands. "You surprise me, boy. I never expected you to give up yore guns. Course, you really haven't, have you? You still got those two around your waist."

"I'll be glad to take care of that." Clay unfastened the buckle and swung the belt with the two guns and bowie knife from around his slim waist. He turned and handed the gunbelt to the cowboy.

The man took them, swinging them over his shoulder, and yelled, "Look out!"

That's when Nestler hit him.

## 3

The big, hard fist, powered by the massive shoulders of the teamster who had spent years loading wagons and driving mules, caught Clay slightly in front of his right ear, just far enough up on his head so that his jaw didn't take the brunt of the blow—his head did. Stars exploded behind his eyes, and he felt himself falling. He seemed to fall forever. He had been standing next to the hitching rail and the blow drove him over it. When he flipped and landed hard on the boardwalk, the hitching rail blocked Nestler from stomping him, a sometimes brutal means of quickly ending a fight by rupturing the internal organs of the opponent. Nestler charged around the rail, cursing, and raised a massive Driver's Boot to crush Clay's chest. Though still groggy from the blow, Clay managed to grab the descending boot, twisting hard, causing the big muleskinner to lose his balance and fall between the rail and boardwalk. The combatants came to their feet at the same time, and Nestler hit Clay again, sending him reeling into the wall of the saloon.

The saloon had emptied, and the shouts of, "fight, fight," echoed up and down Congress Avenue. The audience was a mix of ladies in their finery, with gloved hands clutching their mouths, senators and congressmen, cowhands, teamsters, and shopkeepers.

"Give 'em room," someone yelled. Someone else hollered, "The boy doesn't stand a chance," which was answered by a third person. "I'll take that bet."

The crowd spread out, leaving a semi-circular opening in wide Congress Avenue, extending from boardwalk to boardwalk.

Nestler slammed Clay against the wall and barreled in, swinging successive blows to the boy's head. Clay had regained sense enough to get his arms up, and blocked most of the blows. Nestler swung a deep uppercut to Clay's midsection, but he turned and managed to block the blow with his forearm. Then he struck Nestler with a smashing roundhouse right to the mouth. All of the work with the axe, the fence building, the throwing of cattle at round-up, it all contributed to the broad shoulders that delivered the blow, knocking the big man back and into the street. Blood burst from his pulverized lips. He paused, surprise across his face as blood dripped from his mouth.

Clay followed him into the street, moving away from the confinement of the boardwalk and hitching rail.

While Nestler staggered to his left, Clay followed with a left uppercut to the belly. He could tell Nestler felt it, but the big man charged, wrapping him in the iron-strong clasp of his arms. They encircled Clay's body, hand gripping wrist at the small of the young man's back.

A grotesque grin spread across Nestler's face, exposing crushed lips and bloody teeth.

Clay knew he was in trouble. He had let the man get in too close, and now the breath was being squeezed from his body. He hit Nestler around the ears with a left and then a right, but the big man's head just swung with the blows as he squeezed even tighter. Clay could feel himself getting lightheaded, but with his height advantage, Nestler could not lift him off the ground. In one last, desperate move, Clay dug in a foot and threw all of his weight backwards, drawing Nestler with him, toppling to the ground. As they fell, Clay grabbed the big man by the vest, thrust his left leg up into the heavy body, and pushed. Nestler released his grip and launched over Clay's head, slamming into the dusty street.

Clay was on his feet first and moved into Nestler as he stumbled erect. Though dazed, the older man was an experienced brawler. He caught Clay moving in, opening up a cut over his left eye. Though Clay had no formal training, he remembered what pa had told him: "Take it where they live—hit 'em in the body." He swung another hard right uppercut to Nestler's belly.

The teamster gasped, bending over and staggering back. *If I don't finish him now, I'm done for,* Clay thought. He followed Nestler, pounding, left and right to the belly.

The man was wobbling on his feet. His mind was still game, but his body was running out of steam. Too many beers had taken his wind. As he drew back his right, he dropped his left. Clay saw it. With all the power he could muster from his six-foot-two frame, he smashed Nestler as he was coming in. Clay's right fist caught the man just to the left of his chin. Nestler's head twisted, his eyes glazed over, and his arms dropped. He stood swaying forward and back for a moment until his knees slowly gave way, and he crumpled into the dust of Congress Avenue. A great shout and clapping came from the crowd.

Clay couldn't believe it was over. His ears were ringing, and blood blinded his left eye. He pulled off his bandanna and wiped his face, then held it to the cut over his eye, and looking around for the cowboy he'd given his guns to.

"It is behind you, I am."

Clay turned around, and the young fella was standing there with his Roper and six-guns.

"I'm thinking you destroyed that fellow's meat house."

Clay took his gunbelt and swung it around his waist, fastening the buckle in front and adjusting the holsters. He took the Roper and laid it across his shoulder and grinned. "I'm not too sure whose meat house got torn down. Right now, mine feels pretty shaky.

"Thanks for your help. I'm Clay Barlow." He turned and watched as Nestler's cronies helped him up and back into the saloon. Nestler never looked at him.

The two shook hands.

"I am Michael Patrick Dunbar. 'Tis a pleasure to help." He glanced toward the setting sun in the west. "I'm thinking it's a drink that would do you good."

The crowd had dissipated quickly after Nestler went down. Clay was about to respond.

"Hello, Son."

Clay turned to face the tall, gray-haired man in light gray trousers with a black frock coat and red cravat. Even in the Texas dust, his boots carried a brilliant shine, and his wide-brimmed black Stetson, straight from Philadelphia, sat evenly on his head.

"Hello, Grandpa."

The two clasped hands, and Clay felt the strong tie he had with this man. Though they seldom saw each other now, he had fond memories of when he was young. "Michael, I'd like you to meet my grandpa, Senator Joseph Barlow."

"'Tis my pleasure, Senator. Your grandson holds his own well, I'd say."

"It seems so, Michael," Senator Barlow said as the two shook hands. "I appreciate you keeping the other toughs off Clay while he was occupied. If you're going to be in Austin overnight, maybe I could buy you a drink and dinner tomorrow."

"That'd suit me fine, Senator, if I don't see you sooner."

"Then why don't you meet us at Rock's Restaurant on Pecan? Say about noon tomorrow." The Senator turned to Clay. "Will that work for you?"

"Yes, sir, that'd be a pleasure."

Senator Barlow turned back to Michael. "We'll meet you

then. If you'll excuse us, I need to speak with Clay."

Michael nodded. "It's later I'll be seeing you, Clay." Michael headed back up the street to the Iron Front Saloon.

Darkness was closing in on Austin. Family members hurried home for supper. "Shall we go up to my little apartment, Clay? I'm sure Raymond won't mind setting another plate for supper, and you can stay there for as long as you're in town."

"That'd be fine, if you're sure it won't be a bother. I can just as easily get a room at the City Hotel."

"Wouldn't hear of it."

The two men walked in silence. Once they reached Pine they turned right, then left on Brazos. Facing Pine, at the corner of Pecan, was a two-story building. Across the front window, *Barlow Law and Land* was engraved on the glass. On the south side a set of stairs climbed to the second floor. The senator marched up the stairs to the landing and opened the door.

Raymond waited inside. "Senator, I heard you coming up the stairs. Can l take your coat?"

From the dark landing, Clay stepped into the room behind his grandfather. "Well, I'll be danged, if it ain't young Clay." Raymond stepped forward and grasped him by the upper arms. Raymond, a head shorter than Clay, looked up at the big man, then at the senator. "Aren't you a mite banged up, boy? Looks like you were in a scuffle."

Clay started to grin, but the pain in his face stopped him. "A little disagreement."

"Yep, I can tell that. Hopefully there's another feller that looks worse." Then Raymond went on as if nothing happened. "I'll tell you, Clay, yore ma fed you well. You growed big. He wasn't quite as tall, but you're a spittin' image of your pa." He hesitated for a moment. "I'm right sorry to hear about them."

Raymond's face hardened. In the lamplight of the room, his eyes turned the color of slate. "You did right by your folks, and you showed great restraint. If it'd been me, I'd a hung 'em all."

"It's good to see you, Ray. Thanks."

The senator cleared his throat. Raymond turned to the older man. "Let me take your coat, Senator."

"Thank you, Raymond. Can we add another plate at supper?"

"Yes, sir, there's plenty. I imagine Clay will want to clean up some first?"

"Yes," the senator said. "Clay, Raymond will show you to your room. You have some clothes with you?"

"Yes, sir, I do, but they're in my roll with my saddle."

"Raymond, get one of my shirts and a pair of pants for Clay. They should fit him, maybe a little tight, but I think they'll do."

"Grandpa, you needn't do that. I'll just wash up for now, and go get my roll and saddlebags after dinner."

"Relax, Son. I don't think Raymond will mind getting them later."

"No, sir. Not at all. Follow me."

Clay followed down the hall to another bedroom. He had been here several times when he was younger. His grandfather's little apartment, as he called it, took up the whole second floor of the building. Raymond opened the door and led Clay into the bedroom. Besides the bed, there was a chest at the end of the bed to store bedding, a dresser with a mirror, and a large armoire. Clay stood the shotgun by the side of the bed and removed his gunbelt, hanging it on the iron headboard.

"Thanks, Ray."

Raymond nodded and stepped out of the room, closing the door behind him.

There was a pitcher of water and a basin sitting on the dresser. Clay slipped out of his shirt, pulling it over his head, grimacing at the movement. His ribs and chest were sore from the fight. Nestler had landed some solid blows. He was lucky no ribs were broken. Once his shirt was off, he examined his face in the mirror. Not much there for a woman to like, he thought. Pale gray eyes stared back at him. The cut above his eye wasn't deep and, fortunately, hadn't extended into his thick black eyebrows. Slim always teased him about the big ears, which his black hair tumbled over, but Pa said that was all right—it kept his hat from sliding down over his eyes. Inwardly, he laughed at the thought. Slim and Pa had been good friends and had taught him much.

He poured water into the basin and picked up the washing cloth and began working on his face. After cleaning the cut above his eye, he moved to the rest of his face, removing the layer of Texas dust that had built up through the day. He cleaned around his wide mouth. Ma always said he should have played a brass instrument, since he had the full lips for it. He made a vibrating noise as he blew through his loose lips and laughed. Ma was a sweetheart.

He finished washing his face and rubbed the cleft in his chin. It hadn't concerned him until he started shaving. Now the sharp edge of the razor blade was attracted to the cleft much too often. Clay rubbed his hand across the thick black bristle on his cheek. Seemed nowadays, he almost needed to shave twice a day. He ought to be like a Quaker and grow a full beard. That'd sure save from shaving, but he wouldn't do that, because Ma didn't like beards.

Raymond had brought the change of clothes for him. He slid off his britches and put on his grandpa's. They fit pretty good and were comfortable. A lot of men increased in girth as they got older, but Grandpa was never a man to put on weight. He pulled on the red shirt, pleased that the sleeve length was right, but it was tight around the neck, the upper arms, and the chest. Raymond brought in a set of white suspenders, a black vest, and a black tie. Clay finished dressing and looked at himself in the mirror.

*Not bad*, he thought. *That is, if you discount the eye almost swollen shut.* He tugged the bottom of the vest down and walked into the dining room.

His grandfather sat at the table for four in the sitting room, reading the Austin Democrat Statesman. He looked up from the paper. "Son, you make a mighty striking figure. Put a few years on you, and I can see you in Congress." He shook the paper out, folded it carefully into thirds, and laid it on the side of the table. "I imagine you're hungry after your little workout. Have a seat and let's eat." He raised his sonorous voice slightly: "Raymond let's put the food bag on."

"Yes, sir. Coming up," Raymond replied from the kitchen.

He brought in big steaks, a huge bowl of mashed potatoes, and a large dish of squash. The table was set for three people. After Raymond had brought all of the food, he pulled out a chair and sat down.

"Dive in, boys," the senator said.

Conversation stopped as the three men devoured their food. Clay put a piece of steak in his mouth. It was cooked perfectly.

When they had finished, Clay leaned back in his chair. "Ray, that's the best food I've tasted in a while."

"I enjoy cooking. Maude started my learning shortly after we married."

The senator nodded. "Yes sir, she was a fine lady. I'll always say, it was a special day when the Colemans came into my life."

"Thanks, Senator. She was a shining light." Raymond cleared his throat. "Now, how about some peach cobbler to top off that steak?"

Ray slid his chair back and headed for the kitchen.

"How long has he been with you, Grandpa?" Clay asked.

The older man looked out at the Austin lights and was silent for a moment, deep in thought. Looking back, he said, "I sometimes forget how long it's been. Why, I'm thinking it's been close to forty years."

"Thirty-seven, Senator," Raymond said, walking back into the room carrying a tray with three full bowls of peach cobbler, topped with thick, fresh cream. While placing the bowls in front of each man, he continued, "Your grandpa was a fierce man to see that April. I still remember the day like it was yesterday. The sky was clear, we had a warm breeze drifting up from the coast, and we were backed up against Buffalo Bayou, all seven hundred and fifty of us. And you know what? That blasted Santa Anna, he and his boys was having them a siesta. Can you believe that? Here we were, getting ready to attack, and they were sleeping. Must've been five thousand Mexican soldier-boys out there in front of us."

The senator laughed and said, "Raymond, I think you're exaggerating some. There was only fifteen hundred, though still twice as many as we were."

"Now, Senator, I'm telling this," Raymond said, shaking his gray head. "I swear, he won't let a man tell his own story.

"Anyway, we done marched right up to Mr. Santa Anna's soldiers and danged near killed 'em all. That's where I stuck my pig-sticker clean through a Mex that was about to shoot yore grandpa. In fact, that's how we met."

"He did," Senator Barlow said. "That Mexican captain had his pistol not a foot from the back of my head. I was otherwise busy and hadn't seen him. At least I felt that muzzle blast by my head. There for a moment, I knew I was a goner."

"Otherwise busy, what a nice way of putting it," Raymond said. "You were fightin' like a she grizzly protecting her cubs. It's a good thing I came along, Clay, or you wouldn't be here. That captain still pulled the trigger, but the ball managed to sail right past yore grandpa's head. He couldn't hear much outta that ear for a few days, but that was it, and danged if he didn't end up offering me a job. We've been together ever since."

"If I'd known how ornery Raymond is, I might've had a second thought," the senator said. "Enough of the past—let's finish off this cobbler and get down to business."

Clay barely noticed the sweet goodness of the fresh-cooked peaches and cream. *Now I've got to tell him I'm joining the Rangers. I sure hate to disappoint him.*

## 4

"That was a mighty fine meal, Raymond," the senator said. "Clay, let's adjourn to the couch."

The two men moved to the large, cushioned leather couch. After they were seated, Clay said, "I need to discuss something with you."

The senator stood and moved over to his desk. "Certainly, but first, let me straighten out a mistake I made years ago." He sat in the big leather chair behind his desk and opened the top desk drawer. From it he took a leather folder, laid it on his desk, and opened it.

From where Clay sat, he could see there was only one sheet of paper in the binder. His grandfather picked the paper up, looked at it for a moment, and handed it to Clay. The young man read the paper and looked to his grandfather. "I don't understand."

"Years ago," the senator began, "I deeded what is now your ranch to your father. At the time, I did not want to lose control should he decide to sell it. Therefore, I noted in the deed that should your father try to sell the ranch, it would immediately transfer back to me. That was an error on my part. I should have given it to him with no conditions.

"This contract corrects the error. It supersedes the previous deed. The sale of the property is no longer prohibited, nor does it come back to me should you decide to sell it. This gives you total control, to do with as you desire. I'm getting older, and I wanted to correct this before something happened to me. As you probably are aware, all of the rest of the family is gone. You are the last Barlow."

Clay studied the document. "Grandpa, thank you. But you didn't have to do this. I'm perfectly satisfied with the previous deed."

"I know, but this needed to be done. I am aware of your arrangement with Adam Hewitt, the neighboring rancher. In fact, I approve wholeheartedly. You made a very smart deal with him. It works well for both of you. However, I also know he would like to buy the ranch. This document will allow you to do whatever you feel is right for you."

"I'm actually—"

The senator held up his hand. "Let me say one more thing. I am truly sorry I was unable to come to your aid and assist you in apprehending your parents' killers. Unfortunately, by the time I received the news of their death, I also received the news of you settling the debt. I'm just sorry it was left solely to you. Although, you did quite well."

"Pa trained me. He always said I had natural coordination. He said it was a gift I had to be careful with."

The senator moved back to the couch. "He was right. You come from a long line of Scotsmen who were known for their dexterity with weapons. Handling a gun came easy for your father, as it did for me, your great-grandfather, and now, it seems, for you. Unfortunately, the Barlows are also saddled with a dangerous temper. It doesn't suddenly overcome us, causing us to fly into a rage, but it seethes deep down in our very soul. When it finally breaks free, it is with a cold, terrible fierceness that allows no resistance. From what I've heard, you've inherited it. You must strive to keep it in check."

"I've felt it, Grandpa, and I don't like it. It scares me. It's like I'm losing control, but I'm not. It's almost like I enjoy destroying my enemy."

The senator reached over and grasped his grandson's thick shoulder. "Keep it in control, Clay. It can be used for good, but released too often, it becomes an intoxicant, and you'll find it harder and harder to control. So, enough of that." The senator waved his hand as if brushing aside a cobweb.

"Have you heard your new name?"

Clay shook his head with disgust. "The Del Rio Kid. I had nothing to do with that. I don't even know how it got started."

"Who knows how those things start. It could have been some rummy telling a story in a bar. It sounds catchy, so it stuck. You're going to have to live with it for a while. Hopefully, over time, it will go away. As long as there are no other escapades added to the list, it shouldn't be an extended problem. I'm afraid the fight today may add fuel to the story, though. At least no one was killed. Fortunately, you'll be away from conflict while you study the law."

Clay took a deep breath. He hated disappointing his grandfather. "Grandpa, while I was in Del Rio, I met Major John B. Jones of the Texas Rangers. He offered me a job."

There was silence in the sitting room. The senator stood and moved to the north window of the apartment. The state capital, lighted from within and glistening in the faint moonlight, stood out to the north. He gazed at it for what seemed like hours to Clay. Finally, he turned and moved back to the couch.

"And you are planning on joining?"

"I am."

"I'll not say anything against them. They have certainly brought the Comanche problem under control. They were fierce in the war against Mexico, and now they're battling the border problem.

"However, I had greater hopes for you, as did your mother and father."

It was Clay's turn to move to the window. He walked to the west window where he could see the lights of Austin stopping abruptly at the edge of modern civilization. The dark hill country to the west, was lighted only by the rising moon. That was his country. He'd much rather be out there, sitting near a campfire, than in the biggest, most comfortable home in Austin. The wide open spaces were where he belonged, not in this rushing, noisy city.

He gazed through the window into the darkness. But, on the other hand, he did enjoy studying the law. Finally he turned to his grandfather. "Grandpa, I love this country. I like the wildness of it. I would tell only you this, or Pa if he was here. Though I was scared, hunting those men down and bringing them to justice gave me a feeling I've never had before, a challenge, and something I did well. I want more of that feeling. But I still love reading the law. Why, my copy of the Blackstone Commentaries has been read so much, it's coming apart."

"Come sit," his grandpa said.

Clay returned from across the room and sat back down on the couch, his young-old face a picture of dismay.

"Listen to me, Clay. You're eighteen. You have your whole life in front of you. You are obviously good at law enforcement. You're like your father. He was cool as a March morning facing another man's gun. That's you. It's part of you. That will never change.

"I've been through many more winters than you have. Believe me when I tell you, opportunities seldom come around twice. While you're young, go to New York. Read for the law. Study. Get that behind you, and you'll have something no one can take from you.

"I firmly believe you can make a name for yourself as a Ranger. But if you take a bullet in your arm or hand, you're done. You could join the bar and still become a Ranger. Only then, you'd be better, and with options."

Clay leaned back into the comfortable cushion of the leather couch. *Grandpa makes good sense. A year, two at the most, and I'd be back. With the money I've saved and that coming in from the ranch, I can afford it.*

"Grandpa, thank you. I'm glad I talked to you before I joined. You make a solid argument. Ma and Pa always wanted me to go to New York to study. I've never been there. The ranch is doing well under Mr. Hewitt's management. Thanks to you, I've made my decision. I'm going to New York."

The big gray-haired man clapped Clay on the shoulder. "Son, I think that's a wonderful idea. In fact, there's a man in town— although he'll be leaving in the next couple of days—I'd like you to meet. He manages my legal affairs and investments back East, and his office is in New York City. I've already spoken with him, and he's eager to meet you. He normally has breakfast at the City Hotel. We'll go by there in the morning and see him. I think you two will hit it off. Believe me, you're making the right decision. Texas and the Rangers will always be here. Now, tell me about what happened with the stage, and then why that big galoot started the fight with you."

Clay told him about the attempted holdup, playing down his part in breaking it up. He had just started explaining about Nestler, when a big yawn slipped up on him. He tried, unsuccessfully, to stifle it.

The senator laughed. "Son, you've had a mighty busy day. You can tell me about this Nestler character tomorrow. Right now, I imagine you'd like to be climbing into a bed."

"Yes, sir," Clay replied. "I got a mighty early start this morning. Bedding down sounds pretty attractive."

The two men stood and walked back toward the bedrooms. Raymond was just coming out of Clay's room when he got there.

"I shook out your clothes and laid them across the chair. They'll be ready for you in the morning. Your handguns are laying on the bedside table. I also got a look at that shotgun you're carrying. Tomorrow, you'll have to show me how it works."

"Let him go, Raymond. That boy's just about asleep on his feet."

The men exchanged good nights, and Clay closed the door. As he slipped out of the borrowed clothes, he felt a growing excitement. He had always dreamed of studying the law. He wanted to help people who couldn't afford the cost of a lawyer, and now he'd be able to. After laying the clothes he had been wearing neatly across the remaining chair, he checked his revolvers and moved them to where they would be in easy reach. Yes, he was in his grandpa's house, but he had already learned that evil men were no respecters of persons.

Clay stretched out on the bed and felt the cool Texas breeze waft across his body. Through the open window, he heared a coyote howl, not far away, followed by several barking dogs. The evening honeysuckle shared its nighttime perfume with him. A couple of gunshots rang out, then yelling, from one of the many saloons.

His mind was busy playing with the thoughts of what New York would be like. His last thought, before exhaustion overcame his young body, was of his ma, and how happy she would be to know he was going East to study the law.

HE AWOKE SUDDENLY. He could hear Austin awakening to the light of a new day. It came to him quickly that he had made a decision last night, a decision he had been laboring over for months. The rangers would have to wait. But he would be back, and would be even more effective upon his return.

Throwing aside the light quilt, he tossed his long legs over the side of the bed, stood, and stretched. Raymond had emptied the bowl from last night and brought a fresh pitcher of water, along with a shaving mug, soap, brush, and razor. Clay quickly washed up and, electing to use his razor, pulled it from the saddlebags. He opened it, stropped it a few times on his saddlebag, and laid it on the dresser. First dipping the brush in the water, he spun up a lather in the shaving mug, and began spreading the soap across his face.

The features he covered were sharp and strong. The mirror reflected wide-set light gray eyes watching his rapid, circular movement of the brush, and then the more careful strokes of the straight razor removing the thick, black stubble that covered his face. He thought for a moment about starting a mustache, but decided against it, for now. Diligently working with the straight razor for a few more minutes gave him a clean shave. Face washed quickly, he examined his work.

After getting dressed, he reached for his gunbelt and paused. Thinking better of wearing the belt with two guns, he pulled one of the .44-caliber, Smith & Wesson, Model 3 revolvers from its holster. He broke it open and examined the loads, closed it, and slid it in his left front waist, under his vest. Pulling the vest back down, he looked in the mirror. There was a slight bulge over the grips, but not bad. He wiped his black hat off with the sleeve of his shirt and thought of his pa. This was the hat his pa had given him not too many years ago. It was tight now, but he hated to get another. He looked at it for a moment longer, then pulled it down on his head, adjusted the angle, and stepped out of the bedroom just as the senator walked by.

"Good morning, Son. Glad to see you're ready. The man we're meeting this morning gets an early start on the day."

"Morning, Grandpa."

His grandfather looked him over approvingly. "You make a mighty striking figure." Then he smiled. "Although it looks like that hat is getting a little tight on you."

Clay nodded. "Yes, sir, it is. I'm needing to get another one. I just hate to part with it. Pa gave it to me."

"I understand. Why don't we do this. You'll need some new clothes. We'll drop by the shop that outfits me, and not only get you some suits, but see if they can't fix you up with a new hat. I'll keep your old clothes and your hat here for you, rather than getting rid of them altogether." The senator turned and opened the door.

"We'll not be home for dinner, Raymond," he called out, as they stepped onto the landing and started down the stairs.

Clay marveled at how tall his grandfather used to seem to him. *Now,* he thought, *I'm at least an inch taller.* His mind drifted. *My folks are dead, I've killed seven men, and I'm going to New York. Life sure brings changes.*

They crossed Brazos Street and followed Pecan, turning right onto Congress toward the capital. The senator greeted men as they passed and touched his hat to the ladies. "Never hurts to be pleasant, Son. Even though I'm no longer in the senate, I work with many of these men. Most are good men. Some not so good."

About that time, Clay could see a man coming toward them. He felt a warning from his gut and looked quickly to the senator. His grandfather's face had hardened, and he had adjusted his vest, exposing the handgun grips. Clay could feel the tension come over him, and then the relaxed feeling he always felt just before a fight.

The approaching man was older. His gray hair, falling from under a clean white hat, hung almost to his collar. He was built solid, obviously a hard-working rancher or ranch hand. He continued toward them and then turned and crossed the wide street, disappearing behind a freight wagon. When he came back into view he was past them, continuing down the street.

Clay saw his grandfather visibly relax. "And some, downright mean. "I'll tell you about him sometime, but not now. We're here."

They stopped at the City Hotel. Clay opened the door for his grandfather and followed him inside. The lobby was quiet. Several men sat in comfortable, leather wingback chairs, reading the morning newspaper of their preference. In recognition, they nodded and spoke to the senator as he led the way into the hotel's restaurant. The senator nodded toward two men sitting at a table in the corner and headed their way. Clay looked around and saw Nancy Davis and Dee sitting next to a window with a man about Nancy's age. She waved at Clay.

"Grandpa, there's someone I'd like you to meet. It'll take just a moment."

His grandfather stopped and looked toward Nancy and Dee, held up his hand to the men they were moving toward, and turned with Clay. "Certainly. This can wait a moment."

"Hi, Clay," Dee said, her face beaming with pleasure, as they walked up to the table. He saw Nancy say something to the man, who then stood.

Clay smiled at Dee. "Hi, Dee. Nice to see you." Then he turned back and said, "Grandpa, I'd like you to meet the nice folks that I met on the stage yesterday. This is Nancy Davis and her daughter, Dorenda. I understand everyone calls her Dee.

"Mrs. Davis, this is my grandfather, Senator Barlow."

Nancy Davis extended her hand to the senator. Taking her hand, he removed his hat and inclined his head to her.

"A pleasure to meet you, ma'am. You too, Dee."

"Thank you, Senator," Nancy said. "I'd like to introduce you and Clay to my husband, Niles Davis. We own the Rocking D, over Comfort way."

While shaking hands, the senator said, "Nice to meet you, Mr. Davis."

"You, too, Senator." Niles took Clay's hand. "I reckon I owe you a big debt. No telling what would've happened if you hadn't stepped in. Thank you."

"Mr. Davis, you don't owe me a thing. I did what any man would have done in that situation. I'm just glad I came along when I did."

Nancy spoke up. "No, Clay. You did more than any man. You rode in against six armed killers, and you by yourself. I've seen brave men before, and I know one when I see him. Thank you."

Clay blushed under the praise. "Ma'am, I thank you—"

"No, Clay," Nancy interrupted. "We thank you."

"That's right," Niles Davis said. "I don't imagine it would've gone well with my family if you hadn't been there. Remember what I said. We owe you. Anywhere, anytime. And call me Niles."

Clay was at a loss for words.

But Dee wasn't. "Daddy, this is the man I told you about. He's the one I'm going to marry." She gave Clay a big smile.

Everyone laughed.

"I think I'm a little old for you, Dee," Clay said. He smiled at her. "Though, when you're grown, you're going to be a good catch for some lucky man your own age."

Dee turned to Nancy. "Mama, he doesn't believe me."

"Dee, don't embarrass the man anymore than I have already."

"You better watch out, Clay," Niles said. "I've found out, over these past twelve years, she's a pretty determined girl." He winked at Clay.

The senator chuckled and then said, "Folks, it is very nice to meet you, and to hear the good words for my grandson. However, I do have people waiting on me whom we must meet. If you'll excuse us."

"Of course," Niles said. He took Clay's hand again and shook it vigorously. "Clay, I'm serious. If you ever need anything."

"Thank you, Niles." Clay turned to Nancy and Dee. "Ya'll have a good day, and you be good, Dee."

As they were walking away, Clay could hear Dee say,

"Momma, I'm serious. He's only six years older than me. Daddy's seven years older than you. I'll show you."

The senator grinned at Clay. "Sounds like someone has their hat set for you, boy. It surely does. Now let's get to this meeting. I'm hungry."

## 5

A s they walked up to the table, the two men who had been waiting for them stood. Both were dressed in business suits, their hats on the table, a bowler in front of the older man and a flat straw Nattie in front of the younger.

"Clay, this gentleman is Lionel M. O'Shea.

"L.M., this is my grandson, Clayton Joseph Barlow. He goes by Clay."

L.M. O'Shea looked up at Clay as he took his hand. "Nice to meet you, Clay. My, my. You grow them big in your family, Senator. Ah, yes, this is my nephew and associate Michael Patrick Dunbar. You can call him Mike."

"I think we've already met your nephew," the senator said, taking a seat alongside Clay. Clay looked across at Mike's hat and his suit. "You're looking a little different today."

"So, you've already met?" L.M. said.

"Yes, we have, Mr. O'Shea. We met yesterday," Clay said.

Mike chimed in. "This was the big fellow that was engaged in the sweet science, Uncle, as you can probably tell by that cut over his eye. Although, 'tis sad to say there wasn't much sweet, or science about it. I also had the pleasure of meeting the senator."

The senator nodded. "It was quite a brawl. Fortunately my grandson came out the winner, although I had my doubts at first."

Clay laughed. "You weren't the only one. Getting hit by Nestler's fist was like getting clubbed by a fence post. Fortunately, that hitching rail was in the right place to save my hide. If it hadn't blocked him from getting to me straightaway, while I was still groggy, I might not be here."

Mike winked at Clay. "Laddie, I'd not let him put the stomp on you. Not while yours truly is holding the shotgun, but I saw you coming around. You were ready for him." Mike paused for a second, then turned to his uncle. "We could talk longer about this, but I'm thinking discussing business is on your mind."

"Thank you, Mike. It certainly is." L.M. turned to the senator. "I'll get right to the point. As you've probably read, things are beginning to look grim in the New York and European markets. Inflation has been rampant since the end of the war, and now I see overspending in the railroads. I am extremely concerned in having any investments in the railway system, or in silver. The price of silver has been and continues to drop. As of right now, I forecast a financial disaster looming just around the corner. I have moved most of my investments to a cash position and am recommending my investors do the same."

The senator leaned back in his chair and rubbed his chin. After a moment he said, "If we have a recession, everyone that's carrying debt on their farms or ranches could be in big trouble. We'll see cattle and wheat prices drop drastically. L.M., we could see families losing the homes they fought for, and some died for. Are you telling me it's looking that grim?"

"Aye, that is exactly what I'm saying to you." O'Shea had a tendency to fall back into his Irish brogue when excited. "I'm telling you, not even your Texas will be immune. The entire country it will hit."

The waitress approached the table. The men stopped talking

and gave her their orders. After she had departed, they continued their discussion.

L.M. O'Shea calmed himself and took a deep breath. "Senator, if you or any of your land investors have any debt to the banks, now would be the time to pay it off. Sell what you need to, whether it's cattle, crops, or land, but get out from under the debt. Prices are going to drop precipitously. You won't be able to give a cow away."

Clay thought of the Hewitts. Mr. Hewitt was managing Clay's ranch and running his own cattle there. Was he carrying any debt to the bank in Uvalde? What about the Grahams? They had just bought the bank last year.

"Mr. O'Shea, will this also affect the banks?"

"Aye, Clay. You'll see many banks across this land go out of business, and when they go bankrupt, the families with money in those banks will lose everything."

"But if we start taking our money out of the banks, won't that have the same effect? Won't the banks go out of business, just earlier?"

"Unfortunately, there's not a lot you can do about the result, but yes, to your question. You can leave your money in the bank in hopes it will survive, and probably lose everything, or you can take it out now and contribute to the bank failure—not a pretty choice."

"Thank you for advising us, L.M," the senator said. "You have my authorization to move my funds into a cash position. Any idea how long this recession might last?"

"No, but I do think that with the rampant speculation we've had over the last few years, we could be looking at a deep and fearful recession, possibly even a depression. I would prepare for the worst."

Clay glanced at the Davis family. They were about to leave. "I need to tell some folks."

L.M. responded, "Tell as many people as you can. The more

we alert, the more people we will have financially prepared for this catastrophe."

Clay slid his chair back and stood. He strode over to the Davis family, who had risen to leave the restaurant. "Mr. Davis, could I have a word with you before you leave?"

"Certainly. Have a seat, but please, call me Niles." The family sat back down at the table, and Clay explained what he had been told.

Nancy said, "Clay, are you sure about this?"

"Ma'am, L.M. O'Shea, manager of my grandfather's investments, is sure, and my grandfather trusts him. I reckon that makes me sure. I'm going to clean up my finances before I leave."

Dee looked at Clay, her big blue eyes wide. "Are you leaving Austin, Clay?"

Clay smiled through his concern, his mind working rapidly over the things he needed to do before he left. "I am. I'll be going to New York City to study law, but I'll be back. Now, I've got to get back to my grandpa. You folks stay safe, and do what's necessary to protect yourselves."

Everyone stood. "Thank you again," Nancy said, "for saving our family. You might have saved our ranch for us as well. Good luck in New York."

"Thanks, Clay," Niles said, as they shook hands.

"Hope this was some help. You folks take care." Clay looked down at Dee. "Help your folks—they need you."

Her concerned little face turned up to him. "You be careful, Clay."

The family left the restaurant, and Clay walked back to his table.

He heard the senator saying, "Thank you, L.M. I firmly believe you will not regret your decision."

"I am sure you will be proven correct."

The men stood as Clay returned.

"Looks like traveling together for us is in the cards, Clay," Mike said.

L.M. pulled his gold watch from his vest pocket and opened the cover, checking the time. "We're a bit late." His brows furrowed slightly as he looked up at the senator. "I detest being late, but this was important.

"Joseph," he continued to the senator, "we will be leaving the day after tomorrow on the one o'clock train. Speaking with you has been good. I will move you to a cash position as quickly as I can."Turning to Clay, he said, "Yes, Clay. We will be traveling together back to New York. I look forward to you joining my firm. Now, we must go."

L.M. and Mike rushed from the restaurant. A buckboard waited. Clay watched as they hurriedly stepped up into the buckboard, then disappeared up Congress Avenue.

Clay and the senator walked out of the City Hotel. "That was abrupt."

The senator laughed. "L.M. is like that. When he concludes business, he's on to his next project. He has an appointment with the governor.

"We don't have a lot of time. I imagine you gathered you'll be going to New York with L.M. He'll help you get set up with law classes at Columbia, and you will be working for him. Learn well. He is a shrewd, intelligent lawyer and investor. He can teach you much. Understand, he is a demanding Irishman, but I'm sure that won't be a problem for you."

"Grandpa, I had no idea. I expected to go to New York, try to enroll at Columbia, and find my own job. I don't want to put anyone out."

"I know you don't, Son. He's excited about having you in his office, especially after his nephew told him how you handled Nestler." The senator took Clay's arm. "This way. You need some new clothes."

The men crossed Congress and traveled south.

"Here," the senator said, as they turned into a building with a hanging sign displaying hats. Once inside, Clay could see that not only were hats sold here, but also clothing.

"Senator, how are you, sir? It is always good to see you. And who is this stalwart young man you have with you?"

The short, bald man addressing his grandfather wore spectacles that rested across the bridge of his rather large, red nose.

"Clay," the senator said, "I'd like you to meet Granville Jenkins, the best tailor in the southwest." He turned to the short, chubby man. "Granville, this is my grandson, Clay. He needs a suit or two."

"Mr. Clay, it is a pleasure to meet you," Granville said as he thrust out his pudgy hand.

Clay took the soft little hand in his and shook it, releasing it quickly. "Nice to meet you, Mr. Jenkins."

"Please, call me Granville. All of my wonderful customers do."

The little man grasped Clay by his large biceps and turned him around. "My," he said to the senator as Clay turned, "he's very large." He reached up and brushed his hands along the top of Clay's shoulders. "Senator, I have nothing on the racks that will fit him." He grabbed Clay's waist and pressed in from each side, jerking his hands away as he felt the barrel of the Smith & Wesson. "Armed also."

He shook his head. "Senator, notice his wide shoulders and narrow waist. See how his shirt and vest hang on him. There is nothing he can wear off the racks. If he gets anything to fit his shoulders, chest, and neck, it will hang. Why, it will hang like a potato sack around his waist. Look. Like what he is currently wearing." The tailor placed his hands on his hips and turned to Senator Barlow. "He must only wear tailored clothing!"

Bemused, Clay looked at his grandfather. The older man winked at Clay.

"Well, Granville, why don't you fix him up with a couple of

suits and three or four shirts. He'll need some ties, another hat, and some new boots. Do you think you can handle that?"

The little man frowned. "Senator, I'm hurt. You know, of course, I can handle his needs. Now, let me see, I can have everything ready by"—the little tailor paused, his index finger tapping against his chubby cheek—"I can have everything, hat, boots, shirts, suits, vests, everything ready in two weeks."

At the tailor's estimate, the senator frowned. "I hate to make things difficult for you, Granville, and I know that you're the only man in town that could do this. That's why I always come to you for my clothing needs, but I'm afraid we will need everything, plus a nice traveling bag, by the day after tomorrow morning."

Granville's face turned red, and if it were possible for a man's eyes to bug out, his did. "But . . . but, Senator, in two days? That is impossible! Even if my Grace and Evelyn worked through the clock, we could not possibly have everything ready in time."

*Heck, I can go down the street and buy all the clothes I need. Who cares if it's big in the waist? Anything other than what Ma made me has always been big.*

"I tell you what, Granville, you know how much I like you, and I've recommended you to all of my friends. I'm sure you know that."

"Oh, yes, Senator. I have many important customers because of you."

"Yes. You understand, I wouldn't put you in this difficult circumstance, if it wasn't necessary. You see, my grandson has just come in off the range, and he is leaving on the one o'clock train in two days for Galveston and on to New York City. Now I wouldn't want those New Yorkers to think my grandson is just some backwoods hick. You know what I mean?"

The little tailor thought for a moment, then his frown changed to a big smile. He marched over to his front door and flipped the sign hanging in the window from OPEN to CLOSED.

"Senator, I'll do it. We will close the shop. My girls and I will work through the night, but we will have your grandson's clothes ready, trust me." He looked a little cagey for a moment. "Of course, it will cost a little more than usual, what with me closing the shop."

"Not a problem, Granville," the senator said. "You have no idea how much I appreciate your help. Clay needs to impress those New Yorkers."

"And so he will, Senator. Believe me, he will." The little man turned to Clay. "Now, take your vest off. Let's get you measured, and would you please hand that gun to your grandfather?"

Clay pulled the Smith & Wesson from his waist and handed it to the senator. The tailor quickly went to work taking measurements and asking questions. Thirty minutes later the two big men stepped through the door, closing it behind them.

"Now that was an experience," Clay said.

The senator chuckled. "Granville is an unusual little man, but he is excellent at his work. In fact, I think you would be hardpressed to find a tailor as good as he is in any of the big cities. I have often wondered what brought him out here."

"I'm sure he's good, Grandpa, but I could have gone down the street to the mercantile and bought all the clothes I need. By the way, I need to go over and check on Blue."

"Swing by my office. I should have been at work an hour ago. You can go on down to the stable from there.

"But, as you were saying, you could have gone down to the mercantile and purchased everything you needed. Something you might think about, though, is a man needs to fit into the country he's in. I know you're a good runner. When you are running through the hill country, do you do that in your riding boots?"

Clay laughed. "No, I'd have some pretty sore feet in no time."

"So you change into moccasins. You dress for your needs. That's just one quick example. Son, New York is a totally different place. I understand that clothes don't make the man, but many times a man is judged by his appearance. You need to look similar to the New Yorkers, not the same, because your size will automatically make you different. However, you don't want to look like a cowboy on Madison Avenue. That's what you would have looked like if you had bought your clothes at the mercantile. Buy all you want or need from the mercantile if you're headed out to the ranch. But not if you're headed back East."

The senator stopped and looked directly at Clay. "Do you understand what I'm saying?"

Clay nodded. "I think I do. I also understand I have a lot to learn."

"Yes, you do. You have done wonders, so far. I am very proud of you, but like your grandpa, you still have a lot to learn."

The two men continued walking until they reached the offices of Barlow Law & Land. They stopped in front of the office.

"Thank you, Grandpa. This has been a very enlightening morning. I'm going to go to the stable and make arrangements for Blue. This'll be the first time I've been away from him for more than a couple of days, in the last few years. I've got to make sure he's well taken care of."

"Son, go say goodbye to your horse, but don't worry about him. I have a good friend with a small spread just outside of town. He loves animals, has a good barn, and raises horses. He'll be glad to take care of him. I'll get Raymond to take him out there later this week. Blue will be in horse heaven."

"Thanks, Grandpa. That lightens my mind a lot. He was really the only thing I was worried about. I'll see you later."

The senator stepped inside, and Clay continued to Platt's Livery.

Blue was in the corral when Clay walked up. He whinnied and trotted over to the edge of the corral. Clay leaned on one of the horizontal cedar logs that made up the fencing, reached into his pocket, and brought out the apple he had bought at the restaurant. He held it out to Blue. The horse smelled it for a moment, then pulled his lips back and gently lifted the apple from Clay's hand.

"Never seen a horse that didn't like apples," Platt said, walking out the barn door.

"Yep, he loves 'em." Clay turned to Platt. "Mr. Platt, I need to settle up. I'll pay you for a couple of weeks. Sometime within the next few days, Ray Coleman will be by to pick Blue up."

"You selling him?"

"No. I'm leaving for a year or two. Ray will be moving him out to a horse ranch while I'm gone."

"I know Ray. Two weeks'll be five dollars. I'll see he gets plenty of corn and oats. I'll keep him happy till Ray gets here."

"Thanks, Mr. Platt. That means a lot to me." Clay paid Platt.

"Have a good trip, boy. Maybe I'll see you when you get back." He turned and walked back into the stable.

Clay turned his attention to Blue. He bent over and crawled between the logs. His hands wandered over the animal's flanks and back, then rubbed his withers and neck. The horse turned his head and stared at him.

"Blue," Clay said. "Sometimes it's like you know what's happening." He scratched the broad forehead with one hand, the other resting on the horse's muzzle. They had been through so much together. "I'll be gone for a while, but don't you worry, I'll be back. We still have a lot of country to cover."

The horse continued to stare at him. Clay could feel his heart swelling. *Dadgummit. I'm too old to cry. Get it done.* He rubbed Blue's muzzle one last time, then turned and crawled back through the fence. He remained stationary for a moment. Blue stretched his neck over the corral fence and nudged him in the back. Clay hadn't realized the pain he would feel leaving his horse. Blue was the last tie to the family he had loved. He shook his head and started for the Rangers' office. As Clay turned the corner, one last whinny rang in his ears.

C lay saw smoke rising high, to the east of the Austin depot, and heard the first blast of the train's whistle. He pulled his watch from his vest pocket and checked the time, two o'clock. Only an hour late. "Still can't believe I'm actually leaving Texas for New York," he said to his grandfather.

The tall, gray-haired man watched the train near the station. "You will learn a lot, Son. You'll be entering a new world. Just watch yourself. You can trust L.M., and I believe you will be able to trust Mike, but allow other people to earn your trust. City folk, whether it's here or back East, can be different and the same. Just watch yourself. I have always lived by the philosophy of 'trust no one till they've earned it.' You might do well to adopt that same policy."

Clay pulled two envelopes from his coat pocket and handed them to the senator. "Can you get these messages to the Grahams and Mr. Hewitt? I hate to see them lose money, if this depression hits."

"I'll be glad to, Clay. The next few years will be hard for everyone, but hopefully they'll be able to pull through." The senator grasped his grandson's shoulder. "I'll also make sure Blue is well taken care of. He'll be waiting for you when you get back."

O'Shea and Mike walked out from the station's waiting room. "You are looking much different, Clay. Business attire suits you. I fear you may return to Texas with more than an education," O'Shea said. He winked at the senator.

Everyone but Clay laughed. He smiled and said, "Mr. O'Shea, I'm headed to New York to learn to be a good lawyer. That's it."

"Certainly, certainly, and learn you shall."

The men silently contemplated the train as it was unloaded, and reprovisioned. Once ready, the conductor called, "All aboard if you're going aboard."

Clay turned to his grandfather. "Thank you for your help. If you need anything, you let me know."

"Son, I think that's my line, but thank you. Study law hard, but take the time to also study people. Knowing both will enhance your life tremendously. You take care of yourself."

The two tall men stood a moment longer, hands clasped. Then Clay turned and followed Mike and Mr. O'Shea into the Pullman car. They stowed their bags overhead and found seating. Clay sat next to a window, facing the other two men who were seated facing forward.

Moments later, the whistle blew, and the engine, its wheels first spinning on the hard steel, began to move, slowly at first and then accelerating away from the Austin station. Clay watched his grandfather grow smaller in the distance, then disappear as the train made a turn.

"First time on a train?" Mike said.

"Yep, it sure is."

"You'll be experiencing quite a few firsts on this trip," Mr. O'Shea said. "We'll take the H&TC to Galveston, then we'll sail to New York, on one of the new steamships. It should be a pleasant voyage."

"Never been on a ship before, either. I'm looking forward to it."

L.M. O'SHEA WATCHED the tall young man sitting across from him. He had known Clay's grandfather for many years. In fact, they had first met on his initial trip to Texas, now almost twenty years ago. That had been an experience he was happy not to enjoy again. He had taken a sailing ship from New York to Galveston, followed by a stagecoach to Houston and then Austin. The stage had been miserable. Now he was sitting in a comfortable Pullman car that would take no more than one-tenth the time to get to Galveston.

He continued to examine Clay. The man's young face had a hard set to it. Not what you would expect for an eighteen-year-old boy. The light gray eyes were a unique color, almost piercing when he looked at you. He was a very handsome young fellow. The girls would be all over him. It was hard to believe this well-spoken, handsome young man was a killer.

The senator had explained the boy's background. It must have been horrible to find his parents murdered. But to have hunted down the murderers and faced them with blazing guns, he couldn't even imagine what it took for a young boy to have taken on that task. *And look at his size*, he thought. *My goodness, the boy must be well over six feet tall, and his shoulders are massive.* The well-tailored coat did little to hide the width of his shoulders and huge biceps. The bruising and cut above his eye were the only things to hint he had been in a street brawl just two days ago. And he had almost joined the Texas Rangers and still might, when he returned.

*I just hope he is as smart as he is big*, he continued thinking. *He has a lot of work ahead of him and in a strange environment, but he looks like he could tackle anything. The senator did assure me that he is very intelligent, having read, multiple times, Blackstone's Commentaries. That too is hard to imagine. It will become quite apparent very soon, when I start quizzing him.*

~

CLAY WATCHED the countryside slide by to the rhythm of the clicking rails. The speed amazed him. What would take him several days by horseback was going to be done in hours. The trees began to thin, with wide prairies of tall grass between them. He had never been this far east. Everything was so green. They must get a lot more rain here than in the hill country. As he thought about rain, he watched the big thunderheads growing to the south. He had to shift around slightly. Sitting, the Smith & Wesson had become uncomfortable, tucked into his waistband, but with a little adjustment, he took care of it.

He thought of their stop at the tailor's this morning, before heading for the train. He couldn't believe everything was ready, and it fit so well. He had never worn any clothes that fit him properly, except those Ma made. She sure knew how to sew. But these folks made all those clothes so quickly. Granville even added three more shirts and two trousers, and those socks really felt good in his new boots. He glanced at his new hat, lying on the seat next to him. He hated to give up the hat his pa gave him, but this hat was sure a lot more comfortable. Black, wide-brimmed, with a shorter crown. I won't have to worry about any bullet holes in this hat, he had thought and laughed to himself.

They had been traveling for well over two hours when Clay's attention was drawn to the rear of the car. Two rough-looking men had just walked in. Something about them didn't look right. They were eyeing everyone in the car, and the way they were taking things in, they sure weren't looking for a seat. He leaned forward to Mike. "Don't look around, but we may have trouble."

Mike nodded and adjusted something under his armpit. Clay

hadn't noticed before, but he now suspected Mike was carrying a gun under his frock coat. No sooner had Clay said something, than the two men grabbed seats to hold onto, and the train's brakes locked up.

"This is a holdup!" the men shouted, drawn guns covering the people "Move and you're dead."

Clay had his gun out before the other man's mouth had stopped moving. The robber started to swing his weapon toward him, but it was too late.

Without hesitation, Clay pulled the trigger. He watched the tall man's surprised look as the bullet slammed into his chest. The second .44 American slug smashed the man's chest within inches of the first, the thieve's gun slipping from his fingers.

With the strike of the first bullet, the tall man lurched into his partner, knocking him off balance. From a precarious position, he fired, but the bullet flew wild, out a window, striking no one. Mike had drawn his Remington Pocket Revolver .32-caliber conversion, and his first shot hit the remaining outlaw as he was trying to regain his balance, striking him in the left hand. Clay's third shot struck the man directly in the tobacco pouch stuffed in his upper vest pocket.

"I'm shot," the outlaw cried, clinging to the metal back of the Pullman seat.

"Danged right you are!" shouted a cowboy who drew his six-gun and plowed another round through the stricken man. The cowboy had been sitting under the two men's guns, unable to make a move, until Clay fired. He jumped up and headed for the back of the car.

"Wait!" Clay yelled. "Out the window, I can see more of them up at the baggage car, and there's probably at least two back at the other Pullman car." He reached up and dragged his suitcase down from the overhead storage. Opening it, he pulled out the short-barreled Roper, shotgun shells, and his gunbelt. He fastened the gunbelt around his waist and looped the bag of shotgun shells around his neck. Then he reloaded the Smith & Wesson, dropped it into the empty holster and cocked the Roper.

A drummer stood and said, "I can help." He pulled a long-barreled Colt .45 from his valise along with a box of cartridges.

Mr. O'Shea sat with his mouth agape, shock across his pale face. "Clay, you can't go out there! You and Mike could be shot."

"Mr. O'Shea, we could be shot right here. Those outlaws are probably coming to investigate what all the shooting was. There's women and children on this train. We've got to protect them." He turned to Mike. "Coming?"

Mike popped out the empty cartridge from his pocket revolver and dropped in a fresh one. "Thought you'd never ask."

Clay turned to O'Shea. "Let us know if you see anyone coming in behind us. We're going to clean out the other Pullman, and then check the baggage car."

The four men moved to the back of the car. Mike leaned over and picked up one of the dead men's guns and stuck it in his belt, while the cowboy did the same with the other one. Clay led the way out the back door to the platform between the two cars.

Designating Mike and the cowboy, he said, "You two slip down the side of the car till you get to the rear. Stay on the off side from the baggage car entrance, and stay low, so you won't be seen. As soon as you go in, slide to the outsides of the car, so we don't end up shooting each other. I'll wait for a count of ten, and then we'll go in the front. Good luck."

Clay counted to ten and turned to the drummer. "Ready?"

The man nodded, one small bead of sweat on his forehead the only indication of nerves.

Clay eased the door open slowly and looked in. Two outlaws were busy, one on each side of the aisle, robbing the railroad's patrons. He stepped in just as one of the outlaws hit a woman with the barrel of his revolver, and with the other hand, reached for the lady's necklace.

"I told you everything in the bag. Everything, means every-

thing!" He swung the gun back to hit her again and caught movement, from the corner of his eye, close.

Clay was on top of the man before he could react. He
punched the barrel of the shotgun hard into the man's belly.
When he doubled over, Clay brought the butt down on the back
of his head. The outlaw collapsed in a heap on the floor.

"Don't shoot. I give up," the other man shouted, throwing his
six-gun on the seat beside him, and sticking his arms straight
toward the ceiling.

Clay moved to where the woman was sitting. Silent tears,
mixed with blood from the head wound, flowed down her
cheeks. Clay reached for his neckerchief, then realized he wasn't
wearing one. The cowboy pulled off his and handed it to Clay.

He pressed it gently to the woman's head. "Can you hold this?
There are still more train robbers up by the baggage car."

Her lips pursed and she said, "Yes, I certainly can. Go stop
those animals."

Two more cowboys and two businessmen, all four with guns
in their hands, had stood and moved toward Clay. "We can help."

"Good," Clay said. His eyes had hardened, and he felt the cold
rage deep in his heart. These people were all innocents, bothering no one, and a bunch of no-accounts thought they'd take
what they wanted, something for free.

He took a deep breath. "Tie these two up. We'll head out the
back of the car, slip down the off side from the outlaws, split up,
and come around both ends of the baggage car. As soon as you
get a shot, take it. The lady had it right. These are animals, and
we might as well be rid of 'em."

The men followed Clay and slipped along the side of the
train. They split, half the men going to the front of the baggage
car, and the other group staying with Clay. They could hear
someone saying, "If you don't open that door, I'll use this dyna-
mite. I'd just as soon kill you as not. It'll blow this car half in two.
You heard the shooting. There's folks already dead back there. If

this door and that safe ain't open quick, there won't be enough left of you to be a meal for a buzzard."

"Sir, whatever is in that safe carries a promise from H&TC that it arrives safely. Though you have already killed innocent passengers, I will not brook the thought of opening this door or the safe."

Clay and his men stepped into the open, the large muzzle of the Roper covering the leader. "You fellers are covered. Drop your guns!"

The five remaining outlaws froze, except for the leader. He swung the big .44-caliber Colt Army toward Clay. "Like hell, I will."

Clay watched as the man turned in the saddle to aim at him. It seemed in slow motion. He could see the details of the man's cruel face. The lips were drawn back, disappearing in the heavy mustache and exposing broken teeth, like fangs of a coyote. The man's hat was drawn down where it shadowed his eyes, making them look like dark hollows. But no matter how mean or cruel he looked, Clay knew the outlaw had no chance, yet the man's anger or arrogance made him think he could somehow beat a shotgun leveled at him.

The roar of the Roper coincided with the outlaw leader being blown to one side of his horse, his gun dropping from a limp hand. The horse reared up, throwing the lifeless man from the saddle.

Clay thumbed back the hammer of the Roper, the action throwing one shell out of the chamber and loading another, and swung the muzzle to cover the next man behind the leader.

The other men threw their guns to the ground, yelling, "We ain't shootin'. Don't shoot, don't shoot."

"Get off those horses, now! If anyone of you so much as acts like he wants to ride out of here, we'll empty your saddle."

The five men scrambled to the ground. The cowboys with

Clay had them hog-tied and the horses gathered, while Clay was talking to the agent in the baggage car.

"Mister, could I get your name?" Clay asked.

"Ye-Yes, sir. My name is Marvin Whipple."

"Well, Mr. Whipple, you're a brave man. These men could have blown up that car with you in it."

"Yes, I imagine that is true, but I am paid by H&TC to protect their property and the property of those that use this railroad, and I refuse to be coerced into doing anything wrong."

One of the cowboys came walking back from the engine shaking his head. He walked up to Clay, took his hat off, and wiped the hatband. "These heathens done gone and killed the engineer and the fireman. Shot 'em full of holes."

Clay shook his head, his mind slipping back to the sight of his parents. He looked at the outlaws lying on the ground. They didn't look very tough now. "Which one of you killed the engineer and fireman?"

One of the outlaws turned his head so that he could look up at Clay. "That was Joe Frank, Mister. He's a bad'un. I ain't rid with this outfit long, but it ain't took me long to figger that out."

Clay walked over to the man and stared down at him. "Which one of you is Joe Frank?"

The outlaw wasted no time in answering. "Why, that be him. That dark-featured feller over there with a big ole hole in his belly. You done killed him dead, I reckon. His family ain't about to be much too happy about that."

"I imagine the family of the engineer and fireman won't be too happy, either."

"No, sirree. Reckon they sure won't. But they ain't likely to come huntin' no one. Those Arkansas Blessings hold a grudge so tight, they squeeze the life out of it. They'll hunt you, Mister. I promise you, that is sure a fact."

Clay heard a door sliding and turned to the baggage car, as Whipple slid the door open.

He walked back to the car door. "Mr. Whipple, the engineer and the fireman are dead. Can you drive this train?"

"N-No, sir. I can't. Sorry," Whipple said, as he sat on the edge of the baggage car entry. "I'm a little scared.

"If the conductor is alive, I think he can drive the train, but he'll need someone to load the wood."

A big man, shorter than Clay but heavier, spoke up. "I've worked as a stoker before. I can feed that firebox if you can find an eagle-eye to herd this here train."

"Looks like you men have this under control," Mike said. "I'll find the conductor." He turned and trotted down the side of the train until he disappeared into the first passenger car.

"Let's get these fellers aboard the baggage car. Be sure and search them for any other weapons," Clay said.

The men went to work, none too gently, loading the outlaws into the baggage car. Clay dragged the leader's dead body over to the door. One of the other men grabbed the dead man's feet, and they swung him up and into the car. One of the cowboys inside picked up the man's feet and dragged him into a corner and released him, the dead man's boots making a hollow thump when they hit the floor.

## 7

The conductor walked up to Clay. "Thank you," he said to Clay, and turned to the men unsaddling the horses. "Thank all of you. It looks like you stopped the Blessing Gang." He walked to the baggage car and looked first at the tied outlaws and then the bloody body of Joe Frank lying on the floor in the corner. He turned to look at the Roper in Clay's hand. "From the size of that hole, I'd say that fella was shot by you, Mister. What's your name?"

"Name's Clay Barlow. He wasn't smart enough to put his gun down."

"You got you a big reward coming for this one. This gang has been terrorizing folks around here for a while. I'm surprised the rangers hadn't already hung this bunch."

Clay shook his head. "Split the reward up among the men. This wouldn't have gotten done without them."

"I don't know about that, but I'll get these boys' names and turn them over to the railroad." The conductor looked around. "Now, I understand one of you boys has worked as a fireman?"

The big fellow stepped up. "That'd be me."

"Good. If you men will finish with those horses and load up, we'll be on our way. Someone just give me a wave when everyone is aboard."

The two men walked toward the engine and climbed into the cab. The men with Clay finished loading the saddles and gear into the baggage car.

"What about the horses? This is good stock," one of the cowboys said.

Clay spoke up. "You're right there. Seems outlaws always ride better animals than a cowboy can afford, but there's nothing we can do. We'll have to turn them loose. There are enough farms and ranches around here, they'll find good homes." The men walked back to the passenger cars as the horses slowly drifted away from the train.

Clay unloaded his shotgun and shoved it back into his suitcase, put the suitcase back in the overhead, and dropped into the seat across from O'Shea. Mike was already sitting next to the older man. The drummer, the cowboy, and the other men had returned to their seats as well. The car was alive with conversation, passengers relieving their stress with talking. The train lurched once, twice, and then settled down to a smooth, slow acceleration.

Clay removed his hat and set it next to him on the seat cushion. A welcome breeze flowed through the car as the train gathered speed. The oppressive heat in the car gradually dissipated to a bearable level.

"Thanks for your help," Clay said to Mike.

"Didn't look like you had the need for much assistance. That revolver of yours appeared with wondrous speed, I might add."

"A man can always use help." Clay turned and nodded to the drummer and the cowboy. Like many men, they had been willing to help. They just needed a leader to get the ball rolling. At eighteen, Clay had already learned the importance of quick decisions. Hesitation could often mean the difference between life or death.

He picked his hat up, leaned back and placed it over his face and eyes. The adrenaline was wearing off. He was tired. He stretched his long legs out between O'Shea and Mike. Within moments he was asleep.

∿

O'Shea looked at the man-boy, now relaxed. It was not long ago that the young man was pulling that deadly gun from his waist-band and, without a word, shooting those two men. Not just shooting, but killing them. Mike had told him that he had only hit the man in the hand, but Clay had fired three times, hitting both men in the same location. His bullets had gone unerringly into their chests. Now, two were dead. No, wait, it was three. Mike had told him about the third man at the baggage car. Clay had shot him with the shotgun. What was the name he had heard people using? Oh yes, the Del Rio Kid. How could a soft-spoken, polite young man like Clay, turn so quickly into a cold-blooded killer?

O'Shea had been mesmerized when the shooting started. Clay had moved with such speed and determination. The outlaw had no more than started to speak, when Clay was reaching for the pistol in his waistband. It was like there was no thinking, no deliberating, just action. And his face. Before the man spoke, the boy's face was that of any eighteen-year-old. Well, maybe that wasn't quite true. There definitely was a shadow of hardness, but when that outlaw spoke, it was like Clay's face turned to granite, yet the boy—no not boy, man—was galvanized into action. His eyes had been locked on the outlaw. And then the gun was firing. So fast, yet so sure.

O'Shea felt a shudder pass through his body. He had been out West before. He knew lawmen. Why, he had known Clay's grand-father when he was younger. This call to action must run in the blood of these men. This was the type of man who had opened the West. They believed in justice, but where there were no courts, they meted out justice from the point of a gun or the end of a rope. He, O'Shea, was from a more civilized region. There were police and courts. The evil was still out there, but the average citizen was seldom exposed to it. Of course, when they were, they were mostly unprepared.

The lawyer leaned back in his seat. He watched the peaceful Texas countryside flow by. Without witnessing it, one would never know what violence had occurred only moments before. Would it be possible for him to teach, to control this hard, young man who wanted to become a lawyer? He had promised his friend he would. Now he could only hope he was up to it.

THE TRAIN CAME to a stop at its final destination, Galveston. The sky was dark and cool, damp breezes flowing from the Gulf of Mexico. Clay had been watching the lights go slowly by as they moved through the city to the station.

This had been a more eventful day than he had expected. They had unloaded the outlaws in Hempstead. The sheriff had come aboard and taken his statement, informing him the Blessings family was a vengeful pack, and warning him to stay on the lookout. The interview was quick, taking only a few minutes. Then the train had made multiple stops before finally passing through Houston and arriving in Galveston, where several train executives boarded. They thanked Clay and informed him the railroad had placed a large reward on the capture of Blessing and his gang. He had told them to split it with the other men, Mike included. They refused, insisting on including him in the reward, and in addition, giving each man a lifetime pass on the railroad.

He was just glad the trip was over. It seemed as if he couldn't get away from outlaws. *Maybe I'm destined to be a lawman. Should I even go on to New York?*

"I'm glad that train ride is over," O'Shea said. "That was more excitement than this old heart should have to put up with in one day. Let's get checked into the hotel. We are scheduled to board our ship in the morning."

"I'd say that is a grand idea," Mike said. "Once checked in, it is a fine dinner that tickles my fancy."

"Yep," Clay said. "A meal would sure hit the spot."

The three men moved through the bustling town. Laughter rang out from inside the saloons, and people bustled in and out of the adjacent buildings.

*This place seems huge, and people are everywhere*, Clay thought. He understood that Galveston was the biggest city in Texas. *I've never seen so many people in one place in my whole life.*

After a short walk from the train depot, the men made it to the hotel. They stepped into the lobby. Clay stopped and looked around. Part was caution—he had learned to assess a room as quickly as possible—but he was also astonished at the room's plush appearance. Rich dark-green curtains hung from the tall windows. The lobby alone could seat twenty-five or thirty people in lavish comfort. A huge crystal chandelier hung from the tall ceiling.

Three bellhops dashed up at their entrance into the hotel. "Let us help you with your bags," the first one said.

Mike had been carrying his and O'Shea's large bags, while Mr. O'Shea carried his valise. Clay had his single bag, which was being pulled from his big hand by one of the bellhops.

"Hold on," Clay addressed the man, a man older than himself. "I can handle my own bag."

Mr. O'Shea turned to Clay. "It's their job, Clay. They're only trying to help."

He reluctantly released the handle of his bag to the bellhop. "Guess I have a lot to learn."

"Mr. O'Shea," the clerk said, as they were walking up, "you've returned to our humble hotel. It is good to see you."

"Thank you, Robert, and you also. We need an additional room for Mr. Barlow. Make it adjoining, if possible."

The clerk looked up at Clay. "Yes, sir. Would you sign here, Mr. Barlow?"

Clay took the hotel ledger from the clerk and signed his name, Clay Barlow. The clerk looked down at the ledger, then back up at Clay. "Pardon me for being so bold, Mr. Barlow, but are you the Del Rio Kid?"

Clay looked at the man behind the counter who was staring up at him, almost in awe.

"Mister," Clay's voice was hard and threatening, "I don't like that name. I'd be obliged if you refrain from calling me that. Now could I have my key?"

"Yes, sir. Sorry, sir," the clerk said, a slight tremor in his voice. His hand shook as he handed the key to the bellhop. "Just follow him, and he will take you to your room. Have a nice stay De— Mr. Barlow."

Clay glared at the clerk and waited for Mike and O'Shea to get their keys.

"I'm sorry, Clay. I think the news of the attempted train robbery has already made it around the island. Unfortunately, that ghastly name has been tied to you. I would think it a good thing to be leaving Texas for a while."

As they followed the bellmen, Clay said, "I agree, Mr. O'Shea. I didn't want that name, and I have no idea how it got started, but it obviously did. I'll be glad to leave it here in Texas."

"Also, Clay," O'Shea said in a soft voice, "the bellman will expect a little something for his work. A dime or quarter will be fine. We'll meet downstairs in the restaurant. The hotel has a fine restaurant, and I'm just too tired to go out."

"Thank you." Clay followed the bellman into his room. The man put his case on a stand at the foot of the bed and turned to Clay.

He had dug a quarter out of his vest pocket, and now dropped it into the man's extended hand.

The bellman said, "Thank you, sir," and exited the room, closing the door behind him.

Clay adjusted the Smith & Wesson in his waistband, within easy reach of his right hand. Then he walked over to the window and pulled the curtain back just far enough for him to see. The street bustled with activity. He moved back over to the dresser, poured some water into the basin, and tossed some on his face. He combed his hair back with his fingers, dried his face on the towel hanging by the dresser, and headed downstairs.

He strolled into the restaurant, to find a man standing behind a podium at the entrance.

"May I help you, sir?" the man said.

"I'm looking for L.M. O'Shea."

"And who might you be, sir?"

"The name's Clay Barlow."

"Yes, Mr. Barlow. I can show you to Mr. O'Shea's table. He and his companion have not yet arrived."

The man led Clay to a round table with a fancy cloth on it, lit by an ornate lamp in the center. He held the chair. Clay looked at the man for a moment, then decided he was waiting for him to sit, so he did.

"Mr. O'Shea will be down shortly, sir. Would you care for a drink?"

Clay took his hat off and looked for a place to put it.

"I can take that, sir. Now, your drink?"

Clay handed the man his hat. "Thanks. How about some water? It gets a mite thirsty on that train."

"Water. Yes, sir, I'm sure it does."

The man turned, and with Clay's hat in hand, disappeared into another room. Clay gazed around. *Mighty fancy*, he thought. *I'll probably have to get used to this when we get to New York.*

He felt like he stood out like a sore thumb. He hadn't changed clothes, and in this Victorian-style dining room everyone was dressed for the evening, wearing clothes that no self-respecting cowboy would be found dead in. He noticed several glances his way, and then close head-to-head conversations. He had just about decided that if Mr. O'Shea or Mike didn't show up pretty quick, he was going to be on his way to find a decent place to eat.

"Well, I see you found our table." Mr. O'Shea was closely followed by the man who had led Clay to his seat. The man stepped to O'Shea's chair and pulled it out for him, while Mike seated himself.

"Mighty fancy here," Clay said.

"Get used to it," Mike replied. "My uncle travels in some pretty classy circles, and before long, you'll be right at home."

Clay laughed. "That's hard to imagine."

"Sorry, Clay," Mr. O'Shea said. "I forgot to mention that most people visiting this restaurant are dressed in evening wear."

"Wouldn't have made any difference, Mr. O'Shea. I don't have any."

The older man nodded. "I understand. We'll remedy that when we get to the city. Now, let's order. I'm starving."

Clay glanced at the menu. There were no prices.

He looked over at Mike and tapped the menu. "No prices."

Mike grinned. "When you see no prices listed, that means you're going to pay out the nose."

Mr. O'Shea smiled. "I don't think I'd put it quite as crudely as my nephew, but in essence, he is correct. However, do not worry about the price. I'll be paying for supper."

Clay sat back and looked at O'Shea. "Mr. O'Shea, I carry my own weight. No man needs to buy me any meal, unless I pay him back."

"I understand. However, you are now in my employ, as is Mike. I am paying for everything on this trip. It's not on you. Believe me, you will earn it when we get to New York."

"Listen to him," Mike said. "He's telling you square. Working and going to school will take every minute of your time. My uncle doesn't give money away."

Clay relaxed. "I aim to earn every penny."

"I'm sure you will," O'Shea said.

Dinner went quickly. Mike had talked him into trying the fresh fried oysters. He had tried to persuade him to try the raw oysters.

Clay said, "I don't eat calf fries raw, and I'm not eating these slimy globs raw."

The fried oysters were cooked in a golden-brown cornmeal crust, and, being guided by Mike, he tentatively forked one, dipped it into cocktail sauce, followed with a small amount of horse radish, and slipped it into his mouth with both Mike and O'Shea watching intently. He chewed for a bit and then swallowed.

"Well?" Mike said.

"That was darned good," Clay said, stabbing another one, and following the same routine. Very shortly, he had cleaned his plate.

"So much for oysters," Mike said to his uncle. "I think he likes them. Now we'll see how he likes the shrimp."

He had no sooner said that than the waiters appeared around their table with steaming plates of shrimp. They placed a plate in front of each of the men. The maître d' hovered around O'Shea.

"Mr. O'Shea, I hope you are finding everything to your liking."

O'Shea answered in French. "C'est parfait, comme d'habitude, Jean-Pierre. This is perfect, as usual, Jean-Pierre."

Before the man could respond, Clay said, with a perfect French accent, said, "Oui Capitaine, je viens de l'ouest du Texas. C'est très impressionnant. Je vous remercie. Yes, Captain, I am from West Texas. This is very impressive. Thank you."

Both the maître d' and Mr. O'Shea looked up in surprise.

The maître d' smiled and bowed to the two men. "Thank you,

Mr. O'Shea. It is always a pleasure to see you here." He turned to Clay. "My young gentleman, may I ask your name? I must say, your French is perfect. Where could you have learned it so well?"

Clay smiled at the man. "My name is Clayton Barlow. My mother was French, and my grandparents are from France. They live in D'Hanis, west of San Antonio."

"Ah, yes. I know of D'Hanis. I have some family that lives there. Is it possible you could share your grandparents' names?"

"Certainly, my grandfather is a Chevalier."

The maître d' gasped. "Is he Gabriel Talon Chevalier?"

Puzzled, Clay said, "Yes, how did you know?"

Now excited, the man said, "He is my uncle. My uncle. That makes us cousins. My mother is a Chevalier, your grandfather's sister. Can you tell me how he is doing?"

"He is doing fine. They have a farm and own a general store in D'Hanis. My grandmother is also well."

"Oh, it is so good to meet you." He looked around the room. "I must go. Please, stop by before you leave, so that we may exchange information. I can't wait to tell my mother." He turned to O'Shea. "I apologize for interrupting your supper. Please forgive me."

O'Shea waved a hand. "Jean-Pierre, it is wonderful to see you reconnect with your family. Think nothing of it."

Jean-Pierre rushed off to berate a waiter who had just spilled a tray on a lovely lady across the room.

Mike laughed. "You're full of surprises. Who would expect a cowboy from West Texas could speak French and then meet a relative in Galveston?" He shook his head. "I've got to keep my eye on you."

Mr. O'Shea nodded in agreement. "Your French is very impressive, Clay. Do you speak any other languages?"

"Yes, sir, I do. Languages have always seemed to come easy to me. My ma was French, but she was insistent I also learn Latin. As a young boy, she read to me from *Histories* by Tacitus, *The*

*Conquest of Gaul* by Julius Caesar, which I particularly liked, and *Meditations* by Marcus Aurelius, just to name a few. I learned Spanish and German from the folks I was around most of the time, plus Indian sign language, and Tonkawa."

Mr. O'Shea shook his head. "You are an amazing young man of many talents. I look forward to working with you. Now, let's eat."

The three men dug in to the shrimp, rice, and red pepper beans. It was all delicious. As they were putting down their forks, waiters appeared to take their plates and utensils. Another set of waiters was right behind them, carrying dessert. As each set a bowl in front of the three men, Jean-Pierre stepped to the table.

"Please, let me provide dessert for this evening, on the house." He turned to Clay. "You have brought such wonderful information for my mother. I thank you so much. She would love to meet you, but since she is in Houston, that is impossible. Let me thank all of you with our chef's finest dessert. It is Crème Brûlée à la Vanille Bourbon. Our chef is known for this delicious dessert. Please enjoy."

Everyone acknowledged the offering with a thank you and attacked the Crème Brûlée. Clay couldn't remember tasting anything as delicious as this, allowing it to dissolve on his tongue to savor each bite. When it was gone, even as full as he was, he was sure he could have eaten more.

He leaned back in his chair. "Now that was just about the best meal I ever had."

"That was very good, but wait until New York," O'Shea said. I think you'll enjoy the food." He looked around the table. "We have an early start in the morning. I recommend that we head up to our rooms. Why don't we plan on meeting at four in the morning? We'll grab some coffee and a pastry and take a taxi to the ship."

The three men stood. They thanked Jean-Pierre. Clay exchanged addresses, and his cousin gave him a kiss on both cheeks, which would have surprised him if not for his French family in D'Hanis. The men separated and went to their respective rooms.

Clay was tired. When he walked into the large bathroom, a tub filled with hot water was waiting for him. He shook his head and looked around to ensure his privacy, then took his frock coat off, hanging it on the back of a chair. He pulled out the revolver and rubbed his stomach where the weapon had been chafing.

With only a single, dim lamp on in the room, he walked to the wide window that looked over the Gulf. Opening the drapes, he discovered the window was a door leading onto a balcony. He opened the door and stepped outside.

The moon was up, reflecting off the wide, unbroken expanse of water. It was impossible to tell where sky ended and ocean began. He stood entranced, feeling the moist breeze blowing in from the gulf and hearing the crash of breakers on the beach. His mind traveled ahead of him, creating questions.

What was he getting himself into? How would he fit in with the people of New York City, or Columbia College? Would the studies overwhelm him? Would he be a disappointment to Mr. O'Shea and his grandfather? He took a deep breath, listened to the waves breaking on the beach, and thought, *I'll do my best. That's all I can do.*

He turned back inside, leaving the balcony door and the drapes open to allow the cooling breezes to flow into his room. His only concern now was the nice hot bath waiting for him.

## 8

T he stranger stepped off the train from Dallas onto the Austin station platform, turned back to the steps, and helped an older lady down to the platform.

"Thank you, young man."

"My pleasure, ma'am. May I get you a carriage or escort you somewhere?"

"No, thank you. My son should be here shortly. May I?" She held out her hand, indicating the valise the man had carried down the steps, along with his own bag.

He handed it to her. She took the valise and moved inside the depot. He set his bag down, and took a moment to look around. He had a Western hat and boots, but his suit spelled Yankee. Three toughs who hung around the station when the trains arrived to torment those passengers who looked like easy marks, looked him over. The big man spotted them and drilled them with his light gray eyes. The leader spit, and they moved off to look for easier pickings.

The man thought, *It hasn't changed much.* Then he picked up his bag and headed for the Barlow Law and Land office.

It was late in the fall of the year, and there was a chill in the air, even in the early afternoon. Dust quickly coated his polished boots, blooming up from the dry street with each step. He finally reached the office and entered the building.

A clerk looked up to see a younger man approaching. The man had a friendly face, but there was something about the eyes and the set of his mouth, beneath the thick, well-groomed mustache that caused the clerk to cautiously ask, "May I help you, sir?"

"Yes. I'm looking for Senator Barlow."

"I'm sorry, sir. The senator is indisposed. May I perhaps take a message?"

"No. You may direct me to him."

"Sir? As I said, he is indisposed and is not taking visitors."

"He'll see me. Where is he?"

The clerk became flustered with the man's insistence. "Why, he is upstairs in his apartment. But wait—"

The clerk was talking to the man's back. The big man had spun around and was out the door before the clerk could finish his sentence. He turned and moved rapidly to the stairs, rushing up to the landing and pounding on the door. When the door did not open quickly enough to suit him, his big hand reached for the knob, just as the door jerked open.

"What's the hammering? The senator is—"

Raymond looked up at the man standing on the landing, and his eyes grew large with surprise. "We were expecting you, but not this soon. Come, the senator has been shot."

"Who's raising all the ruckus out there?" boomed from the senator's bedroom, just as the two men walked in.

The senator was propped up on pillows in bed, with papers scattered all around him, bandages across his chest peeking out from his nightshirt's collar. He lowered the paper he had been reading when Raymond led the way into the room. "Well, Raymond, who?"

He stopped when he saw the man behind Raymond. It was a face he would never forget, changed but yet the same.

"Clay?"

"Hello, Grandpa." Clay crossed the room in three long strides. He stopped at the side of his grandfather's bed and thrust out his hand.

The old man took it, fighting back tears that welled up in his eyes and threatened to break loose. Something that he hadn't done since his son and daughter-in-law were so brutally murdered. It took him a moment, but his self-control won. "Son, you're a sight for these old eyes." He took Clay's hand in both of his, wincing slightly from the pain in his chest. "You have no idea how good it is to see you. Are you hungry? Raymond can throw something together in the kitchen."

"I'd be glad to, Clay."

"Ray, if you don't mind, all I need is a glass of water. Its been a long, dry trip."

Raymond spun around and disappeared from the bedroom. The senator, after a long moment, released his hand, and Clay looked around the room. Finding a chair, he slid it up next to the bed and sat down. "What happened?"

"Somebody shot me. It was two—no, wait, three—weeks ago, right outside on the steps. I'd worked late in the office. It must have been close to nine. Raymond had already come down earlier to tell me supper was ready, but I had an important case I was working on and lost track of time. When I realized how late it was, I locked the door and headed up the stairs. About halfway up, I heard something and turned around to look. I imagine that must have saved my life."

Raymond came back in with a tray and set it on the side of the bed. A glass of milk and a thick roast beef sandwich rested on the tray, along with a glass of water and a quarter of an apple pie. "Never knowed you to turn down food. Thought you might be hungry."

Clay grinned at Ray. "Guess I've never been accused of being a picky eater. Thanks, Ray." He took a sip of the milk and picked up the sandwich and took a big bite. "That's good. Texas beef. I've missed that. Thanks, Ray."

"Can I finish here?" the senator said.

Ray turned and left the room, muttering something that was unintelligible.

"Anyway, whoever it was, and I think I know who that could be, took two shots at me, hitting me with both. Then he took off. Lucky for me, he didn't wait around to see how successful he was. He put two bullets in my back. One round was high, but the other just clipped my lung. It was touch and go for a while, maybe a week. But I've always been lucky.

"Now I just have to get out of this blasted bed. Raymond is worse than a nurse. I know because they had one here the first week. He hovers over me, making me take some of the most gosh-awful medicine you've ever tasted. So anyway, enough about me. Tell me about you. I didn't expect you back this year. Did you get finished?"

The senator took a deep breath.

Clay could tell that the excitement and the explanation of what had happened had sapped the man's strength. While his grandfather had been talking he had been eating and had finished his sandwich and half the pie. Between bites, he said, "That's a long story, Grandpa, and we have plenty of time for me to tell you everything. I just want you to know I'm back. I don't yet know what I'll be doing, but we can talk about that too." He finished the food, then stood and picked up the tray.

"You get some rest, and I'll be back later to fill you in."

The senator nodded. "That might be a good idea, Son. It's good to see you back in Texas." He closed his eyes and was immediately asleep.

Clay eased from the room and took the tray into the kitchen, setting it down on the counter. "Ray, you have any idea who could have done this?"

He nodded. "I have an idea, but I don't know for sure. The senator has been at odds for several years with a rancher between here and San Antonio. He fought a case in court against the man and won it. I'm surprised there hasn't been a shooting before now. Although, I always thought it would be face-to-face."

"Well, who is it?"

"Now, don't you go flying off the handle," Raymond said. "You've got too much at stake to do something stupid."

"I just want to talk to the sheriff, see if he has found out anything, or see what kind of leads he might have."

Raymond looked at him for a moment. Then nodded. "Like I said, he has a ranch, south of here, toward San Antonio. There was a lawsuit over water rights, and he lost. He killed the man that brought the lawsuit. He's not hanging from a rope or in prison, because it was a fair fight. He's been gunning for your grandfather for years. It looks like there'll be a gunfight every time the two of them meet on the street."

"I think I know him, a stout fella, two or three inches under six feet. Wears a white hat and has long gray hair."

"That's him. Name's Jedediah Jenkins. Has a fairly nice ranch, but when your grandpa won the water rights case against him, losing that water forced him to move almost a thousand head of cattle off the adjacent land. He was madder than a bee-stung bear. But like I said, I never pictured him as the kind of man to be a backshooter."

"I think I'll just ride down and ask him," Clay said.

"Best not do that. He's got some cowboys that are about as mean as he is. Could be dangerous. In fact, why don't I ride down there with you?"

Clay shook his head. "No, you need to be here to look out for Grandpa. If you weren't here, it wouldn't surprise me if the scum that did this made another try."

Raymond thought about it for a moment. "I guess you're right. I just hate to see you go down there by yourself."

"Don't worry about me. I can take care of myself."

"You're probably right. We heard back here about the attempted train robbery. I guess those boys picked on the wrong train."

"My old stuff still in the bedroom?"

"Yep, though I don't know if it'll fit you."

"Ray, I haven't changed much."

"Don't kid yourself, Clay. You've filled out quite a bit in these two years, but don't listen to me. Go see for yourself."

Clay went into the bedroom where he had stayed before. He walked to the dresser and opened a drawer. There were his clothes, clean, folded, and ready for him. He took off his frock coat and unhitched the shoulder holster. Thanks to Mike, he had learned the convenience of a shoulder holster. It sure beat having a gun barrel shoved by your leg, the grips poking you in the belly anytime you tried to sit down.

He laid the shoulder holster on the bed, pulled his boots off, undressed, and pulled on the britches. They fit perfectly, just like he had never left. He picked up the black-and-white checked shirt and slid it over his head, but couldn't pull it down over his arms and chest. He wrestled with it for a moment, then pulled it off. He stood there for a moment looking into the mirror. His muscles rippled across his chest. To him, his biceps and chest didn't look any bigger than they had when he left, but the shirt proved him wrong. The clothes he had purchased in New York had been tailored, so he wouldn't have noticed the gradual changes. He put the Eastern shirt back on and slid the Western brown vest over it. He couldn't button the top buttons, but that was fine. He'd wear it open. Then he stomped his boots back on.

Opening his bag, he took out the Roper and his gunbelt. With the rag he carried, he gave the Roper a good wipe down and checked its loads, then pulled out the bag of shells and laid them next to the shotgun. Picking up the gunbelt, he swung it around his waist, buckling it tight. He pulled each Smith & Wesson Model 3 from its respective holster, broke it open and checked the loads. Closing them, he spun the cylinders, dropped each into its holster, and drew several times. During those lonely times at the ranch, he had perfected drawing and shooting with his left hand. He wasn't quite as fast with his left, but he was deadly accurate— that's what counted.

Clay pulled the dark brown frock coat from his traveling bag. It would do. He looked at it for a moment, then took it off and laid it across the bag. Now, he picked up the shoulder holster with the pocket pistol, hung it across his shoulders, and fastened the buckle. He had gotten used to having it. It wouldn't hurt. He laughed to himself. He had enough hardware to start a war. He picked up his hat and put it on.

He man walked out of the bedroom to find Raymond sitting on the divan reading the paper. "Ray, where's Blue, my saddle, and all my gear?"

Ray looked up from the paper, precisely folded it into thirds, and laid it on the side table. "When I picked up Blue, I left everything at the livery. Frank has it all, saddlebags, rifle, bedroll and slicker. Tell him who you are, and you can pick everything up. If you want to get Blue, he's lording it out at Jethro's ranch, The Bar Three. He's the one your grandpa was telling you about, Jethro Bates. He has a few head of cattle, but mostly he raises horses, good horses. This depression ain't hurt him a bit. Everybody needs a good horse.

"He's not but about ten miles out of town, to the west. If you were headin' back out to your place, you'd go right close to it. I imagine ole Blue'll be glad to see you."

"Thanks, Ray. No more than I'll be to see him. Tell Grandpa I'll be back in a few days. Probably shouldn't say anything to him about where I've gone. I don't want to upset him."

"Shaw, boy. You think I could keep anything from that old

codger? He'll wring it out of me before you're astride Blue. He'll be fine. You just watch yourself."

Clay said, "I'll do that," and stepped out the door. From his position on the landing, he could see over most of the buildings. The afternoon sun cast shadows on the eastern slopes of the hills. A light west wind brought the cedar smell to him off those hills. It's good to be back, he thought, as he descended the stairs and stepped out, stretching his long legs toward the stables.

He walked into the livery as Platt walked out of his office.

"Can I help you?"

"Mr. Platt, don't know if you remember me, but my name's Clay Barlow."

"Senator Barlow's grandson."

"Yep, that's me. I need to pick up my gear and rent a good horse from you. Might be gone for several days."

"Sure. I've got your gear in the office, and I owe you some money. When you left your horse here, you paid me for two weeks. He only stayed for three days. Ray picked him up and took him out to Jethro's. Let me get that for you, and then we'll get you a horse."

"Thanks, Mr. Platt, but that won't be necessary. You never know when I might be short. I'll just bank it until then."

"Well," Platt said, drawing the word out, "I can do that, but I sure wouldn't want it to be said that I ever tried to cheat a man. No, sir, I wouldn't want that at all."

Clay nodded. "I understand. If you'd feel better about paying me back, then that's fine, but I was very serious. A man never knows when the tide might turn."

"That's true. You can plan on leaving your animals here anytime you like. Now let's find you a good piece of horseflesh."

They walked out to the corral. Several horses stood three-legged in the afternoon sun. Occasionally, they'd swish their tails to chase the flies away.

"Now that buckskin gelding's a stayer. He's a cutter too. He can turn on a dime and give you nine cents change. You'll find him a little feisty. Hasn't been run for a while." A grin tugged at the corners of his mouth, but he managed to control it. "That'd be a buck a day."

"Dang," Clay said. "Mr. Platt. I just want to rent him, not buy him. If I kept him for a year, I would've spent enough to buy two good horses."

Platt turned and spit. "Tell you what I'll do. Since you're the senator's grandson, I'll let you have him for eighty cents a day and throw in some oats to take with you."

Clay frowned. "Look here, I just got back from the East and I'm danged near broke. I hate spending so much, but I'll give you seventy cents a day, if you'll throw in those oats."

"Boy, I'm gonna be losing money on this blasted horse at that price. I never seen anyone drive such a hard bargain, just to rent a horse. You've got yore own blanket, saddle, and bridle, so I ain't making any money there." Platt kicked a horse apple across the corral, making the horses jump and look at him indignantly for disturbing them. "Here's what I'll do. Now this is my best offer. I'll toss in some oats, and I'll let you have that fine piece of horse flesh for seventy-five cents a day. That's my bottom offer."

Clay stuck out his hand. "Deal."

Platt tilted his head sideways so he could look up at Clay out of one eye. "Why do I feel like I've come in last at a one-legged sack race?" He put out his hand and took Clay's. "Deal," he said and turned his head and spit. "Yore stuff is at the back of my office. You want to go get it? I'll get this jughead roped and ready." He picked up a lasso from the corral fence and swung out a loop as Clay went back to the office to get his gear.

Clay had saddled the buckskin, slid the Roper in one scabbard, and the 1866 Winchester in the other. "Thanks, Mr. Platt."

Platt walked over to the gate and flipped the gate loop off the fence, holding the gate so that only the buckskin could get out.

"Shore nuff," he said," hiding a big grin as Clay swung his leg over the back of the buckskin.

The horse stood still for a moment, then bowed his back, went straight up, and came down on stiff legs. Clay could feel the jar all the way to his head. Then the horse started crow hopping around the corral.

"Ride 'im, boy," Platt shouted.

Passersby stopped to watch the entertainment. Clay stuck to the buckskin. It felt good. This was one of the things he had missed while in New York. The horse finally worked out the vinegar, then Clay walked him to the gate. "Thanks, Mr. Platt."

The older man grinned. "Anytime. He is a little feisty, like I said, but he's got a lot of bottom."

Clay nodded and trotted the horse down the street, turning him west on Pecan. Once over the creek bridge, he leaned over the buckskin, and nudged him in the flanks. "Let's go, boy. Let's see what you've got."

# 9

The buckskin slowed to a natural walk after running for three miles. Clay rocked along, enjoying the sights of the hill country. He had been gone for almost three years. It was good to be back, although he wished he'd gotten a heavier coat. The medium-weight frock wasn't built for this kind of travel. He'd get him a heavier coat when he returned to Austin.

He rode steadily west. The foothills reached up to the sun as it drifted lower in the west. He was hoping he'd reach Williamson Creek before dark. Time drifted by, and, rounding a bend in the road, he could see the dark outline of trees ahead. That would be the creek. Clay nudged the buckskin into a lope, then slowed him as they neared the creek. He kept a close lookout. Not everyone you met out here was friendly. Entering the trees, he slowed the buckskin more, to a walk. The pecan trees were losing their leaves and dropping nuts all over the ground. The sound of the shells crunching under the horse's hooves would carry quite a distance.

He rode the horse down the slope to the creek. Once in the water, he stopped and allowed the animal to drink. It was almost dark under the thick stand of pecan and oak trees that followed along the shallow stream. The few trees that had completely lost their leaves stood like stark skeletons against the purple sky.

After allowing the horse to finish drinking, Clay started him out of the water and up the sloping western bank. Before topping out again, he stopped, just so he could see over the rise. Being late in the day, deer were scattered on the narrow flat, cropping at the thick covering of chickweed. He watched them for a few moments and then eased up the crest and out of the protection of the creek. Immediately, heads popped up from the chickweed, and the deer watched him intently. Assessing he was no threat, they went back to feeding, occasionally looking up to watch his progress. He rode out of the flat and up the hill, watching for the turnoff.

He caught a glimpse of a faint trail leading off to the south. Stopping the buckskin, he assessed it. The trail was as Ray had described, faint, running south from the road, just east of a lone red oak. He turned the buckskin down the trail and started him at a fast walk. The ranch should be no more than a mile from the road.

Sure enough, just as it was getting almost too dark to make out the dim path, he saw a light through the scrub oaks. He rode into a clearing that started roughly seventy yards or so from the house. The clearing was a rough circle, with the house, corral and barn, and bunkhouse, located in the middle. It was dark now, so Clay stopped at the edge of the clearing.

"Hello, the house," he called. This was Texas, not New York City. Out here in the hill country it was necessary to announce yourself. Folks, for good reason, could be almighty edgy at night.

The door of the ranch house opened, and light flooded the yard. A man stepped onto the porch. "Ride on in and state your business." The Winchester cradled in the crook of his left arm was handy for quick use.

Clay rode up to the cedar hitching rail, just to the right of the front door. "Howdy. Name's Clay Barlow. Reckon you're keeping a horse of mine. Ray Coleman brought it out a couple of years ago."

Clay heard a long, loud whinny from the barn. The man on the porch let out a big belly laugh that echoed across the hillside.

"I think Blue heard ya," the man said. "Let me grab a lantern, and we'll mosey out to the barn, and you two can get reacquainted.

"My name's Jethro," he said as he stepped out of the house carrying a kerosene lantern."

Clay swung down from the buckskin and, led the horse, stopping at the trough for another drink, then entered the big barn.

"Here," the man said, "let me take care of your horse. You go say howdy. I think he's anxious to see you."

Blue's head was sticking out of the third stall, his neck stretched toward Clay. The roan nickered a greeting as Clay walked up and scratched the big horse between his ears. "How you doing, boy? It's been a long time."

Jethro had pulled the gear off the buckskin after leaning the rifle and shotgun in a corner. "Lot of hardware you're carrying here."

Clay turned to look at Jethro and the buckskin. "Times are when it comes in handy.

"I can take care of the buckskin, you don't have to do that."

"Son, I hanker after working with horses. Been doing it since I was knee-high to a grasshopper, and I reckon I'll be doing it just before they toss dirt in my face. You relax yourself and take care of ole Blue. He's missed you.

"Looks like this is one of Platt's horses. I'm headed into Austin in a couple of days. You want I should return him for you?"

"I'd appreciate you doing that, if it wouldn't be too much trouble."

"No trouble."

Clay went under the rope tied across the stall. His hands traveled across the horse's withers and down his back. Then he reached down and pulled up Blue's front hoof and examined the leg. He moved around the horse to check all of his legs, arriving back on the other side of the horse's neck. He continued patting and rubbing. The horse had turned his head back and was snuffling Clay's coat pocket.

"You looking for something, boy?" He pulled an apple out of his pocket and handed it to Blue. The horse took it and noisily crunched, making it quickly disappear. He immediately stuck his nose over by the coat pocket again.

Clay laughed. "Don't get greedy, Blue. That's all there is for now. You ready for a ride? You look like you've been well taken care of."

Jethro was just finishing rubbing down the buckskin. He put some oats in the feed bin and walked around the end of the stall, fastening the rope. "Exercised him every week. He's in good shape. You got you a strong, mature horse that has quite a few years left, lot of bottom in him."

Clay rubbed Blue's nose one more time, then swung under the rope, facing Jethro. "I appreciate you taking such good care of him. He's a fine horse."

"Been my pleasure. Now, why don't you toss your stuff in the bunkhouse and meet me up at the house. I think the boys may have saved you a piece of venison."

"Thank you, Mr. Bates. I'll be right up."

"It's Jethro."

Clay nodded, grabbing his saddlebags, guns, and bedroll, and headed for the bunkhouse. He walked in and looked around. There was a big pot-bellied stove sitting in the middle of the one-room structure, with wood stacked in the box next to it. Three bunks lined the west wall, and three the east. He had his choice, since only two bunks were being used. He picked one, set his gear on the bunk, then headed to the house. He was mighty hungry.

He stepped into the house and, as he was removing his hat, was hit full in the face by the aroma of fresh fried venison.

"Come on in, boy," Jethro said. "Grab a chair. Clay, this here is Mrs. Bates." Jethro indicated the gray-haired lady with the kind face, working at the stove.

Clay nodded to her. "Pleasure to meet you, ma'am."

She smiled, then said, "Sit down young man. You don't want this venison to get cold."

Clay pulled out a rough-cut cedar chair from the long table and sat.

"Those three towheads at the end of the table are Joe, Jack, and Jim."

The three boys nodded to Clay, the youngest grinning, while the older two each gave him a more serious look with their nods.

Jethro continued. "These two fellers been with me darn near as long as I can remember. This 'un"—he pointed out the older man—"is Ab Ivy, and the one next to him is Sheldon Wells. Everybody calls him Shelly."

Before Clay could say anything, Mrs. Bates set a big plate of venison and mashed potatoes in front of him. She put a large glass of milk next to his plate and said, "Biscuits are on the table. Don't be shy."

He smiled at her, reaching for a couple of biscuits. "When it comes to eating, ma'am, I've never been accused of that."

Mrs. Bates returned to the table and sat at the opposite end from Jethro. She watched Clay as he worked through the venison and potatoes. Finally, she asked, "Ray came out a couple of months ago. He was telling us how you were finishing up your schoolin' in New York City. What was it like back there?"

Clay reached for another biscuit, put it on his plate, and leaned back in his chair. "Well, ma'am, it is nothing like I expected. Sure, I thought it would be big, but I had no idea. It was nothing to see buildings of three and four stories high. Before I left, they had just finished the New York Tribune building that was nine stories up, and that didn't include the clock steeple that towered above the building. I read, counting the steeple, that building was two hundred and sixty feet high!"

"Shaw," Ab Ivy said. "I ain't never heard of no building being that tall. Why, it would fall down, just from it's own bigness."

"Ab Ivy, you just shut your face," Mrs. Bates shouted down from the end of the table. "Let the boy talk." She shot her attention back to Clay. "What'd the women wear?"

"Ma'am, as I was saying, that city is hard to imagine. But it wasn't just the building, it was the people. I've never seen so many people crammed into a small space. Around eight o'clock in the morning, people were shoulder to shoulder going to work."

Clay paused for a moment, took a sip of his milk, and then continued. "I can't say I know a lot about women's clothing. I'll tell you this, they are wearing a lot of silk and light wool, except in the winter, when they go to a heavier wool. One thing you can't miss"—Clay looked around the table at the men—"is the big bustle. They've gotten huge."

The boys at the end of the table, where their mom sat, started giggling. She glared at them for a moment and silence quickly returned.

"Anyway, they're wearing a lot of browns, yellows, and light green. Some of them are might pretty."

Ab Ivy, with a glint of humor in his eye, spoke up again. "You talking about the dresses or the girls?"

At that question, the boys broke out laughing.

Mrs. Bates glared at him. "Ab, if you were younger, I'd send you off to bed right now."

"Yes'm, you just might, but I ain't," he answered. After which he wiped up some gravy with a biscuit and stuffed it in his mouth.

Jethro cleared his throat, and everyone looked up at him. "Clay, how's the depression going back there?"

"Hard, Jethro. There are thousands of people out of work. Bread lines stretch around the block. Businesses have shut down.

A lot of folks, if they have any money, are outfitting and heading west. It's sad to see all the kids on the streets. Several organizations have banded together to help them, but it appears to be an impossible undertaking.

"I understand it's been hard here in Texas?"

"Sure has," Jethro replied. "Lot of folks have lost their ranches, a whole passel of banks have gone bust. We were luckier than most. When Ray came out with Blue, right after you left, he let us in on what was coming. We had a note at the bank but was able to sell some stock and pay it off. We've weathered pretty fair."

Everyone had finished eating. "Boys, help me with the dishes," Mrs. Bates said, as she stood.

The men also stood, and Clay said, "Thank you, ma'am. That's the first supper I've had back in Texas. It was mighty good."

Mrs. Bates actually blushed. "Why, thank you, Clay. You come by anytime."

Jethro and Clay moved to the fireplace, while Ab and Shelton said their goodnights and headed for the bunkhouse. The fireplace felt good on this cold night. Clay turned to Jethro. "I'm going to head on back to the bunkhouse. I've got a long ride in the morning, but I sure appreciate your hospitality. I'll be leaving early, so I need to settle up with you for keeping Blue."

Jethro nodded. "All settled. I've been looking for a long time to pay back the senator, and Blue weren't no trouble."

"Jethro," Clay said, "I appreciate your kindness, but I take care of my own debts. Now, how much do I owe you?"

After studying Clay for a long moment, Jethro said, "I reckon you do, Son. Why don't we make it fifty bucks? That should do it."

Clay shook his head. "I've never had such a hard time paying a man in my life. It should be five or six times that much."

Jethro thought for a few moments. "Son, make it one fifty, but I'll not take a dime more."

Clay took three fifty-dollar gold pieces from his coat's inside pocket and dropped them into Jethro's hand. He grinned down at him and said, "You drive a hard bargain, Jethro." Then he shook the man's hand. "Thanks for taking care of Blue. That horse means a lot to me."

"Anytime."

"Well, I've got to get some sleep. I feel like I've been riding a train for the past month." He headed for the door. "Thanks again, ma'am. Nice to meet you, boys."

He stepped out onto the porch, caught his boot on a loose board, and slammed the solid cedar door closed as he was falling. At that same instant, the slap of a bullet hitting the door behind him was followed by the echoing roar of a rifle from the blackness beyond the house. Clay lay prone on the porch. Cedar splinters stung the back of his neck.

The lights inside the ranch house went out. Clay remained motionless, listening. He wanted to move, but it would take a while for his eyes to adjust. He felt sure the shooter was at least seventy yards away, because that was the distance that had been cleared off by Jethro.

"You all right, Clay?"

He didn't answer. He wanted the shooter to think a hit had been scored. The forty-four was in his left hand. *I must have slipped the rawhide and drawn while I was falling*, he thought. *I didn't even notice. I guess all that practice paid off.*

Just as he started to make a move, he heard hoofbeats to the north. Coming off the porch in a run, he raced to the edge of the trees. Once protected by the dark, dense cedar, he stopped and listened. Only the faint sound of gradually fading hoofbeats came to his ears. He waited for a few more moments, then called back to the house. "I'm fine. Sounds like he's gone."

Jethro came outside, rifle in hand. "You all right?"

"Yes, sir, just fine. Could you bring a light? I'd like to look around."

Clay stepped out from the tree as Ab and Shelton came running up. "Why don't you boys hold up. When Jethro gets out here, I'd like to look around, see if I see anything. Too many of us might wipe out the tracks."

"Good thinking," Jethro said, walking up with a lantern. "Boys, why don't you go on back to the bunkhouse. We got it here."

The two men turned and headed back to the warmth of the bunkhouse. Jethro had moved a short distance back into the trees. He bent over and picked something up. "Look at this, Clay. Looks like from one of those newfangled Winchesters."

Clay walked over and took the cartridge from Jethro. "You're right. That's a .44-40 centerfire. As far as I know, the only rifle that fires that is the Winchester 73. Not many of those around these parts, yet. Good rifle. I wouldn't mind having one. I just wonder who could be after me? I haven't even been back a full day."

The thought of his grandfather shot and lying in bed came to mind. "Jethro, back in Austin, the senator has been shot."

"What? Is he alive?"

"Yes. He's alive. He was lucky, but they shot him twice in the back. He's still in bed, but doing well. Ray is taking good care of him."

"Who in this world would shoot the senator?" Jethro said.

Then, in the light of the lantern, Clay saw the man's expression change, and a knowing look crossed his face. "Do you have any ideas who could have shot my grandfather?"

"Let me think on it." Jethro leaned over with the lantern and started moving slowly down the trail. "Look here." He pointed to the hoofprints in the dirt alongside the trail.

Clay moved up to the prints. Even in the faint light of the lantern, they were clear, fresh.

"Look, boy." Jethro pointed to one of the tracks. "The left fore hoof. Looks like there's some kind of old cut to the right of the frog. Must've been pretty bad as big as it is." Jethro continued to follow the tracks with the lantern, Clay alongside. The two men stopped and moved back to where the horse had been standing, careful to remain clear of the tracks.

"You notice how wide those prints are?" Clay asked.

"Yep, a deep-chested horse, big. Funny thing, looka here. That feller done mounted from the off side. Don't see that too often. And look at his tracks. Those boots are round-toed, with a thick, short heel. Not something you'd see a cowboy wearing.

"I had a thought of who might've shot your grandpap, but this don't mesh with my thinking. Course, could be two different men."

Clay and Jethro started back toward the bunkhouse. "Jethro, who do you have in mind?"

The two men reached the bunkhouse and stepped inside.

## 10

The pot-bellied stove was giving off welcome heat in the cold bunkhouse. Ab and Shelly were seated near their bunks at a small table, playing a game of checkers, their rifles leaning against the wall but within reach.

"Find out anything, Boss?" Shelly asked.

"Big horse. Has an old injury on his left fore hoof to the right of the frog. Funny thing is the rider. He ain't wearing proper boots. Looks more like sodbuster boots, with a round toe and low heels."

"I'll tell you what," Clay said, "he may be wearing farmer's boots, but he can shoot. The only reason that bullet missed my head was my stumble."

"Even then, it ain't missed by much," Ab said. "Look at yore hat."

Clay pulled his Stetson off and took a deep breath. His hat was sporting a hole just below the edge of the crease, near the top of the crown. He turned it around and looked at the exit. The exit hole was a little lower than the front, indicating his head was tilted in the fall when the bullet went through his hat.

The men had gotten up from their checkers game and were gathered around Clay, looking at his hat.

"Whoo-wee," Jethro said. "Clay, you was just about a goner. If you hadn't of stumbled, boy, why—"

"Believe me," Clay said. "I've got the picture. That fellow ruined a good hat. He owes me."

Ab and Shelly returned to their checkers game, and Clay tossed the hat over on his bunk. He turned back to Jethro. "You said you had someone in mind for Grandpa's shooter?"

"Let's sit." After pulling their chairs up close to the stove, Jethro said, "There was a man, a few years back, that had a lawsuit over water rights."

"Jedediah Jenkins," Clay said. "Ray told me."

"Did he tell you that before the lawsuit, he and the senator were long-time friends?" At the look on Clay's face he continued. "I thought not. They'd been friends for a long time. In fact, all three of them, the senator, Jenkins, and Ray, were running buddies for a while, after the war for Texas independence. But the lawsuit sure ripped that blanket. Reckon I never knowed a man to be so mad. I guess the loss of the water rights tore Jed up, and to have it come from a friend made it a mighty nasty pill to swallow. Why, to this day, when they meet on the street, he'll cross over."

"I saw that. A little over two years ago, when I was about to leave for New York, Jenkins was coming toward us in Austin. Grandpa tensed up, in fact he adjusted his gun, but Jenkins made no move other than to cross the street."

"Yessir. That's what I mean. Jed's been festering over that loss for years. I've been waiting for him to blow his top and come after your grandpa. But he ain't never worn no sodbuster's boots, and he has no reason to shoot you. Also, it's hard for me to picture Jedediah shooting any man in the back. He's the type of feller that meets a man face-to-face."

Clay thought for a moment, then said, "That's where I'm

headed. I want to talk to him myself. If it was him, he needs to be stopped. No one gets to backshoot my grandpa and get away with it."

"You ride easy, Clay. Other than the sodbusters, he's well thought of by the folks down that way. His men like him, too. He's bought horses from me. Strikes me as an honest feller, hard but honest. I think it's a case of two good men gettin' crossways."

"Didn't that good man kill the man he lost the lawsuit to?"

Jethro nodded. "He did, but that weren't all his fault. The other feller goaded him into it, claiming Jenkins was a liar and a cheat, and he said the truth come out in court. Well, if you knowed Jedediah Jenkins, you'd knowed he wouldn't stand for that kind of talk. The two men pulled leather in the saloon. Jedediah was faster."

"I'll talk to him," Clay said. He yawned and stretched. "I'm thinking I'd better hit the sack. It'll be an early morning."

"For all of us," Jethro said. He nodded at the cowboys, who were putting up the checkers and getting ready for bed and walked out the door.

Clay moved the rifle and shotgun from the bed and laid his bedroll across the top. He pulled his boots off and took off his gunbelt, hanging it on the end of the bunk. The cowboys had noticed when he had taken the frock coat off and exposed the shoulder holster. He pulled the pocket pistol from the holster and hung the rig next to the gunbelt.

"Ain't seen a rig like that before," Ab said, indicating the shoulder holster.

"Picked that up in New York. Folks don't go around heeled, least not so a man can tell. I sort of got used to it. Hate to get rid of it.

"See you boys in the morning," Clay said, as he started to swing his legs into bed.

Shelly had been looking at Clay off and on the whole evening. "Clay, you mind if I ask you a question?"

"Ask away."

"There's a Clay Barlow that has a ranch north of Uvalde. Would that be you?"

"I reckon so, Shelly."

"Would it of been you that happened up on that stage robbery, out west of Austin, a couple of years ago?"

"Yeah, that was me."

Shelly leaned forward. "You didn't happen to get a look at the owlhoots that done that holdup?"

"No. I didn't." The realization came to Clay that Shelly could be the brother of the man riding shotgun, Cleatus Wells. "Was Cleatus your brother?"

"Nope, but he was a mighty fine cousin. I've been hankering to know who killed him for these past two years. I even run into Whip Bingham and talked to him. 'Bout all he could tell me, was that the man who shot Cleatus was really fast and had hair so blond it was almost white."

Almost white, Clay thought. Whip didn't tell me that. He just said he was blond. That reminds me of the fellow that almost drew on me in Brackett. It was when I was hunting the killers of my folks. What was his name? He was the son of the marshal. Davis. That was it, Cotton Davis. His hair was so blond it was almost white. There can't be two men like that.

"Think about somebody?" Shelly asked.

"What? What'd you say, Shelly?"

"There for a minute, it looked like you was thinking. Did you think of somebody?"

"No . . . No, I was just thinking about the holdup. Sorry about your cousin, Shelly. But boys, I've got to get some sleep. See you in the morning." With his last words, he swung into bed, and pulled his blanket up over his shoulders.

∾

WHEN CLAY OPENED HIS EYES, it was still dark. There was a little moonlight seeping into the bunkhouse, and he could make out Ab, in his red long johns and boots, tossing kindling on top of the hot coals in the pot-bellied stove. He swung out of bed, grabbed his pants, and slipped them on. Next, he stomped his feet back into his boots, slipped the shoulder holster on, and shoving the pocket pistol back in place, fastened his gunbelt.

"Morning, Ab," Clay said.

Ab mumbled some unintelligible word and set a coffeepot on top of the stove. The fire had started, so he picked up several more pieces of firewood and tossed them into the stove. Shelly had gotten out of bed, slipped his boots on and headed outside. A few minutes later he was back.

Clay pulled his coat on, picked up his guns and gear, and headed for the door. "Adios," he said. He stepped to the door, cracked it, and looked around. It was still dark, and Clay felt naked coming out of the bunkhouse. He headed for the barn.

Blue had heard him and was looking toward the door when Clay walked in. He unfastened the rope across the stall and led the horse out into the center of the barn. There, he saddled him up, slid his rifle and shotgun into their scabbards, and swung up onto the blue roan. Just as his right foot hit the stirrup, Jethro walked in. He had something wrapped in a towel.

"Figgered you'd be heading out early. I'm like you, not much for goodbyes. The missus saw you go into the barn and whipped you up a little something to keep you going."

"Thanks, Jethro. Tell her I'm much obliged."

"I'll do that, Son. I sure will. Now, do you know where you're going?"

"I'm headed south, looking to find the ranch of Jedediah Jenkins. I should hit it before I reach San Antonio."

"Let me give you a mite finer directions. You're looking for the Lazy J. Leaving here, head a little west of south. You'll cross Slaughter, Bear, and Onion Creeks. Next, you'll come up to the

Rio Blanco. Cross it and bear a little more west. You'll see high bluffs ahead, four, five hundred feet. Just before you get to those bluffs, you should hit the Lazy J. Now, you stay safe and keep your eyes open. I doubt that shooter from last night will give up, whoever he is."

"Thanks again. You've been a big help." Clay leaned over and shook the man's hand, then straightened and nudged Blue through the barn door and turned left, headed southwest. "Adios, Jethro."

Dawn was breaking, bringing life to the countryside. Blue stepped gingerly in the cool morning. No sooner had they moved back into the trees and brush, than a covey of quail burst in an explosive launch from under the horse's front hooves. He shied to the right as the birds, surprised in their ground roost, flew in all different directions. Clay fought him for a moment, got the horse under control, then leaned forward and patted Blue's neck, talking to him. "Easy, boy. You've had scarier things than a covey of bobwhites happen to you. Although, they scared me some too." He chuckled to himself and scanned the broken hills. They were covered with tall bunch grasses, interspersed with thick islands of ashe juniper and oak, the trees making persistent claim to their rocky real estate in these rugged hills.

He scanned the slopes around him, checking his back trail, determined to see the backshooter first. The sun had leaped well above the flatter land to the east, bringing welcome warmth to the chilly morning. "Great country, Blue. It's sure good to be back." He, like many riders, often talked to his horse.

Since there was no trail in the direction he was going, he worked his way through the rocky terrain, staying in shadow as much as possible. At this speed, it would take him all day to reach Jenkin's Lazy J. If he was lucky.

Though his eyes were alert, his mind wandered back to New York. It had been a good time for him. The crush of people had initially assailed his senses, but in no time he grew used to the loss of personal space. Mr. O'Shea had taught him much. He had learned from the classes he took at Columbia, but his real education came from dealing with O'Shea's business and clients. Investing had been a foreign language to him when he first arrived, but he quickly began to learn the nuances and, being a voracious reader, developed an uncanny ability to predict what the market would do.

Mike provided a training he hadn't expected. He taught Clay the sweet science of boxing. Clay took to it like a bird dog to hunting. For him, it came naturally.

Over the next two years, Mike, along with some of his friends, taught Clay the ins and outs of not just boxing, but skull and knuckle fighting, back-alley survival. Clay even earned a few dollars in the ring, never losing a fight. He might have continued, but L.M. found out and put a stop to it.

The battles in the ring were refreshingly clean compared with some of the legal battles he learned to fight. It was during his training that his love of the law began to wane. Oh, he still believed in justice, now even more, but too much of what he had seen, both in school and in the trenches of Mr. O'Shea's office, left him feeling like he needed to take a bath. He was having doubts about being a lawyer. Maybe he was more effective on the point of the spear, as a Ranger.

The sun had long passed its zenith. Shadows were beginning to lengthen. He had already crossed the three creeks Jethro had told him about and was watching ahead for the Blanco river. He had kept a sharp lookout for the backshooter, but had seen nothing, and was still alive. He eased Blue through a notch in the hill and found himself staring down on the Blanco.

Here was one of the reasons he loved the hill country. Many rivers and streams in Texas tended to be muddy or dark. Not so here. The clean water, originating from springs back up in the hills, and flowing through limestone, had a clear green-blue cast to it, and the water was always cool, even in the hottest summer.

He admired the view a while longer, then urged Blue down to the tree line paralleling the river on both sides. He pulled Blue up alongside a hackberry tree and stopped. The tree was covered with red, ripe hackberries. He ate a few. A little dry but sweet. Moving deeper into the trees, he stopped next to a low-limbed pecan that was still clinging to some of its fruit. Clay popped a couple of pecans out of their husks, cracked them against each other, and picked the meat out. This was a bountiful time of year.

A memory flashed of the times when he and his ma would go down to the Frio. He would climb the pecan trees and jump on the bigger limbs. The nuts would rain down. They had spent many an afternoon picking up pecans and filling empty potato sacks. Sometimes the Hewitts would join them, and they would have a picnic.

Clay finished the pecans and eased down to the river's edge. It was shallow here, with a small sandbar. He let Blue walk into the water, stand, and drink. At the horse's first steps into the water, the fish dashed away, clearly visible, coming from under and around the bigger rocks that lay on the bottom.

After Blue finished, they crossed the Blanco and climbed the opposite hillside. Once in the shade of a large oak, Clay dismounted and allowed the animal to munch on the bunch grass. Cattle were grazing across the open patches, content to fill their bellies this fall afternoon. He pulled his binoculars from his saddlebags and examined the cliffs behind the next hills. That was what Jethro had been talking about. He wasn't far from the Lazy J and his confrontation with Jenkins. Nothing in sight but cattle, he stowed the binoculars back in the saddlebag, fastened it, and swung up onto Blue.

They eased through the hills, keeping a lookout for any movement. What was it Pa used to say? "Complacent travel could be hazardous to a man's health." That was sure a fact in this country. He topped the last hill and looked across a pretty valley. It was probably two miles wide and covered in grass. This time of year the grass was brown, but still nutritious for livestock. Cattle covered the valley, feeding leisurely in the sun. To the north there was an unusual stand of trees. Big live oak and pecans, maybe a red oak or two. Behind the trees he could see smoke rising in the almost calm air.

He turned and pulled the binoculars out again. Close study allowed him to see glimpses of broken outlines of buildings. Blue's head jerked up and he looked behind him. Clay heard hooves scraping against rocks. There were at least two horses. Looping the binoculars over the the saddle horn, he reached for the Roper.

"Probably a good idea to leave that gun in the scabbard, Pard-ner," a coarse voice said.

## 11

Clay looked over his right shoulder. A man stood next to a large boulder, his rifle trained on him. About that time another man rode up from his left, leading a horse.

The man on the ground said, "Get a nice view of the ranch? Them glasses sure help, don't they?"

"What'd you catch here, Dutch?" the mounted cowboy said.

Clay had said nothing. He started to turn Blue where he could see the man on the ground without twisting around.

The man called Dutch waved his rifle barrel. "Whoa there, Mister. Why don't you just keep facing west. We'll be headed that way shortly. Heck, looks like I caught a big ole snoop. You know, like them peepin' Toms you read about in the city?"

"I'm not snooping," Clay said. "I'm just trying to find the Lazy J."

"You shore nuff found it, Snoop," Dutch said. "Heck, bring my horse over here. Let's get him down to the ranch and let Mr. Jenkins have a chat with him. He likes snoops, wouldn't you say?"

Heck guided the horses over to Dutch, released the reins to Dutch's horse, and covered Clay with his sixgun. "Why, I reckon he does. He's got himself a special place to bury snoops. So, Mr. Snoop, you got a name?"

"The name is Clay Barlow. I've got a ranch west of here on the Frio."

"Well, I'll be danged!" Dutch said. "A real gunfighter. Keep him covered, Heck. This feller's supposed to be faster than greased lightning. Hand over your guns, Del Rio."

Clay turned in the saddle so that he could look into Dutch's eyes. "I don't like that name."

"He don't like that name, Dutch. You best be careful. He is dan-ger-ous. Yes sirree. Like Dutch said, Mister, hand over your pistols, slow like."

Clay grasped the two Smith & Wesson's with his thumb and forefinger of each hand and slipped them from his holsters. Dutch eased up close enough that he could take the revolvers.

"Okay, Del Rio, let's head on into the ranch. Mr. Jenkins will be tickled to meet you."

Things are going from bad to worse, Clay thought. He rode forward and put Blue into a lope. His move surprised the two cowboys. Dutch was still trying to get the two revolvers in his saddlebags.

"Get on after him, Heck. I'll be along shortly."

When Clay saw Heck draw within a length, he nudged Blue in the flanks, leaned forward, and said, "Let's run, Blue."

The horse leaped forward. Heck was again surprised, and the big roan quickly pulled away from him. Dutch was bringing up the distant rear.

Clay knew it was dangerous to approach the ranch house like this. Some itchy-fingered cowboy could loose a round at him. With the first shot, everyone would turn loose. He turned down the wide path to the ranch house. Big sycamore trees overhung the road, keeping it shaded most of the year. He raced into the ranch yard, the south wind blowing the dust away from the house, and covering Heck and Dutch. Jed

Jenkins walked onto the big veranda, as cowhands came trotting from the corral, barn, and bunkhouse, to see the excitement.

"Thanks for covering my rear, boys," Clay said to the two stragglers as they finally pulled up next to him. "Mr. Jenkins, how do you do? I am Clay Barlow."

A look of surprise crossed Jenkins' face.

Heck blurted out, "We caught him snooping around the eastern edge of the valley, Mr. Jenkins. Thought we ought to bring him to see you."

Jenkins' frown was so intense, it caused the two thick, white eyebrows above his hard hazel eyes to come together, forming one long white line. "Looks like he brought you two to the ranch. Not the other way around. Makes me feel real safe."

The two cowboys looked sheepish. Finally, Heck said, like he had just thought of it, "We took his guns."

From the tall veranda, Jenkins could see Clay's rifle and shotgun. Clay's coat had flung open from the wind, and as he pulled up, the man could see the shoulder holster under his left arm as well.

"I've got to say, boys, you did a real good job. From where I'm standing, I can see a rifle, a shotgun, and a revolver. Now, tell me again, how you took his guns."

The cowboys on the ground were roaring with laughter and slapping each other on the back. Clay just sat on Blue, a calm countenance, surveying the ranch. From where he sat, beside the big, stone ranch house, he could see the corral, a massive limestone barn, and a bunkhouse. Hay was packed in the loft and stacked almost to the roof on one outside wall. The bunkhouse, also limestone, looked large enough to house fifteen to twenty men.

Heck took his hat off, his voice almost a whine. "Mr. Jenkins, he was snooping. Why, he was looking at the ranch with them binoculars hanging on his saddle horn. So we took his sidearms, two Smith & Wessons. We figgered, since we was with him, he wouldn't have no chance to use them long guns."

"You were with him?" Jenkins shook his head. "You men need to stop talking. Give this man back his guns. Then you two go over to the corral and get a couple of fresh horses, since you've worn these out, and get back on the range."

Dutch rode up to Clay and gave him back his guns. His head was down, but as Clay took the revolvers, he saw Dutch's eyes. The man was furious.

*I'll have to remember him,*" Clay thought. *He could be trouble.* Clay dropped the two revolvers back into the holsters and faced Jenkins.

"Are you the grandson to Senator Barlow?" Jenkins asked.

"Yes, I am."

"Then your parents were killed by outlaws about three years ago?"

"That's right. Except they weren't outlaws. They were cold-blooded killers."

"Yes, I heard. I am sorry about your loss. Your father was a fine man. I knew him when he was young.

"Get down. I let no man go hungry at this ranch. Come in."

"Mr. Jenkins. You may not want me in your house."

The cowboys had started to disperse. When they heard his refusal, they stopped and returned to listen.

"Then tell me, why are you here?"

"Have you heard my grandfather has been shot?"

Clay saw the look of surprise the man exhibited. If he had already known, he should be in New York, onstage.

"No, I haven't. What happened? Is he all right?"

Clay leaned his left forearm on the saddle horn. "Mr. Jenkins, he has two bullet holes in him. If by all right you mean, is he alive? Yes. But he is definitely not all right. He was shot in the back, twice. Luckily, he's recovering, but slowly. I've been in New

York for the past two years. He was shot about a month ago, three weeks before I returned. I'm just thankful he is still alive."

Clay saw a look of relief slip across the man's face, and then it hardened.

"I've asked you once. Why are you here?"

The cowboys had moved closer.

"Mr. Jenkins, I just have one question. Did you shoot my grandfather?"

Murmuring went throughout the crowd of cowboys. Hard faces glared at Clay.

"And what if I did?"

Clay, his voice calm and cold, said, "That would mean that I have to take you in to stand trial."

Jenkins returned the hard look. "Are you a lawman, boy?"

Clay held the man's stare. "I'm an officer of the court, but more than that, I'm his grandson, and I aim to take care of the man who shot him, whether it's prison or a bullet."

"Boy, I've got fifteen cowboys standing here. They'd fill you with so many holes, your belly would be showering beer before you emptied the mug."

"First thing, I don't drink beer. Second, believe me, I'd have two bullets in you, dead center, before any one of them would clear leather."

The door slammed behind Jenkins, and a young woman, no more than Clay's age, if that, stepped from behind the man. She was a lovely young girl, filled out in all the right places. Soft, auburn curls fell around her green, flashing eyes. In her small, steady hands she held a big double-barrel shotgun that seemed to dwarf her, the muzzles trained on Clay's chest.

"Think you could beat this, Mister?" she said.

Clay eyed the big muzzles staring at him. Then he looked at her face. Framed in her red hair, her skin looked like cream, soft to the touch, but her green eyes were hard as flint. "No, ma'am. I sure couldn't. Because I'd never draw on a girl." He folded his arms and looked back at Jenkins.

"Mr. Jenkins, I need to know. Did you shoot my grandfather?"

The older man reached out to his daughter, gently taking the shotgun away from her and carefully lowering the hammers.

"Daddy," she said, "you don't deserve to be talked to like this."

"This man is trying to find the coward that shot the senator, Lisa. I don't blame him." Sadness had replaced the anger in the rancher's eyes that Clay had seen with the first accusation. "No, Clay. I did not shoot your grandfather. You can ask anyone here. I haven't left the ranch for a couple of months. Though he and I have our differences, I would never shoot him."

Clay looked at the man closely. Jethro was right. This man would never be a backshooter. He tilted his hat to the young woman. "Sorry, ma'am." Looking back at Jenkins, he said, "Thank you, Mr. Jenkins. Sorry to cause a problem here. I'll be going."

Clay started to turn Blue to leave the yard when Jenkins spoke up. "Clay, get down. It'll be dark soon. Spend the night with us. We have plenty of room. Anyway, I'd like to hear more about how Joe is doing."

Pulling Blue up, Clay said, "Thank you. It's been a long day, but I brought accusations into your home, and I certainly don't want to create anymore discomfort." These last words were directed to Lisa.

She spun around and opened the door. "Whatever Daddy says is fine with me." The door slammed behind her as she charged back into the house.

"Put your horse up, and come on in," Jedediah Jenkins said to Clay, motioning toward the barn and entering the house.

Clay walked Blue over to the trough and stepped down. The cowboys all disappeared back to the jobs they had been doing. He stood by while the horse drank. This is a fine ranch, he thought. Looking around, he could tell that Jed Jenkins knew what he was doing. The man was putting a lot of hay away for the coming winter. He was well prepared. The buildings were all in good shape, painted and repaired where needed. It took a good man to get cowboys to climb down off their horses and do work that had to be done standing on their feet.

Blue stopped drinking and Clay led him into the barn. He examined the building as he walked back to an empty stall. After stripping his gear from the horse, he carried it over to the saddle rack, tossing the saddle across, putting everything else next to it. Seeing a brush, he picked it up and started currying Blue.

"That feel good, boy?" Clay said. "Aren't you special? You get to stay in a barn tonight. You've been spoiled here lately. Reckon you've been in a barn way too long." The horse snorted and shook his head, as if he understood. Clay continued to work, taking long strokes over his back and sides. Suddenly Blue's head jerked up and to the right, his ears forward.

Clay also heard the scuff of boots in the barn. He turned his head to look over his shoulder, and saw a huge man, wearing a long, leather apron and carrying a pair of farrier tongs in his left hand, standing behind and to the other side of Blue. The man's arms looked to be twice the size of fence posts, and he was at least as tall as Clay, only bigger. He carried more weight in his shoulders, chest, and belly.

Clay nodded, and said, "Howdy." Then he went back to rubbing down Blue.

"I like a man what takes care of his animal," the big man said. He said no more but stood and watched Clay.

Clay continued, working where he could keep an eye on the blacksmith. Time ticked slowly by, and the man kept standing there. Finally, Clay straightened, then, placing his hands at his hips, he bent way back, his back popping in the process. "Ahh," Clay said to no one in particular, "that felt good." Then he went back to work.

"I don't much like people threatening the boss," the man finally said.

"Yep," Clay said, and continued to work on Blue.

"The boss is a fine man."

Clay moved to Blue's front, where he could keep an eye on this stranger. It sounded like he might be leading up to something, something not so good. From the look and sound of him, he must be German.

"He took me in when I was a young fella, and my folks were killed by Comanches. I been working for him ever since. Ya, he treats me mighty well."

Clay said nothing. He figured that this huge German would get to the point eventually.

"Now, you seem like a nice young fella. But you caused Mr. Jenkins and Miss Lisa to be upset. No. That is not good. Miss Lisa was even bringing out the shotgun. Ya, a lesson I must teach you." The man had placed the tongs on a shelf and was rolling up his sleeves.

"Wait a minute," Clay said. "I have nothing against you. Heck, I don't even know you." Clay was frustrated now. There was no reason to fight this man. Everything had been solved. "Sure, I came here to talk to Mr. Jenkins, but just to question him. In fact, he invited me to dinner. Does that sound like an angry or insulted man?"

"The boss is a good man. That is something he would do for any cowboy. I don't much want to do this, but you got to learn your lesson. Come out here and take your medicine like a man." The big man motioned for Clay to come out from behind Blue.

"This doesn't make sense at all." Clay walked out from behind Blue and into the center of the barn, facing the man. He had never backed down from a fight, but this was senseless. He and Jenkins were all right. Clay believed the older man when he said he had not shot his grandfather. Jenkins had even invited him for dinner and to stay the night. Now this big hulk wanted to fight him? "Is there anything I can say to convince you this isn't necessary? I don't know you. Things are fine with Mr. Jenkins. What else can I do?"

"Just walk on over here. I won't hurt you bad, but you got to learn not to upset Mr. Jenkins or Miss Lisa."

Clay shook his head. What kind of crazy place had he ridden into? He wasn't afraid of the big man. He thought for a second. Well, maybe a little, but he felt sure he could win. It was just going to hurt a lot, for both of them, for no reason. *Okay,* he thought, *I can't get around it.*

He unbuckled his guns, took the frock coat and the shoulder holster off, and laid them across his saddle along with his hat. He rolled up his sleeves, and though he exposed powerful forearms and biceps, they were almost dwarfed when compared with the blacksmith's.

"Mister, if you're going to make me fight you, which understand, I don't want to do, at least tell me your name," Clay said.

"Ya, that is reasonable. My name is Gunter Schmidt. I know your name. It is Clay Barlow, and Mr. Barlow, I am going to give you a whipping, but not too much." With that, Gunter hauled off and slammed Clay in the chest with a mighty blow.

Clay rolled head over teakettle out of the barn and into the yard. He lay there a moment, sucking hard, trying to get his lungs primed. Gunter walked calmly out to the yard and stood watching Clay, his hands resting on his hips.

"Mr. Barlow, are you going to lay on the ground, or will you now get up and take your medicine?"

With the sound of the heavy blow on Clay's chest and his rolling into the yard, cowboys came running, yelling "fight!" in delight. This was a terrific way to break up the monotony that could set in around the ranch.

Clay, lying on the ground, leaned back on his forearms, and said, one last time, "Okay, Gunter. You whipped me. I told you, I have no reason to fight you. Why don't we chalk it up to a win for you, and call it a day?"

The cowboys were standing around Clay laughing, which didn't go over too well for him, but he still didn't see any sense in fighting this man.

"No, Mr. Barlow. One blow is not a whipping. When I'm done with the whipping, I'll know when to stop, but like I already told you, I won't hurt you bad."

At Gunter's statement, the cowboys' laughter filled the yard. Somebody yelled, "Yeah Mr. Barlow, he won't hurt you too bad." At that statement, the cowboys roared, slapping each other on the back.

Clay shook his head and stood up. "Well, if you're dead set, there's nothing I can say, but I'm sorry about this. I'm afraid you're going to get hurt." Clay took his shirt off and handed it to the nearest cowboy. "You mind hanging on to this for me? I only have a couple with me, and I feel certain this one would get torn to shreds."

The cowboy took it. "Your funeral, feller. I've seen Gunter fight before. I wouldn't want to be on the receiving end of his right, and come to think of it, his left either." The cowboys around Clay all chimed in in agreement.

Clay didn't have anything on under his shirt, exposing his muscles as his body moved. The years of work, and his additional training in New York, had built him up and thickened his back and chest. The men standing around Clay looked at him and back at Gunter. They immediately started placing bets.

## 12

"Okay, Gunter. I guess this is something that must be done," Clay said, moving forward.

The big German stepped toward Clay and swung a powerful right. Had it connected, that would have been the end of the fight, but Clay, watching the right, moved his head slightly, and felt the breeze of the massive fist as it sailed by. He stepped in and slammed a left, right, left combination to Gunter's solar plexus, and stepped back unscathed. Gunter stopped for a moment, watching Clay.

Gunter took a deep breath. "Good," he said. "You hit good."

This is going to be a long fight, Clay thought. Those were hard punches. Any other man would be on the ground gasping for air. Clay moved cautiously around the man, then stepped in and hit him again, this time with a left jab that bloodied Gunter's lip. The cowboys were cheering Gunter on. The blow to his lips quieted them, at least for a few moments.

Hearing the commotion, Lisa and Jenkins stepped out on the veranda. After hearing the door open and close, Clay could hear the talking on the high porch.

"Daddy, why is Gunter fighting Barlow?"

"Sugar, I have no idea, but Gunter is pretty protective of us. Barlow riding up here like he did, may have set him off."

Lisa moved up to the railing, next to her father, placing her delicate hands on the rail. "Aren't you going to stop it?"

"I will if it looks like it's gone too far. But let's see what young Barlow is made of first."

*Great. I feel like a gladiator at one of those old Roman coliseums.* He had danced away from Gunter. The big man walked toward him, both hands up. Clay feinted a left again at Gunter's mouth. Both of the man's hands came farther up, and Clay hit him hard in the belly, using all of the power in his right arm and shoulder. The big man smiled and hit him with a roundhouse left that sent Clay staggering across the yard, fighting to keep his balance.

He could feel the eyes of Jed and Lisa Jenkins on his back. *I hope you're enjoying this. It's time to get serious.* With that thought, he tucked his chin into his shoulder and stepped into Gunter, hitting him again in the stomach. This time he didn't get away scot-free. Gunter caught him with the left on the right side of his head.

Colors exploded through his eyes. Both ears sounded like steam whistles were going off in his head. Gunter moved toward him and hit him in the chest again. This time Clay was ready. It sent him a couple of steps back, but he didn't lose his balance, and he danced to Gunter's left, closing and driving another left to the big man's bleeding mouth. This one hurt, he could tell. Gunter stopped for a moment and spit blood on the ground, then wiped his lips, looking at the back of his arm. He looked up at Clay, a look of surprise and determination, and started moving toward him.

THE TWO BIG, bloody men had been trading blows for almost twenty minutes. Clay had felt the ground on his back three times, and Gunter had yet to leave his feet. But Clay could see the man was tired. He could feel it in the blows he was taking. They hurt, but not as bad. He could also tell that Gunter was not only physically tired, but tired of fighting him.

The cowboys had grown quiet. They were watching two good men go at each other for no reason they knew. They, too, were ready for it to end. Had it been a prize fight with professionals they would still be screaming for blood, but Gunter, a friend, was getting chopped to pieces. Granted, he had knocked the other man down several times, but the man wouldn't stay down, and it was obvious he knew what he was doing.

He had just hit Gunter on the cheekbone, opening a deep cut. Clay stepped back and dropped his arms. "So, Gunter, have you given me a good enough whipping? I sure hope so, because I'm tired of this, and I'm aching all over."

The big German stopped, looked at Clay for a moment, and dropped his arms. He grinned through broken and bloody lips. "Ya, I'm thinking you have been whipped enough. My face is feeling not too good."

"Good," Clay said. He walked up to Gunter and stuck out his hand. "Friends?"

The cowboys were in total silence, watching the two bloody and bruised men. They waited.

Gunter said, "Ya, we be friends. Only you be nice to Mr. Jenkins and Miss Lisa." The German stuck out his hand. Clay's big hand disappeared in the grip of the blacksmith's.

The normally quiet and taciturn cowboys broke out into a big cheer, clapping and slapping Gunter and Clay on their backs. Then they turned to more serious business, divvying up the money, arguing about who had won or lost.

Clay turned and looked at Jenkins and Lisa.

Jenkins gave a slight nod "See you for dinner," he said, and turned and opened the door for Lisa. She held Clay's gaze for a moment and, turning slowly, stepped inside. The door closed, and Clay looked around.

The cowboys were all moving back to their jobs, each in animated conversation. Gunter had headed for the trough and now had his head submerged in the water. He raised his head, blowing air and slinging water like a horse. Clay laughed and walked over next to him. The water had settled down, and he could see his bruised and bloody reflection. He looked at it for a moment, took a deep breath, and plunged his head in. Once out, he wiped the water from his eyes. Gunter handed him a towel.

He looked at the clean towel and felt his dirty, bloody face. "I'm going to get this mighty dirty," he said to the German.

"It is no problem. It will come clean. You go ahead and dry yourself off. You made a good fight."

Clay let out a dry chuckle, then said, "I don't think my body appreciated it."

"The body heals. A good fight cleanses mind and the body. Makes you feel good. Like a man should." Gunter clapped Clay on the back, almost knocking him into the trough, then walked back into the barn.

Clay wiped his face, drying his hair, then combing it back with his hand. Rubbing his chest and shoulders with the towel, he glanced at the ranch house. There was a quick movement by a side window. It looked like Lisa moving back. Interesting. He picked his shirt up from the top rung on the corral and slid it on over his head before he walked back into the barn.

CLAY KNOCKED on the screen door. From inside came the gruff call, "Come on in."

He walked through the door and looked around the sitting room. The walls were solid white blocks, packed with a hard gray sealer between them. The walls were at least two feet thick with the windows doubling as gun ports. *This place is a fortress.*

The room had a huge fireplace against one wall. Over it hung the widest set of longhorns he had ever seen. A long, padded cowhide couch sat to one side, with three deep easy chairs, also covered with cowhide, facing it. Against the back of the couch, a clean, long, waist-high, iron-legged table stood.

"We're back here," Jenkins called.

Clay walked past the couch and chairs to a door set in back of the house, and stepped into a huge kitchen. In the middle of the kitchen sat a pecan wood table that looked to be built for at least twenty people. Jenkins was sitting at one end.

"Come on in and have a seat. Here, by me." The man indicated a chair next to him, on his right.

The table was covered with an assortment of food, duplicated every five feet or so. Cedar framed chairs with cowhide bottoms lined the table. Clay moved to the chair next to Jenkins, pulled it out and sat.

Jenkins eyed his bruised face, one eye swollen, and a large bump on his forehead. "I've seen worse after Gunter finished with someone," he said.

"Does this happen a lot?"

Jenkins laughed, then said, "Not often. Most people are smart enough to shy away from him."

"Yeah. Guess that doesn't say a lot for me," Clay said, and then grinned, wincing slightly from his sore cheek.

"So what started it?"

Clay shook his head. "Danged if I know. I was just giving Blue a rubdown, and he walks up to me and says he's got to teach me a lesson for upsetting you and your daughter."

"Yeah. He is protective of us. I took him in as a young boy. He is very devoted. Which is good, and sometimes not so good, but it looks like you came out of it with no severe damage."

"From your perspective."

Jenkins laughed out loud. "Yes, from my view."

Clay turned serious. "Mr. Jenkins, I may have brought danger to your home."

Jenkins faced sobered. "What do you mean?"

"Someone is dogging me." Clay told him what had happened at Jethro Bate's home, the gunshot, the farmer's boots, and the marked hoof.

"Don't worry about it. We keep a pretty good guard up around here, night and day. Though this is the eighteen seventies, there are still a lot of desperadoes in this country, and the occasional renegade Apache raid. That's one of the reasons we have so many men. We've had a tough time supporting this many, what with the depressed beef prices, but we're still managing."

A young Mexican girl ran out the other door that came from the yard, directly into the kitchen. A moment later, the ringing of a forged, large, triangle dinner bell carried across the yard and into all corners of the ranch. It seemed she rang it forever, but finally, the loud ringing ceased, and the sound of the striker being hung on the triangle could be heard. The girl came back into the kitchen, followed by a stream of cowboys. Everyone seemed to have their place, and they went straight to it. In only a couple of minutes the table was surrounded, with only the chair at the opposite end of the table empty. The girl was going around the table filling coffee cups.

"Don't wait for me, boys. Dive in," Jenkins said. Immediately, the energy picked up. Cowboys were reaching, utensils were clanging, and steaks were disappearing. "Go ahead, Clay. After your workout today, you must be pretty hungry."

Clay grabbed a couple of biscuits from the huge platter that had been set in front of him. The cowboy to his left handed him another big platter containing steaks. He forked one and put it on his plate as Jenkins was handing him a big bowl of mashed potatoes. "It must take half your budget just keeping these men fed."

Jenkins nodded, chewed a piece of steak, and then said, "You have no idea."

The meat was delicious. With the tension of confronting Jenkins, and then the fight, he had not realized how hungry he was. He joined in the celebration of food with the other cowhands. All that could be heard was the clinking of utensils and the women talking.

Clay glanced up the length of the table. Lisa had sat down and was eating. She seemed to be enjoying the sight of the men devouring their food. Gunter was sitting next to her.

Jenkins leaned forward. "Lisa was just a little girl when we took Gunter in. They became fast friends. He's a good man. He's a little slow, but an excellent blacksmith. I'm glad we have him here."

Lisa got up and helped the Mexican cook and girl clear the table of food and set seven apple pies on the table. Each pie was cut in quarters. Jenkins and Clay got a piece and went to work. When Clay looked up moments later, all the pie tins were empty.

"We've got a little orchard planted up on top of the bluff just behind us," Jenkins said, around a large piece of pie he was chewing. "It provides peaches, apples, and pears. We dry a lot of 'em. Makes a nice addition to meals. Keeps that cowboy sweet tooth calmed."

The two men finished and Jenkins stood. "Boys, finish up, and then those of you going on watch tonight keep a sharp eye. We might have a backshooter slipping around the ranch. He's already taken a shot at Clay, here. If you see him, don't ask questions, shoot. Looks like he's pretty slick." He then spoke directly to Lisa. "Make sure you keep the women folk inside as much as possible. No evening ride today."

Lisa shot him a petulant look, and started to say something, then waited. The men were leaving, each one saying good night to her, the little girl, and the cook, as they passed.

Clay rose after Jenkins stopped speaking to the men, and Jenkins said, "Come with me into my office." After the sitting room and the kitchen, Clay expected a large office. He walked into a small room that provided only enough space for a narrow book case, a desk and chair, and two other chairs facing the desk. It had a window looking out over the corral and part of the barn.

"Have a seat." Jenkins opened a drawer of the desk and took out a box of cigars, opening it and extending it toward Clay. "Smoke?"

"No, thanks," Clay said, relaxing in his chair.

"So you came here to take me into custody or to shoot me?"

Clay thought for a moment. "If you were guilty of shooting my grandfather, then yes."

"That takes a lot of grit, boy."

Clay said nothing, just sat and looked at the man.

"I'm not sure whether I like you or not. You're certainly like your grandpa, you have a presence about you, and you're brash." Suddenly, Jenkins slammed his fist down on the desk. "But nobody rides into my ranch and threatens me. You understand me? Nobody!"

Clay never broke his gaze with the man and said nothing.

"You know I could have you strung up right now? My men wouldn't hesitate, even after the fight, and, let me tell you, that fight sure didn't go the way I expected it to. I figured Gunter would beat the holy stuffin' out of you."

It looked like the man was working himself into a heart attack. *What is going on? I know Jed said he had a hot temper, but he seemed so easygoing earlier.*

"But he didn't. And to top it all off, you lead a bushwhacker to my doorstep, to my family. Maybe I should have you strung up on one of those big pecans. That way the backshooter will see you, an' we ain't gonna have to worry about the likes of you, no longer."

*Enough*, Clay thought, and stood up. "Mr. Jenkins, it's obvious to me that I misunderstood your intentions. I don't believe you shot my grandfather, but I can see, though you keep it hidden well, that you are an angry, bitter man. I'll get Blue, and we'll be off your ranch before dark."

The man's face was almost scarlet. He stood and pointed at Clay, shouting, "You say that to me, after eating under my roof? By Henry, I may just have you hung."

Clay felt the cold come over him. "You don't want to do that, Mr. Jenkins. I think you've got some good men here, though I can't understand why they'd work for you. You wouldn't want them hurt, and I promise you, if you send them after me, they might get me, but you'll be digging more than one grave. Now, I'll take your leave. Thanks for the meal." He stepped through the door to see the lovely Lisa standing just outside.

"Mr. Barlow, he isn't always like that, only occasionally. He's a good man with a bad temper. If you wait, he'll be fine in a few minutes."

"Ma'am, thank you for the fine dinner." He tipped his hat and walked out the door and down the steps, wondering what had just happened.

He thought back to the statement his grandfather had made: "some, downright mean." He was puzzled, how could any man be so nice, yet so volatile? Gunter certainly liked him, and his ranch hands seemed to. Did he keep that side hidden, only to have it break loose occasionally? Well he'd never know, because he was getting the heck out of here.

Gunter was waiting in the barn.

Clay stopped. He held his hands up palms turned toward Gunter. "Gunter, I don't feel like another fight."

"No fight. I am just sorry you must leave. You seem to be a good man, and Mr. Jenkins, he is a good man. But sometimes he lets loose his temper. Sometimes he even gets mean with his horses, and I must stop him. Since Mrs. Jenkins died it seems to be worse. He loved her very much. She was a good lady." A piece of furniture crashed in the house and Gunter looked in that direction.

"Will the women be safe?"

"Oh, yes. He would never touch a woman. He has demons that afflict him."

Clay shrugged. "Well, I'm glad you're not out here waiting to whip me again. I don't think I could handle another whipping from you."

Gunter grinned. "Yah. I have never been hit as hard as from you. I don't think I want to whip you no more."

"Wait," Gunter said. He came back with a heavy, wool poncho. "You take this. You'll freeze in that coat."

Clay looked at the poncho. "Gunter, I can't take that."

"You take it. It was made for me by the cook. It is warm, but too small. It'll fit you."

Clay took the poncho. It was thick and heavy, hanging down to his thighs. "Thanks, Gunter. Let me pay you for it."

"No. Friends. Maybe you help me sometime."

Clay swung up onto Blue and stretched his hand to Gunter. "I think you are a good friend. If you ever need any help, get in touch with me, either in Austin or at the ranch. Adios." The two men shook hands, and Clay rode out of the barn, still unable to understand Jenkins and his apparent change.

Lights had been lit inside the house. Clay could make out the man standing in his office. He shook his head in puzzlement as he rode past. A small figure came from the shadows. It was Lisa.

She handed Clay a package. "There's two steaks, bread, and a pie. Hopefully this will keep you going for a while. I'm sorry for the way Daddy acted. You've got to understand this isn't him."

Clay said, "Thank you."

She continued. "When I was still small, before Mother died, Daddy was having headaches. As much as he hates doctors, he finally went. The doctor told him he had a growth in his brain, and there was nothing that could be done. Here lately, it has gotten worse. I'm afraid for him."

"What about you and the other women?" Clay asked.

"He would never hurt us. It's just difficult to see this happening to him. He has been such a good father, and your grandfather was one of his best friends. That has been such a terrible hurt, but you've got to believe, he did not shoot your grandfather. He hasn't hardly left the ranch for months. I think he's concerned about being out alone in his condition."

She paused for a moment, looked around at the house, and said, "Maybe we'll see each other again, under better circumstances." With that, she spun around and quickly disappeared in the shadows along the side of the house.

Clay turned and carefully placed the food in his saddlebag. He didn't want to smash the pie. "Come on, Blue let's see if we can find a safe campsite before it gets too dark."

## 13

They lost the light crossing the wide pasture. Now under the trees, it was hard to see to the next tree trunk. Clay let Blue pick his way through the trees and brush to the Rio Blanco. He brought them to a gently sloping bank that led down to a shallow crossing over the river.

Once in the river, Clay allowed Blue to drink. This would take care of the horse's water needs until the morning. They came out the other side, stopped for a moment, and listened to the night noises. A couple of coyotes were serenading the star-studded sky, sounding more like a dozen than only two. An armadillo snuffled nearby in his relentless search for any complacent beetle, grub, or worm that might be in range. The forlorn hoot of an owl nearby announced his coming hunt for prey on his soundless wings.

Blue moved farther into the trees. The noise was atrocious. The ground was covered with dry leaves, and it was impossible to move quietly through here. They entered a small clearing was surrounded by vines and covered with thick grass. "This is a good place, Blue. Nobody can get close to us in these leaves."

Clay pulled his gear from the horse, took his rope from his saddle, and staked him out in the clearing. Then he spread his bedroll on the grass, and in moments, he was stretched out. "Let me know if you hear anything, fella."

He pulled the warm poncho over his blanket and, using his saddle for a pillow, leaned back and relaxed. It had been an interesting and confusing day. Tomorrow, he would be back in Austin and continue his search for the backshooter. He heard something small trotting through the leaves. It passed on the upwind side, never slowing. Probably a red fox.

It was warm under the blanket and poncho, a long day coming to an end. An early start and some hard riding tomorrow should put them in Austin before sundown. He yawned once and was sound asleep.

LARGE RAINDROPS FALLING on leaves woke him from a deep sleep. Only it wasn't raining. He could hear Blue contentedly cropping the bunch grass. He opened one eye and saw another big brown eye staring at him, only this one was fifteen feet up on a tree limb. A red fox squirrel sat on his haunches chewing on a pecan. The cuttings fell continuously, raining down on the dry leaves. He laughed to himself. *Too bad it isn't rain. Moisture is always welcome.*

He threw the poncho and blanket back and sat up, stifling a groan. His body was sore all over. Gunter's whipping had his body aching in places he didn't even know he had. Turning his boots over, he beat them out, then ran his hand down in them. The last thing he wanted was to start his day with a scorpion sting or spider bite. Boots empty, he pulled them on and stood up.

Blue was giving him an impatient look. He had slept longer than expected. He wanted to get an early start. Pulling out his pocket watch, he checked the time. It was after seven o'clock. Past time to get moving. He strapped on his shoulder holster and then his gunbelt, checking each of the three weapons. He picked up the frock coat, slipped it on, and followed it with the poncho. The morning was cold and the poncho felt good. *Thanks, Gunter.* Clay bent over and picked up his hat, looking at the entry and exit hole. He was a lucky man. A few inches lower and Jethro would have been throwing dirt in his face. But he wasn't one to dwell on such things. He brushed his hair back with his hand, slapped the hat on his head, and walked over to Blue.

"How are you doing this morning, Blue?" he said, pulling the stake from the ground and coiling the rope. "We'll be on our way just as soon as you get some water." He walked the horse back to the river and let him drink his fill. While Blue was drinking, he moved upstream, laid down on the sandy bank, and quenched his own morning thirst. When they were finished, Clay led Blue back to camp.

After getting the horse saddled and ready to go, he pulled the package that Lisa had given him out of the saddlebag. Resting safely on top was the apple pie. Seeing that, his mouth started to water. He pulled out his knife and cut the pie in half. *Who said you can't eat dessert first?* he thought. He laid the pie on a nearby log, wrapped the rest of the food in the cloth, and gently returned it to the saddlebag.

"Let's get moving, Blue." He picked up the pie from the log, stepped into the stirrup, and swung his leg over the horse's back. He sat there for a moment, still in the trees, listening to the sounds of the outdoors. He could hear the cattle lowing on the other side of the Blanco. Bob-white quail were greeting the day with their distinct call. The squirrel had run down to the ground, picked up another pecan, and returned to his perch on the limb, raining mast to the ground. "This is the life. I love the law, but I don't know if I can give this up."

They moved out of the trees and pushed forward, a long day ahead. Clay kept to the lower side of hills, careful not to silhouette himself on a crest or ridgeline. Keeping his eyes moving, he enjoyed his breakfast of apple pie. *That was mighty good. Thank you, Lisa.*

The nights were downright cold, but the days could still be hot. So it was with today. He had shed the poncho earlier and tied it across his bedroll. The last creek had been a welcome cooling, but now the Texas heat had returned. They had just moved around a rocky edge of a prickly-pear covered hill and through a thick patch of dark green cedars when movement on the far slope caught his eye.

He pulled Blue up at the edge of a large, bushy green cedar tree, reached into his saddlebags, and pulled out his pair of binoculars. He looked over the area where he had noticed movement. Nothing. He decided to wait in the shade of the cedar. Suddenly, a large tawny mountain lion appeared from behind an outcropping of rocks, waited for a moment, and effortlessly jumped up on a big boulder. Clay watched the cougar for several minutes.

Since he had the binoculars out, he scanned all the visible hillsides. He made a second pass, then a third. The tawny cat sat motionless on the warm boulder. On his fourth pass, his eye caught something out of place. Knowing that the eye can sometimes identify a distant object easier if focusing a little to the side, he moved his eyes away from the area he was scanning. With that small shift, a horse's hoof came into focus. Now, he looked directly at the hoof and could make out the indistinct outline of the leg, but the rest of the animal was hidden behind a small thicket of oaks. While keeping his eyes on the spot, he reached down and pulled his 1866 Winchester Yellow Boy from the scabbard, laying it across the saddle. The horse hadn't moved.

It now became a waiting game. The catamount couldn't be more than fifty yards from, and a little below the horse, sitting relaxed on the boulder, its black-tipped tail swishing rhythmically back and forth. The cat had no idea anyone was around, which was pretty amazing, as alert as the animal normally was.

The cat laid down and started cleaning itself, starting with the left front paw. He worked on it for several minutes before he moved to the right one. Clay stayed still in the shadows, waiting. This could be the case of first to move dies.

The hoof moved, then the whole right side came into view. He could see the stirrup and the leg of whoever was on the horse. The cat disappeared soundlessly. He continued to wait. The water of the shallow creek, below the hill, gurgled pleasantly. He could occasionally hear the splash of a bass striking a bug on the water's surface. Sweat dripped from his forehead into his left eye. He ignored it. His nose itched something fierce. *That's right. Itch now, while I can't scratch you.* He kept his eyes on the leg.

He heard the bass strike again, and, at the same, time the horse moved up ever so slightly. Clay could see the full length of the rider. And he had a rifle pointed directly at him! Clay dropped his binoculars, and threw himself out of the saddle, his rifle in his right hand. The last view of the man, as he was leaving the saddle, was a puff of smoke from the rifle muzzle. He hit the ground and pushed farther under the thick cedar. The shot echoed through the valley, bouncing from one hill and then the other. Clay wormed a little farther forward and watched the horseman. He hadn't moved. Now it was time to wait, again. It was too long a shot for his rifle. If he had a Sharps or a Spencer, he could take the man out of his saddle, but not with the Winchester. So he did the only thing he could do, he waited.

He lay on the rough ground with rocks gouging into his thighs and belly. Two hours had passed, and the man had not moved. The sun was hot on Clay's back. Thirst gnawed at the back of his throat.

And then the shooter moved.

He walked his horse out from behind the oaks and slowly started working his way across the wide, shallow canyon. The man's horse stepped easy, missing rocks and moving around cactus.

Clay carefully extended his arm. Shoving the rifle farther under the cedar, this would be close-range, handgun business— he slipped the pocket pistol from under his left shoulder. The smaller version of the Smith & Wesson .44-caliber rested lightly in his big right hand. He watched the man ride toward the cedar. The horse slowed, then stopped. The man sat loose in the saddle, the reins in his right hand along with the pistol grip of the rifle, the forearm resting in the crook of his left arm, ready for immediate action. The man's face was tense with concentration. He was close enough for Clay to see the man's features through the interlaced limbs of the brushy cedar tree. The man was older. White had taken over the brown of his hair, and his flop hat was set jauntily on the right side of his head. His beard was the same shade as his hair, tobacco stains running from his mouth to below where his chin should be.

*Don't look him in the eyes. Not this close.* The man wore bib overalls and had farmer's boots on. The bass in the river made another loud splash.

"Must be a lot of bugs on that there creek, wouldn't you say, boy?"

*The man was talking to him. Did he see him?*

"That big bass, he's been tearing it up. I reckon yore probably dead. I just don't miss with this here Winchester '73. At least I didn't until I come to Texas. That ole gramps of yours oughta be dead. If he hadn't turned, he would be. Can't believe I put two of these little lead pills in him, and he's still kicking. But it did what I wanted. It got you back to Texas. You ought not shot my boy. That was right hard to take. That train was owned by a bunch of Yankees. It shouldn't made no never mind to you.

"I thought I had you the other night—don't rightly know how that happened. But anyway, I got this here rifle off a drummer that tried to sell it to me. Never buy a thing if you can just kill a feller and take it, wouldn't you agree?"

Clay lay still, watching the man through the cedar, as he prattled on.

"Well, I ain't seen nobody, 'cept maybe an Injun play dead as long as you have. Reckon I'll just come around there and get me that fine head of hair you have. It'll look mighty nice hanging across my saddle."

The man clucked a couple of times, and his horse picked his way around the cedar. Clay lost sight of him but could hear the horse. At the same time, he heard a rock grate on the opposite side of the cedar—behind him. Clay only had a moment to relax back to the ground, the Smith & Wesson under his body in his right hand.

Rocks grated again. "Well sir, ain't this nice? All stretched out here ready for the preacher. You just shouldn't have shot my boy. And with a shotgun. That's just no way for a Blessing to die. Why, looky here. You got a fine pair of boots. Looks like just my size. Reckon that coats a mite big, but it'll do."

Clay's hat lay over the side of his head and face. Gravel scraped again. The man was right on top of him. Clay felt the muzzle of the Winchester as Blessing pushed him in the side with it. He remained limp.

"What's this?" the man said. "Looks like a mighty fine hat."

The pressure of the rifle against his side disappeared. He could smell the unwashed man's odor mixed with stale tobacco, strong in his nose. He felt a large hand grab his left shoulder and pull hard.

Clay flexed his right shoulder and violently torqued his body to rotate, at the same time bringing the revolver out from under his chest. His eyes met the wide, cold gray orbs staring at him from the man's startled face. He thrust the muzzle against the older man's forehead.

"If I were you, Mister Blessing, I'd drop that Winchester, or you're going to find your hair parted with a forty-four."

"Now, hold on, Sonny. You just stay nice and relaxed. I wouldn't want you to accidentally put too much pressure on that there trigger." Blessing slowly squatted down and laid the Winchester on the rocky ground, the muzzle of Clay's revolver never leaving his forehead. "No call to get twitchy here, boy. I'm doing what you said."

Blessing looked up at the Smith & Wesson, his gray eyes crossing. "That there is a fine pistol, boy. Mighty fine. Why I'd love to know where you got one like that. Maybe I can get one."

Clay stood, never removing the muzzle from the man's forehead.

"You sure are a big feller. Reckon yore ma fed you mighty well. Joe Frank's ma fed him well, too. She set a big store by her boy. I'd almost say he was one of her favorites. She is shore unhappy now. She shore is. Breaks a man's heart to see her carry on so."

"You talk a lot, don't you?" Clay said, slowly backing away from the man.

"That's been said, all right. But I find if you carry a conversation on with a man, it helps pass the day. Now, take you, for example, it looks like you ain't much for makin' conversation. That makes it might tough on you, makes the days longer and more lonesome. Why, I can be by myself and—"

"That's enough. You carrying any other weapons?"

"Why, no sirree. I ain't got nary another thing on me. You can search if you're a mind to, though you won't find nothin'."

"Turn around. Now lay down on the ground, facedown. Spread your legs, and stretch your arms straight out from your sides."

The old man looked hard at Clay. His friendly talk belied the cold anger that flowed from his old gray eyes. He smiled, the smile not moving past his lips. "You're mighty untrusting, I'd say. That ground is almighty hard on an old man. I'd sure be obliged if you wouldn't make me do that."

Clay moved the forty-four to his left hand and slipped the leather thong off the hammer of the Smith in his right holster.

"Tell you what we're going to do, Mr. Blessing. Before you lay down, unfasten that bib and let it and the back straps fall. Then pull up your shirt. Once that's done you can lay facedown."

"Now, look, boy, I—"

"Do it, now!"

The older man glared at Clay for a moment, then unfastened the front of the bib overalls and let the straps fall over his back. When he released the bib, it fell past his waist. The cap and ball pocket pistol that had been hidden in the bib of the overalls continued, clattering to the ground. Clay, keeping his revolver on the man, moved forward and picked up the pistol.

"Down!"

The man knelt and stretched out on the ground. Clay moved up to the man and started at the back of his neck, pulling a knife out of its holster, from where it was hanging down under the back of his shirt. He moved to the man's waist. A pocket had been sewn inside the right waist. He found a double-barrel .44-caliber derringer in that pocket. He tossed the knife and derringer in a pile, well to one side and out of reach of the man. The man's legs were clear. Clay moved the pocket pistol to the pile.

"Take off your boots and toss them over here."

Now it was the old man's turn to be silent. He glared at Clay for a moment, then pulled first one boot off and then the other to toss them to Clay.

Clay was almost overcome from the stench inside the boots, but he found a knife in the left boot and another derringer in the right boot. He tossed the booty into the pile with the others and kicked the man's boots back to him. "Put them on and stand up."

The man did as instructed, fastening the straps of his overalls when he stood. Clay moved to the man's horse and searched his saddlebags. He found two new issue Colt .45-caliber Army revolvers along with at least two hundred rounds of ammunition. He held one of the Colt Army revolvers up. "Where'd you get these? From that same drummer?"

## 14

T he man said nothing, just stared at Clay.

"You've gotten almighty quiet, for a talkative man." Clay pulled the saddlebag off the man's horse and laid it in front of Blue's saddle. "Sorry, Blue. I know these things are heavy, but it won't be too long."

"Sit down, right there," Clay said, indicating with his revolver's barrel the rocky ground where the man was standing. Once Blessing was seated, Clay walked over to the cedar, where he had been lying, and pulled his Yellow Boy from under the tree. Moving to his right, he picked up Blessing's Winchester '73. He walked back to Blue and slid the Yellow Boy into its scabbard. With the rawhide strip Blessing had threaded through the saddle ring on the rifle, he hung the Winchester on his saddle horn and looked around for his binoculars, spotting them near where he had fallen. He picked them up and examined the lenses. Everything looked good. Clay slipped them back into his saddlebags, and then walked over to Blessing's horse, and lifted his left fore hoof. Sure enough, there was an old cut to the right of the frog. Releasing the horse's hoof, he patted the animal on the neck and pulled a piggin' string from Blessing's saddle. He turned and walked back to him.

"You've got a choice. You can ride your horse with your hands tied, or I can hog tie you and sling you over the saddle."

The man stuck out his hands.

Clay slid his Smith & Wesson back into the shoulder holster and reached for the man's hands. Sure enough, Blessing grabbed at Clay's right thumb to twist it back, throwing all of his weight into the move. Clay braced himself, grabbed the man's wrist in his big hand, squeezed, and twisted. Blessing let out a yelp, going to his knees.

"All right, all right. You can't blame a man for trying."

Clay turned him loose and motioned for him to stick out his hands. The man shoved his hands toward Clay. After he had him tied, he walked back to his horse and built a loop with his rope. Taking the loop, he dropped it over Blessing's head.

"What's this?" Blessing asked, grabbing the rope and starting to shove it back over his head.

Clay yanked it tight, pulling the man off his feet, and causing a coughing spree. "I'd suggest you leave it alone. Now, get on your horse."

Clay could see that the man was frightened at the possibility of his hanging and let him sweat. He stepped into the stirrup and swung his long leg over Blue. "Now, Mr. Blessing, this is a fine cow horse. So should you decide to take off, I'll just loop this end of the rope over this here saddle horn, and he'll sit back when it comes tight. Now, I don't know if that would break a man's neck, but it would sure hurt, so I'd recommend you stay real agreeable. Understood?"

Blessing nodded his head.

"Sorry," Clay said. "I can't hear you."

"Yes! Yes, I understand. But listen here, boy, this ain't no way to treat a man twice yore age. I'd expect a mite better treatment. I would for sure."

Clay shook his head. "Sounds like you've gotten your voice back, Blessing. How about doing us both a favor, and keep your mouth shut."

It was late in the afternoon when Clay and his prisoner rode up to the Colorado River on the south edge of Austin. He waited until a loaded wagon crossed the single-lane bridge and had passed him, before continuing across. After crossing the river, he rode up Brazos Street until Cedar and turned left.

The sight of a man on horseback with his hands tied and a rope around his neck began to build a crowd that followed them.

"Ain't this a shame, folks?" Blessing said, speaking to his growing audience. "This here big ole boy done trussed up a poor old man, like myself, who never done harm to no one in his whole, complete life."

The crowd began to murmur amongst themselves. Clay heard one woman say, "For heaven's sake. That is not Christian. Why, to put a rope around a poor, sickly old man and ride him down the street in public is shameful." He could hear other people agreeing with her. One of the people who heard her was Blessing.

"Yes, ma'am. It is truly shameful. Why, I was just riding along minding my own business, and this here young feller rode up like he rightfully owned the world, and he threw down on me. Me, a God-fearing man—amen. Then he tied me up and put this frightening rope around my neck. Why, if I even fall off my horse, it might break my neck. And me, honest as the day is long."

They finally reached the Rangers' office at the courthouse.

"Stop here," Clay said.

Blessings pulled up. "About time. You pert near wore out this old man."

Major Jones was standing on the steps of the Rangers' office. He looked around at the crowd.

"This looks familiar, Clay. Do you like audiences?"

Clay swung down from the Blue's back. "No, sir. I sure don't. I guess they're just drawn to backshooters."

"Now, see here," Blessing said. "You ca—"

Clay gave a sharp tug on the rope around Blessings neck. "If you want me to drag you off that horse with this rope, then keep talking."

Blessing shut up, but the crowd gasped. Clay heard a woman, possibly the same one he'd heard before. "That is horrible. Is Major Jones going to allow that? Why, I'll go to my minister. No, I'll go to the mayor."

"Why don't you take the rope off his neck?" Major Jones said. "Between you and me, I understand why you've got him tied up like that, but it doesn't go well with the tame residents of Austin."

"Is the jail here?" Clay said.

"Yes, it is. It's run by the local police and located on the back of this building."

"Thank you," Clay said. He walked over to Blessing and pulled him out of the saddle. The man staggered when his feet touched the ground.

"Oh, look, that poor man can hardly walk. I would imagine that big man has beaten him."

As Clay was slipping the rope from around Blessing's neck, the man turned to the crowd. "Yes, Dear Sister. He has treated me brutally. It is even hard for me to breathe. I must have several broken ribs." At that, Blessing coughed and gasped from his pain.

"You better get him inside," Major Jones said. "With his performance, they'll start throwing money at any moment."

Several rangers were standing at the top of the steps. They were all chuckling and making comments, each obviously happy they weren't the brunt of the crowd's dislike.

Clay took Blessing by the arm to guide him back to the jail. The man stumbled. The gasp from the crowd was audible, and Clay caught the sly look on the man's face. Blessing leaned toward Clay and whispered, "They love me, Barlow. I won't be in jail long."

"I'll tie your horses to the hitching rack," Major Jones said.

"Thanks, Major," Clay replied, walking Blessing around to the jail entrance.

Pulling the jail office door open, Clay shoved Blessing into the room.

"Here now," a man dressed in a blue uniform, standing behind a long counter, said. "What's this?"

Clay walked up to the counter and released Blessing. "This man needs to be incarcerated, Officer."

"What's the charge?"

"Two charges of attempted murder."

Blessing leaned over the counter. "Pardon me, Captain, but I ain't attempted any murder on nobody, not here, not now, not ever." He looked the jailer in the eye and whined. "My eyes ain't what they used to be, I admit that. I shoulda been more sure of what I was shooting." With that statement, he cut a hateful look at Clay. "But, I truly thought I was shooting at a deer, him being so far away and all."

The jailer looked at Blessing, obviously enjoying his rank increase, and then up at Clay. "I don't recognize you. What department are you with?

"I am Clay Barlow, Officer . . ."

"Scott."

"Officer Scott. My grandfather is Senator Barlow, and I am an attorney."

"So, you don't carry a badge of any kind? If that's the case, it's just your word against his. He'll be let off. There's no sense holding him and the city feeding him."

"Officer Scott, I am an officer of the court. I bring this man to you because he tried to kill my grandfather and me. Almost three years ago, I killed his son, and now he is attempting to seek revenge. This will be decided in court and not here, not based on your opinion."

The jailer looked at him for a moment, clearly about to argue, then thought better and said, "Fine, sign him in here. You need to stay in town for the trial. Of course, you'll lose. It's just your word against his, but that's up to the court."

"Is it possible, Captain," Blessing said, "for me to get a message to my family? They're in Arkansas, and I'm sure they're powerful worried about me. I don't want to keep my dear, sweet wife in the dark as to what has become of me."

"Sure, I'll get something sent as soon as you're booked."

Clay filled out the paperwork. Realizing he didn't know Blessing's full name, he looked up and said, "What's your full name?"

"I'm rightful proud to say my ma named me Washington Jefferson Blessing. I go by Mr. Blessing."

Clay wrote down the name and continued to fill out the paperwork. The jailer untied Blessing, handing Clay the piggin' string. "Austin's courts are pretty fast. I'd expect the trial within a couple of weeks, so stay in town."

"My address is on the paperwork. Notify me of the trial and I'll be here." Clay started to walk out of the jail, then turned back to the jailer. "What about his horse and gear?"

The jailer continued to fill out papers without looking up. "Where is it?"

"I left it tied up in front of the Rangers' office. It's a tired little bay."

"I'll get to it in a spell."

Clay nodded. "I understand you're busy, but we've had a long ride, I'm sure he's thirsty."

This time, the jailer looked up in frustration. "Look, Mr. Barlow, I'll take care of that horse as soon as I can."

Clay turned and walked out of the jail. He took a deep breath. What a relief to be away from Blessing, the murderous windbag, and that jailer. He looked around. The crowd was gone. He walked down the side of the building to the Rangers' office entrance and went in. The major was nowhere to be seen.

One of the rangers pointed to the back office. "He's back there."

Clay knocked on the door. "Come in," he heard called through the closed door.

He opened the door and walked into the office. The major looked the same as he had almost four years ago, slim and confident. He was of average height with dark hair, eyebrows, and mustache. His mustache was thick and angled down past the corner of his lips, to end in points. His dark, piercing eyes added to the man's confident air.

"How have you been, Clay?"

"Fine, sir. I have been reading of your exploits. It seems, you've been a busy man."

"Don't believe everything you read, Clay, but we have been busy. We yet have much to do. But tell me about yourself. I understand you are now a lawyer."

"Yes, Major. I trained and began my practice in New York and intend to continue here in Texas. Unfortunately, it seems circumstances have kept me busy."

The major nodded. "Yes, I heard about the senator. Is this the man that shot him?"

"Yes, sir. He tried to kill him, but lucky for the senator, that didn't happen. Blessing was hoping my grandfather's death would bring me back. What he didn't know was that I was already on my way."

Clay continued the story, telling Major Jones everything. When he had finished, the major leaned back in his chair.

"I must say, Clay, you stay busy. Now that everything seems to be under control, do you plan on continuing as an attorney?"

Clay let out a big sigh. "Major, I feel I should. I do like the law. I enjoy helping people. That part is gratifying."

When he paused, Major Jones stepped in. "Being an attorney

is an honorable profession. Your grandfather is a good example. I'm sure it can be quite rewarding. As an attorney, you will find many ways to serve this great state of Texas. Service to something other than himself is the greatest thing a man can do. If you've found your calling as an attorney, then God speed. However, I believe I hear doubt in your voice. If that's the case, then search your mind for the truth.

The major leaned forward, closing the distance between them. "You are a born lawman, if I've ever seen one. In Del Rio, when you brought those killers in, alive, that had murdered your family so vilely, I knew you were a different breed. A man that could control his emotions. We need men like you." He took a deep breath and again leaned back in his chair. "You can make a great difference here. But I will understand, and recognize that Texas has gained a great attorney, if you should decide to follow that path."

He chuckled and smiled at Clay and stood. "Sometimes I get a bit long-winded. Please forgive me."

"No, sir," Clay said, standing also. "I appreciate all the advice I can get. My surprise is that it seems I still have a decision to make."

"Well, let me know. Now I must get back to work. Keep me posted on the status of the upcoming trial. I'd like to know the results."

The two men shook hands, and Clay walked out of the office. He nodded to the rangers in the outer office and went out the door. Blue was waiting patiently at the hitching rail, along with the little bay. Clay untied both horses and swung up onto the Blue's back. Leading the bay, he turned Blue down Cedar to the livery. "Just a few more minutes, boys and you'll be getting a drink, a rubdown, and a good supper. Reckon the jailer won't mind at all."

～

A FREEZING WIND blasted from the northwest, driving sleet and fine snow against the office windows. The searching wind from the blue norther found its way through cracks in the walls. The stoves were fighting a losing battle against the cold. A small ridge of snow and sleet had built up inside from the crack under the front door.

Clay sat at one of the desks in the Barlow Law and Land office, studying a land agreement made with a bank and a farming family. The bank was about to call the loan, but wanted to make sure the agreement would stand up in court, since the banker felt the owner might sue. The depression was contributing to many families, both farmer and rancher alike, losing their homes.

The front door banged open, letting a blast of frigid wind and sleet blow into the office. Andy, the schoolboy employed by the senator, charged in, turned, and, fighting the wind and snow piled at the base of the door, wrestled it closed.

"Mr. Barlow," he said to Clay, "it is danged cold out there."

Clay looked at the chilled boy standing in front of his desk with a handful of mail. "Two things, Andy. One, don't call me Mr. Barlow. I'm Clay. The second thing, if your ma hears you saying dang, you'll be eating your meals standing."

The boy grinned at Clay. "Your danged right, Clay! That's the reason I don't say it in front of her."

"You're dripping on the mail." Clay reached for the mail and Andy handed it and court affidavits to him, then stood in front of the stove with his hands steaming above the top. Clay thumbed through the envelopes. Most of it was routine, none of it addressed to him. He set it aside to take up to the senator when he went up for lunch. It had been two weeks, and his grandfather was recovering nicely from the gunshot wounds. His wind was still limited. Just going up or down the stairs caused him to stop and catch his breath, but the doctor said, in time, he would recover completely. Clay wondered if a man in his sixties could ever completely recover.

"Andy, when you were at the courthouse, did you hear anything about the Blessing case?"

"I went to the prosecutor's office. I knew you'd be interested." He beamed with satisfaction, knowing he had gotten information for his new hero, Clay Barlow, the Del Rio Kid.

"Well, are you going to keep it a secret?"

"Oh. No, sir. The prosecutor said to tell you the case is scheduled in two weeks. He said it got set back, and then used some legal mumbo jumbo that I didn't understand. November twenty-third is what he said."

"Thanks, Andy. You did good."

He grinned at Clay, then turned back to face the stove, his backside steaming.

Clay looked at his calendar. November twenty-third would be the week before Thanksgiving. *Good,* he thought, *then Blessing will be finished. Over and done with.*

"Did you hear anything of interest at court or at the post office?"

"No, sir. Wait, there was one thing. The sheriff was talking to one of his deputies at the post office. They were talking about bank robberies. The sheriff was saying that the number of robberies was up. He wondered why the rangers weren't doing anything about them." Andy crinkled his face in a quizzical frown. "I don't much think the sheriff likes the rangers, do you?"

"I really don't care what the sheriff likes or dislikes. Was that it?"

"Well, no, sir. He did say that there had just been another one robbed." The boy took his wool hat off and scratched his head. "I know he said the name. He even said the sheriff there was killed. Oh yeah, Uvalde. It was Uvalde, and the sheriff's name was Haskins. That's it, Haskins. I knew I'd remember. My ma says I'm good with names. Clay?"

He had jumped up and was pulling his coat on. His face had hardened. He turned gray, steely eyes on the boy. "Andy, did they say if anyone at the bank was hurt?"

"Uh, gee, let me think. They did mention that a banker was shot, but I didn't hear if he was killed or not. Mr. Barlow? Is anything wrong?"

"Andy, you've done good, but I want you to stay here, in the office, until Ray comes down. Can you do that?"

"Yes, sir, but it's almost lunchtime. Ma will worry if I'm not home for lunch. Especially with the weather like it is."

"You'll be fine. I'm sure Ray will be down soon. You take care, Andy."

With his last words, Clay stepped out in the freezing sleet and snow. He pulled the door closed and dashed to the stairs, raced up them, and burst through the door.

## 15

Clay rushed into the apartment to find himself staring into the muzzle of his grandpa's new Remington Model 1875 nickel-plated revolver. When he saw Clay, the older man immediately lowered the muzzle and relaxed. "What's wrong?"

"The Uvalde bank was robbed. Sheriff Haskins was killed, and a banker was shot. You know the Grahams. They bought the bank after Houston went to the pen. If either of them was in the bank, they could have been murdered or injured. I've got to go. I've got to find out."

The senator had risen. "Good gosh, Clay. Look outside. No one should be out in this weather. There's no telling how long it will last. To get to Uvalde, it'll take you at least four days, and that's in good weather. It's insane to even think about going."

"Grandpa, I understand your concern, but I'm going." Clay had gone back to his room, stripped and slipped on a pair of wool long johns. He looked through his clothing and took out a pair of heavy wool pants tossing another pair on the bed.

His grandfather had followed him in, Raymond right behind him. "Raymond, tell this young fool he has no business out in this weather. He thinks he's going to Uvalde, but he's just going to end up one big block of ice, and Blue too."

Raymond looked at Clay's face for a moment. "Senator, ain't no use. The boy has made up his mind. Just look at him. He looks just like his pa, or you, when you've made a decision. Mark my words. He ain't changin' his mind."

The senator continued. "Clay, what are you going to do? The robbery was probably weeks ago. The robbers have already escaped. You have no chance of finding them, so you're just going to ride to Uvalde, say hello to your friends, and ride back? There's a norther going on out there. It's liable to drop into the teens tonight. You and your animals don't stand a chance."

Clay kept on packing. He pulled out his bedroll, and this time he took his soogan. He tossed an extra blanket in it before he rolled it up with his slicker. Then he turned back to the closet and pulled out the heavy coat he'd worn in New York and laid it on the bed. His grandfather looked at it.

"You're joshing me, right? You think that'll keep you warm out there? Not even a little chance." He let out a big sigh, and said, "All right. Raymond, get my big buffalo coat."

"Yes, sir." Ray said and dashed back to the senator's room, returning with the buffalo coat. He handed to the senator.

"If you're dead set on doing this, Son, then take this coat. It'll keep you warm in some mighty cold weather, but it's heavy. I'm guessing just that coat alone weighs twenty-five to thirty pounds. But it's cut so it'll lay over your legs. You'll get warmth and so will Blue."

Clay finished packing. "I just need enough to get to Uvalde. I can buy whatever else I need from the Grahams' store."

He turned to the bedroom door, as ready as he could ever be. Ray had taken his saddlebags and filled them with food. The senator stepped aside and Ray entered the room to pick up Clay's bedroll.

"You've got a lot of weight, here," the senator said. "Blue will have a heavy load. You need to take another horse with you."

"That's a good idea, Grandpa. I'll buy one from Mr. Platt."

"No, take one of mine. Take Pearl. You've ridden him, he knows you, and he's big, fast too. Tie a couple of wool blankets over him. That'll help whichever one you're not riding to stay warmer."

"Thanks, Grandpa. I know Pearl means a lot to you. I'll take care of him, as best I can." He shook hands with his grandpa, then shrugged into the buffalo coat, and looked at his gear.

"I'll help with the gear," Ray said. He had left the room for a moment to slip into his sheepskin coat. Now, he reached down and picked up the saddlebags, along with Clay's Winchester.

"Thanks, Ray." Clay turned back to his grandpa. "I almost forgot. Andy is alone in the office. He said his mom would worry about him if he's not home for lunch."

"I'll go down with you two and relieve him until Ray gets back. Don't worry."

Bundled up, the three of them made their way down the stairs, the senator waving as he turned in the opposite direction from them. Reaching the small stable door, the two men pushed inside, the wind, sleet, and snow following them.

Platt stepped out of his office. "I hope you fellers ain't planning on headin' anywhere today. This here norther is way too frosty to be out in." He looked at the gear they were carrying and Clay's buffalo coat, and shook his head. "Reckon you boys have lost your minds."

"Mr. Platt, I need Blue and my grandpa's Pearl. We'll put the bags and bedroll on Blue. If you'd fasten a couple of blankets on Pearl, to keep him warm, I'll shift them to Blue when I switch horses. I'll also need a bag of oats."

Platt looked at Clay like he was crazy.

"Ray, thanks for your help. I've got to be on my way. I don't have to tell you, but take good care of Grandpa."

Clay pulled off his gloves and the men shook hands.

"You take care, Clay. I don't envy you. Good luck." Ray turned and opened the small entry door in the barn, stepping out into the wind. He pulled it to and Clay went back to saddling Blue.

He put the bit under his shirt for a few minutes to warm it, before he put it in the horses mouth. By the time he finished with Blue, Platt walked up with Pearl.

"How you like it?" Platt asked pointing to the two heavy blankets draped over Pearl.

Clay walked to the white horse and examined the rig. Platt had a double-blanket rig that had a cinch strap around Pearl's neck and chest, and one fastened around his belly. The straps passed over and through the blankets so the upper portions were pulled close around Pearl, while the remainder hung free, covering his back and legs. He examined it closely.

"It looks like the blankets will stay on even if the horse is running."

"That's the idea, Clay. I thought of this years ago but have used it only a couple of times. It should work for you. Now, here's another set of straps you can use when you've stopped. Give each horse one blanket, fasten 'em, and they'll be fine through the night, or at least better. Although, I don't think anything or anybody, including you, will be fine through this night."

"Young feller, you ain't got a lick of sense if you take off in this. There'll be livestock dead overnight."

"It's something I've got to do, Mr. Platt. Thanks for your help." Clay swung up on Blue, while Platt walked over to the big swinging doors. He managed to get one of them open, against the driving wind, enough for Clay to ride out into the white misery. He needed to make one stop before heading for Uvalde.

Clay tied the horses to the hitching rail outside the Rangers' office. The wind threatened to knock him from his feet as he carefully climbed the icy steps and pushed through the door. Papers flew from the desk, and the ranger behind it cursed and leaped up to grab them. Clay closed the door quickly and said, "Is Major Jones in?"

The ranger—Clay didn't know him—motioned with his thumb toward the back office. Clay shucked his gloves and the buffalo coat, and laid them on one of the chairs, along with his hat.

A voice inside the office called, "Come on in, Clay."

He walked inside, and Major Jones waved him over to the desk.

"What in blazes are you doing out on a day like this," he asked.

"Major, I just heard about Uvalde. Sheriff Haskins was a friend, and so are the Grahams who own the bank. I've got to get over there and make sure they're all right."

"It'll be terrible travel, Clay."

"Yes, sir. The reason I'm here is to find out if you have any further information as to who else might have been hurt?"

"No. Sorry. I'm afraid I know no more than the sheriff."

"All right. I've got to be on my way. The horses are standing outside. Don't want to leave them still too long."

"Are you going after the robbers?"

"I hadn't thought of it, but I might. Depends on what I find out."

"I thought so," Major Jones said. "Be careful. If you can, bring them in. Now get out of here before your horses freeze, and good luck."

"Yes, sir." Clay spun around, picked up his gear, and put it on. This time he took a kerchief out of his pocket and tied it around his face. After putting his hat on, he put another kerchief over the top of the hat and his ears, tying it under his chin. He nodded to the ranger at the desk and opened the door. From the corners of his eyes he could again see papers flying off the man's desk. He closed the door quickly and carefully moved to Blue's side. Once there, swinging into the saddle, he adjusted the buffalo robe over his legs, and with Pearl in tow, headed Blue for Uvalde.

They crossed the Colorado River on the one-lane bridge. The river was freezing along the shorelines. He'd probably have to break ice for himself and the horses to drink. The sleet had stopped and the wind was slowing, but the snow was getting heavier. It was hard to believe that yesterday, it was warm under a clear sky. Texas weather, he thought, shaking his head in disgust.

They continued along the road to San Antonio. He planned on cutting west of the city, so he didn't waste time going through it. But he was getting way ahead of himself. He would consider himself lucky if he made it to San Marcos tonight. If he could make it there, he'd be able to put the horses up in the livery and get a hotel room. He certainly couldn't travel in this at night. He pushed on. The road made traveling easier. Blue and Pearl slogged on through the freezing cold. They had been on the move for two hours when they came to Grass Creek.

Clay could tell Blue was tiring. It was unusual for the big horse, but he was carrying much more weight than normal, and the cold was sapping his strength. He rode into the dry creek bottom and checked both directions for ponds of standing water in the creek. Downstream, about twenty yards, was a wide pool, bank to bank. He dismounted and led the two horses across the river rocks, to the pond. The water was shallow and already freezing around the edges. Steam, from the warmer water, rose to meet the snowflakes.

He pulled his Winchester out of its scabbard and using the rifle butt, broke the ice from the edges, so that the horses didn't have to walk out into the frigid pond. They both immediately moved up and thrust their noses into the cold water, blew, and started drinking. Clay knelt between them, took off his glove, scooped several handfuls, and drank it. Cold, but good.

He needed to switch the gear and blankets between horses.

Fifteen minutes later, the blankets were on Blue and the gear on Pearl. He mounted Pearl, and, leading Blue, he headed south.

It was dark when he rode into San Marcos. He rode down the main street, looking for a livery. He passed a hotel, and next to it an eating establishment. Midway through town he found the livery. It was closed. Clay rode up to the doors, threw the pin, and holding onto one side, backed Pearl up sideways. Once he had the door wide open, he rode the two horses into the dark cavern. He dismounted and swung the door closed. The wind was letting up. Thank goodness, he thought.

Clay struck a match and made out a lantern on a post. He took it down and lit it. After a few moments it cast a bright circle of light. He led each horse into a stall and started stripping gear.

A back door opened, and footsteps crunched on the dry hay.

"Howdy, Mister, mighty cold tonight. Name's Tater. Got that name from my ma, cause I love sweet potatoes. How long you plan on staying? Till the storm's over?"

Clay had everything off the two horses. He nodded to Tater. "What's your surname?"

"Well, don't rightly know what a surname is, but my first name is Franklin, and my last name is Coke, but everybody calls me Tater."

Clay nodded. "I understand, but would it be all right with you if I called you Mr. Coke?"

"Well, nobody ever called me mister, but shore, that would be fine."

"Good. Mr. Coke, I'll be leaving in the morning. Can you give me a hand rubbing down these horses? Let's be sure they're both dry. Then, if you have a couple of dry blankets to toss on them, I'd be much obliged. If you don't have any oats, there's a bag of them with my gear."

After the horses were finished, Clay walked to his gear and extracted the Roper. "Mr. Coke, do you mind if I leave my things right here? I'll be leaving early in the morning. I might as well go ahead and pay you now. You might still be sleeping when I leave."

"Sure," Coke said, "you can leave everything right there. Four bits for both horses ought to do it. You might have to break the ice in the trough in the morning. I reckon it's gonna be mighty cold."

Clay pulled out fifty cents and gave it to the man. "I saw a restaurant by the hotel. Would you recommend it?"

"If you're hungry, I'd sure recommend it, seeing as it's the only one open this late."

"Great, thanks. I'll be at the hotel."

"What's your name, Mister?"

"Clay Barlow."

"The man looked at him for a moment. "You the feller whose folks were murdered over near Uvalde, three maybe four years ago?"

Clay sighed. "Yes."

"Then that means you're the Del Rio Kid. Mighty pleased to meet you. I understand folks couldn't even see your hand move, and then your gun was a blazin'."

Clay turned for the door and said, his words as cold as the wind blowing through the cracks, "I don't go by that name." He pushed through the door into the chilling night air. Carrying the Roper and his saddlebags, he made his way to the restaurant. The warmth hit him as he passed through the doorway. He closed the door quickly to keep the cold out and surveyed the room. There were five tables, each with a tablecloth that had begun its life white. The chairs were rough-cut cedar, smoothed out enough to prevent getting splinters in your rear when you sat in them.

Two men occupied one table, their coats lying in the empty chairs. They looked up when Clay entered. The older one seemed to take Clay's measure, then went back to his supper. Clay took off the buffalo coat. By the time he got it off, he had already begun sweating. He laid it across one chair, and stood the Roper up against the coat, in easy reach.

The waitress came out from the kitchen with a coffeepot and a cup. "Hi. All we've got left is beef stew. I do have some home-made bread I can throw in." She set the cup down and started to pour.

"No thanks, ma'am," Clay said. "Don't drink it. Beef stew sounds mighty fine."

She nodded and went back to the kitchen.

"Bad night to be out," the older man said.

Clay looked over. "Yes, sir. It is mighty cold."

"Staying the night?"

"Yep. Too cold to travel. Reckon there ought to be a room at the hotel."

The other man nodded over his coffee cup. "Yes, sir. There sure is. I'm the night manager. When you get finished, just come on over. I'll fix you right up." The man took one more sip of his coffee and said to the other man, "Night, Sheriff. See you tomorrow."

The sheriff nodded. "Tomorrow."

The woman returned from the kitchen and placed a big bowl of thick, steaming stew in front of Clay and several thick slices of bread. He immediately started eating. The stew and bread disappeared quickly. The woman came back out.

"Care for some more? Don't cost no more."

Clay grinned at her. "Maybe another bowlful would be nice. That was mighty good."

"Glad you liked it. One thing I like about stew in the winter, it sticks to your ribs and heats you up." She picked up his bowl. A couple of minutes later she was back with the bowl, along with more bread and a large bowl of bread pudding. "A little something for your sweet tooth."

"Thank you, ma'am."

She nodded and returned to the kitchen.

The sheriff glanced over at Clay. "Mabel likes a good eater. So, where are you from?"

Clay slowed his eating with the second bowl of stew. Between bites, he said, "That's hard to say. Right now, I guess you'd have to say Austin."

"I'm Sheriff Bob Nelson. I missed your name."

"Didn't mention it, but I'm Clay Barlow." Clay watched the sheriff for a reaction. There was none.

The sheriff turned his chair toward Clay and leaned back. "You planning on staying in our little town for a while?"

"No, Sheriff. I'm headed for Uvalde."

"Uvalde. Understand they had a bank robbery?"

Clay nodded as he finished off his stew. He pushed the bowl aside and pulled up the bread pudding. He could smell the cinnamon. He loved bread pudding. He shoved his spoon into the pudding and glanced to the sheriff. "Yep. Had a friend killed there."

"Really, who might that be?"

"The sheriff. Sheriff Haskins."

"Yeah. He was a passing acquaintance, but I never like to hear of a lawman killed."

"Sheriff, it's my understanding the one that killed him had blond hair, almost white. You seen anyone like that around here?"

"I hadn't heard that description. Come to think of it, I have seen a feller like that. Woman moved here maybe two, three years ago. Moved in with her divorced sister, Mrs. Wilma Norton. The two of them take in sewing and mending, laundry too. Right nice ladies. They also take in boarders. Her name's Davis. She's got a son that comes through occasionally. Don't know his name. Did hear his ma call him Cotton once."

The spoon that was headed for Clay's mouth stopped. That was the fella that braced him and backed down in Brackett.

## 16

"Sheriff, do you know if he's here now?"

"Haven't seen him for several weeks. I did notice he didn't seem to mix with folks when he was here. Just kinda kept to himself."

Clay nodded. "He may be the killer. His father is the marshal of Brackett. I had a little run-in with the son several years ago. But I can't imagine he would've turned outlaw while his father is still marshal."

"He ain't," Sheriff Nelson said. "Been several years, but I heard he was tossed off a horse. Ended up with a broke neck." The sheriff picked up his cup of coffee. "So Mrs. Davis is the marshal's wife. I'll be dogged. She never mentioned it."

"Sheriff, if he's the man, he's almighty dangerous. I know of at least two men he's killed. I imagine you know Whip. The stage driver. Whip said he's the fastest he's ever seen."

"Well, Mr. Barlow, I've been a sheriff for quite a few years. I've found that a shotgun can take care of the fastest man. I guess you've learned that too." The sheriff indicated Clay's Roper leaning against the buffalo coat.

"It certainly can make a difference." Clay laid a quarter, dime, and nickel on the table and stood. "Sheriff, I'm heading to the hotel, and I'll be leaving for Uvalde early in the morning. When I finish there, I'll come back through San Marcos. If you go after this Cotton Davis, assuming he's the right man, he rides with a gang, so be careful."

"Don't worry yourself, young fella. I've been over the mountain, but I will be cautious. See you on your return."

Clay stood, gathered up his goods, and headed for the hotel.

Little time passed before Clay was in a snug room on the second floor of the hotel. The wind had died down, and so had the sleet and snow. Quickly getting undressed, and with the pocket pistol in his hand, his gunbelt on the chair, and the Roper leaning against the wall next to his bed, he crawled between the stacked heavy quilts.

The sheets were icy, but the weight of the warm quilts was reassuring. Straightening his legs, he stretched out to his full length, and his feet slid out from under the covers. *Dang,* he thought. Turning diagonally across the bed he could just barely keep his feet covered if he stretched out. *When I have my own home, I'm going to build a bed long enough for me.* With that thought, he rolled over and was sound asleep.

HE HAD LAID his watch on the chair with his guns. No light come through the frosted panes of the window. Stretching his arm out from under the warm cover, he picked up his watch to check the time. It was so dark in the room he couldn't see the face. The bed felt good, and his room was freezing. Both good reasons to stay in bed, but not good enough. He threw the covers back, jumped out of bed, lit the lamp with a match from his vest hanging on the back of the chair, and dressed quickly. He thrust his feet into his cold boots without bothering to go through his normal ritual of checking for stingers or biters, too cold for them or him.

After he dressed, he checked his watch—four o'clock. Good, he wanted to get an early start. He'd grab some breakfast, make sure the horses were fed and watered, and hopefully be out of here by five.

HE HAD TAKEN it slow in the miserably cold weather. San Marcos was no more than seven miles behind them when daylight began breaking timidly over the stark white landscape. Nothing moved, except for him and his horses. He had met no one, nor had he seen any animals, no cattle, no deer, not even a squirrel when he crossed the last creek. There was no wind. It was as still and white as a frozen, uninhabited wasteland. He rode on.

About nine, he stopped and changed horses. He managed to break through the ice so they could get a drink, and was soon on his way. Finally, early in the afternoon, he saw a stage in the distance. Drawing near, he moved to one side of the road and waited.

His chilled face broke into a grin when he saw the driver. It was Whip. The stage pulled alongside and stopped.

Whip unwrapped the long towel from around his face and neck, leaned over the side, and said, "You folks might as well get out and stretch yore legs. We'll be stopped for a few minutes."

The door opened, and several men stepped down from the stage. One of them turned his face up to Whip. "Driver, I've an appointment in Austin with the governor. I expect you to keep this stage moving."

Whip spit a long stream of tobacco juice, turning the snow-covered ground into a brown blob. "Mister, I'm driving this here stage, and I reckon it'll get there when I do. Now if you'll stop jawing we'll get outta here a lot quicker." He turned to Clay and gave him a big grin. "Boy, you pick the best days to go for a ride across the country. Trying to get you a little fresh air?"

Clay smiled. "I was just minding my own business, when it looked like I might get run over by an ornery old stage driver, so I reckoned I best get out of the way."

Whip threw back his head and roared. In his crusty voice, he said, "Yeah, and it's a danged good thing you did. I ain't run me over any slick city boys lately, so I'm thinkin' it's about time."

Clay laughed, and said, "Yeah, I'm beginning to feel like one. How've you been doing? Looks like the arm is working well."

Whip swung his arm in a circle, almost knocking the fella riding shotgun off the stage. "Yes sirree, it's working mighty fine. Boy, what are you doing out on a God-forsaken day like today? You ought to be curled up in front of a fire, doing what lawyers do."

"I'll tell you, Whip. I would be, but I got word that the Uvalde bank was robbed and the sheriff killed. The sheriff and those bankers are my friends. Thought I'd go down there and see if I could be any help."

"That's fine, Clay. I was through there a week ago. The word is both the sheriff and the banker was shot by a blond-headed feller."

"Did you hear the name of the banker that was shot?"

"Sorry, Clay, I ain't heard a name. But as I was saying, folks claimed none of the rest of the robbers did any shootin'. Just him, and they said he didn't hesitate, just shot the sheriff, before he even had a chance to draw. I'm thinking that's the same guy that tried to rob us and killed Cleatus. He's one mean hombre."

"The guy that robbed the stage, was his hair almost white?"

"Yes sirree, so blond it was almost white."

"Listen to me," Clay said, "I think I know who it is. His name is James Davis, but everyone calls him Cotton because of his hair. His pa was marshal in Brackett several years ago. If you come across him, go to the law. He's extremely dangerous."

"I'll keep an eye out." Whip looked around at his passengers. "All right, folks, let's get loaded. We're burning daylight."

"I'll be seeing you, Whip," Clay said. He touched his hat in salute and nudged a tired Pearl forward.

LATE IN THE afternoon of the fourth day, he rode Blue into Uvalde. The trip had been hard on the horses and him. The first day of the four, had been short. Though hard at the time, it turned out to be the easiest. Then it got worse. They covered fifty miles the second and third day.

Clay had pushed the horses hard, wanting to be past San Antonio by the end of the second day. It didn't happen. The cold was relentless, sapping the horses' strength, even as he drove them forward. He gave it up. In the dark, on the west side of San Antonio, he stabled the horses and found a hotel room for himself.

The next evening, he reached D'Hanis and spent the night with his grandparents. They were thrilled to see him, and he them, but he was so tired his eyes were closing even as he ate. They sent him to bed. He got an early start the next morning, only to find the ground thawing, and the mud clinging in heavy clumps to the horses' hooves. The last thirty miles proved the most exhausting. But now he was here.

It hadn't changed much. If anything, the false cedar fronts of the buildings had just gotten grayer. The snow had disappeared, and the ground had changed from white and hard, to heavy, thick mud. Both animals were near exhaustion.

He rode them straight to the livery stable and pulled up to the trough—no ice to break. The horses drank while he went inside. "Mr. Johnson, you here?" he called.

"No sense yelling," Johnson said, coming out of his office. He walked down the steps and stopped. "Why, I'll be hornswoggled if it ain't Clay Barlow. Young feller, you've grown an almighty bunch. Let me get a good look at you." He walked over to Clay and looked him up and down. "Boy, you stand a long way from the ground. I've got to say, you look different." He stuck out his small, gnarled hand. "But, it's good to see you."

Clay smiled at the livery owner. The man never aged. He remembered him looking the same when he was a boy. "It's good to see you, Mr. Johnson."

Then Clay sobered. "I understand there's been unwelcome excitement around here lately."

Johnson shook his head. "Who'd ever believe it? Sheriff Haskins shot dead in the street, and old Mr. Graham shot and barely holding onto his life. And him a gen-u-ine hero to this town."

Wrinkles of worry invaded Clay's face. "How's he doing?"

"He's a tough ole man, he is. He's hanging on. The doc says he should be dead, but he's still here. Don't know how or why, but he is."

"Where is he, Mr. Johnson?"

"Why, Son, he's at the doc's. You remember where that is?"

"By the sheriff's office, and up the stairs."

"You mind taking care of my horses and gear? They've come some long hard miles and deserve some special care."

"I'll see to 'em. The Grahams are always talking about you. They'll be mighty happy to see you."

Clay took off running, his big, wooly buffalo coat billowing out from his side as he hurried through the mud to the doctor's office. The Grahams had been like family to him when he was growing up. In fact, Mr. Graham had given him the Roper when he was in pursuit of the outlaw gang that had killed his parents.

He ran up the stairs, the building vibrating at each step from his weight. He pushed the door open and stepped into the doctor's front office. Mrs. Graham and the doctor were staring at the door when he burst through. Her expression went from startled to recognition, and she dashed into his big arms, sobbing against the buffalo robe. They stood there for a few moments until she regained control of herself and stepped back.

"Clay Barlow, I knew you'd come just as soon as you heard. Why, my goodness gracious sakes alive, you had to travel in the terrible storm, but I'm so glad you're here and safe."

Clay grasped her arms. She seemed so small and frail. "How's Mr. Graham?"

Doctor Taylor spoke up. "It's good to see you, Clay. Mr. Graham is not doing well. I'm surprised he has lasted this long. He took a bullet to his midsection. I had to operate and clean things out, but there was a large blood loss. It's a miracle he's still with us. Now, it's looking like he might make it if we can get him through the infection. Right now, he's burning up with a fever."

Clay took off the heavy coat and laid it in a chair. "May I see him?"

"Of course," the doctor said.

As they entered the back room, Mrs. Graham took Clay by the hand and led him to her husband. "Clay Barlow is here, dear. He rode all the way in that terrible norther, just to see you. He is such a sweet boy."

Graham opened his eyes, and in a hoarse voice said, "Hello, Clay. It's good to see you. I can't believe how big you are. It must have been all that hard candy."

Clay looked down at the haggard, fever-racked body "It's sure good to see you, Mr. Graham. Sorry you're not feeling good, but I understand you're getting better."

Graham smiled. "We'll see. I'm tired now. Think I'll get some sleep. Good to see you, Clay." The wounded man closed his eyes and was soon snoring lightly.

The doctor motioned them out of the room. "At this point, there is not much we can do. Keep him warm, hydrated, and fed. We just have to wait until the fever breaks. The Good Lord's in control now."

Mrs. Graham looked reprovingly at the man. "Doctor Taylor,

He is always in control." She turned to Clay. "Come, Mr. Graham is in good hands. You come with me to my house and we can talk."

The two walked in silence down the stairs, and across the street to the general store, which the Grahams owned, and into the back. He followed her upstairs to their modest home.

"Please, Clay, sit down, and I'll fix us some hot lemonade."

"Thank you, ma'am." He remembered Mrs. Graham's lemonade during the summer. It was so good with the sugar cookies she always made. He laid his coat on a chair and took a seat at the little table. These were frugal people. Though they owned the biggest store in Uvalde, as well as the bank, they lived like everyone else.

She brought in the hot lemonade and poured a cup for each of them. After setting the kettle on the iron trivet, she turned back to the kitchen, and returned with a plate of sugar cookies. "I seem to remember you liked these sugar cookies."

He stood as she returned and sat. "Thanks." he said, a smile playing around the corners of his mouth as he took his seat. "I haven't had one of these in years." He picked up a cookie and took a bite. "Tastes just like I remember." Then he grew serious. "Mrs. Graham, what can you tell me about the robbery?"

She placed her hands in her lap. "It was horrible. We've had the bank for three years, now. Since, well, you know. Nothing like this has ever happened. I was in the store and Mr. Graham was at the bank. I happened to notice five men ride up to the bank. I didn't pay them any mind until two were left outside watching the horses, and the other three went inside." She lifted a small handkerchief and dabbed at a tear trying to escape from her right eye. With a big sigh, she continued.

"I heard a shot and a scream. I ran to the door just as they were running out. The sheriff had been at the barber shop next to the bank. He still had the sheet tied around his neck. Three men came out of the bank and the blond-headed man saw the sheriff wrestling with the sheet, trying to get to his gun, and shot him. Killed him right there in the street. What a horrible thing."

She stopped, taking a sip of her lemonade. "Mr. Graham wouldn't open the safe. That's why the blond man shot him. He told him to open the safe, and my brave husband said no. He said that money belonged to the citizens of Uvalde. He was entrusted with it, and he would not be the one to give it up to a thief. That man cursed him and shot my poor husband without a second thought." She dabbed at her eyes again. "They took the teller's money. That was a little over two hundred dollars. Then they dashed out of the bank, leaving Mr. Graham lying in a pool of blood."

She took a deep breath and looked up at Clay. "And how are you doing? I heard you are a New York trained lawyer now. That's just wonderful. We both are so proud of you."

"I'm doing fine. Thank you. Which direction did they head when they left town?"

"Why? You're not planning on going after them, are you?"

She looked at the hard eyes and determined set of his jaw. If possible, the mustache even gave him a fiercer look. "Oh, Clay. You're a lawyer now. You should leave this up to the lawmen."

"Mrs. Graham, the rangers are spread too thin to be able to deal with the robbery of a bank in a little town like Uvalde. I have a good idea who is leading this bunch, and I aim to find him and put a stop to this thievery and killing. Now, do you know if anyone noticed which way they were headed when they left town, or did anyone hear them say anything that might be of value?"

"I'm sorry, Clay. I don't know. The teller, old Mr. Simpson, and Mrs. Percy were the only other ones in the bank. Have another cookie."

Clay took another cookie—they were really good. "I suppose Mr. Simpson is in the bank. Could you tell me where I could find Mrs. Percy?"

"Yes. She lives in a small house on the south side of town. It's the one with all the roses."

"I remember the house. Though I can't say I remember her."

"She's always been a quiet one. Keeps to herself."

Clay stood. "Thanks for the information, Mrs. Graham. I'll go talk to them right now."

She remained seated. "It's so hard. We've been in Uvalde for all these years, even through the war and the Comanches and Apaches. Nothing like this has ever happened." She looked up at Clay.

*She looks old and tired,* he thought. *I have never seen her like this before.*

"Ma'am, Uvalde's been lucky. There's bad people in this world. Most folks, even out here in the West, are lucky enough to go through life without running into them. But then you do. Hopefully it won't happen here again. Now I need to talk to those folks. Maybe they saw or heard something."

Mrs. Graham stood. "While you're in town, you're welcome to stay here."

"Thank you, ma'am. I'll be in and out a bunch and don't want to disturb you. I'll stay at the hotel, but thank you. That's mighty nice of you."

Clay excused himself and headed down the stairs. He heard Mrs. Graham close her door as he was entering the general store. He questioned the lady who worked in the store with no positive results. Stepping outside, he looked up at the sky. The sun was breaking through the overcast. Hopefully, tomorrow would be warmer. The buffalo coat was welcome, but he found it bulky and restrictive.

He looked south, down the street, and saw the little home that should be Mrs. Percy's. He needed to interview her, but first, he wanted to talk to Mr. Simpson at the bank. Maybe the teller might remember something that could be helpful.

## 17

C lay walked into the bank. Simpson was alone at the teller's cage. "Evening, Mr. Simpson."

The man acknowledged him with a nod. "Long time no see, Clay. How can I help you?"

Clay shoved his hat to the back of his head and leaned on the teller counter. "Mr. Simpson, do you remember anything about the bank robbers that might have stood out, or maybe they said something that could be important?"

He scratched the bald spot at the crown of his head. "You got to remember, I was staring down the barrel of a big Colt .45. I wasn't thinking much about trying to record information. I was just thinking about not being ready to die. The blond fella was the only one that did any talking, and that wasn't much. He just told Mr. Graham to open the safe."

Simpson shook his head. "I couldn't believe what I was hearing when Mr. Graham told him no." The man looked up at Clay. "He had a gun pointed right at him and he said, 'No.' Now, what kind of guts does that take? If I'd had the combination I'd been spinning that dial like a roulette wheel. That's when the blond shot him. He didn't say anything, just shot him. They were wearing masks, and there's no way I could see his face, but I'd swear he was smiling when he pulled that trigger. One of the other robbers shoved a sack at me and told me to empty the cash drawer. I wasted no time in doing it."

"So you didn't notice anything?"

Simpson looked at the ceiling for a moment, rubbing his chin with his thumb and forefinger. "Come to think of it, the feller laid the bag on the counter, and then shoved it to me with his gun hand. It looked like his right arm was stove up, maybe broken at some time or other. He couldn't extend it full out, had to twist his body to get it to me. Same problem when he was reaching for it through the bars. Fact is, he was a little slow, and the blond fella, sounded like he was the boss, yelled at him. He said something like, 'Come on, Shad, let's go.' That's all I remember. I'm just glad to be alive. That blond fella acted like he liked to shoot people."

"Thank you, Mr. Simpson. You've been a big help. Has anyone investigated the robbery?"

"Well, the deputy has, if you want to call it an investigation. Don't seem like he's done much since the sheriff was killed. Sheriff Haskins was a good man."

Clay nodded in agreement. "Yes, sir. He was indeed. Thanks again." He left the bank and turned left to head south to Mrs. Percy's. Upon reaching her house, he tried his best to clean his boots on the edge of her steps. They were covered with mud from the street. He pulled out his Bowie and scraped the glue-like mess from the soles of his boots. After getting them as clean as he could, he wiped the knife off and slid it back into the scabbard, walked onto the porch and knocked at the door.

An attractive lady of middle age answered the door immediately.

"Yes?"

"Ma'am, I'm Clay Barlow. I'm looking into the bank robbery. Would you mind if I asked you a few questions?"

"Why, certainly. Do come in out of that frigid air."

Clay looked at the spotless living room behind the lady. "Ma'am, my boots are awfully muddy. Would you mind stepping out here on your porch? I know it's cold, but I don't want to mess up your floors."

She looked down at his muddy boots and laughed. "Come in this house. I raised a bunch of boys. They're all gone now, but a little mud doesn't frighten me, and take off that coat. You'll roast in here."

Clay walked in, closed the door, removed his coat, and stood on the entryway. "I can just stand here, ma'am. No need to track this mud into your home."

"Goodness, young man. Come in and sit down. Don't worry about the mud. It gives me something to do. Since Mr. Percy died, and the boys are gone, I have so little to do around here. Now, please, sit."

Clay walked in and sat on the couch she indicated. She sat in a wingback chair across from him, clasped her hands in her lap, and leaned forward. "Call me Norma. What can I do for you?"

"I'll get right to it. Is there anything you can remember about the bank robbery?"

"Wasn't that horrid? Poor Mr. Graham getting shot. I just wish I'd had a gun. I would have certainly given those boys what for."

"Did you say boys, ma'am?"

"Yes, I certainly did. Of course, they were men, but they weren't much older than you."

"Are you sure, Norma? I know that during something as scary as a bank robbery, we tend to not be quite as alert."

"Of course I'm sure. I raised six boys. I know a boy when I see one. They carry themselves different than a man. They don't have the self-confidence that comes with experience. A woman notices such things. I feel so sorry for their parents, to have worked all those years raising your children only to see them turn out as lowly bank robbers. It just must be heartbreaking."

"Yes, ma'am, it must be. Did you happen to notice anything else?"

"As a matter of fact, I did, two things. The leader had hair so blond it was nearly white. He was a hard one. If he isn't stopped, he'll continue killing.

"And one of the other boys had an injured right shoulder. An old injury, but injured nonetheless. He favored it, and his movement, or range was limited. He's right-handed, too. Must be difficult. If he was planning on working cattle, he couldn't throw a loop at all."

"That's pretty observant."

"Yes, well, Mr. Percy owned a ranch. I sold it and moved into town after he died, and just before the depression, thanks to the Grahams. Mr. Graham visited me and suggested I sell. He said the market was about to drop. A big ranch stepped in and bought it. I'm so glad they did. I would have lost it in the depression. The Graham's are such a blessing."

Clay noticed it was getting late, and he wanted to talk to the deputy before he headed to the hotel.

"Can you think of anything else, Norma?"

She thought for a moment, then shook her head. "No. That's all I can remember."

Clay stood, picked up his coat, and walked to the door. "Thank you, ma'am."

She followed him. "I hope I've been some help."

"You've been a big help. You have a keen sense of observation. Thank you."

He left her smiling as she closed the door. He stepped off into the mire and marched up the street to the sheriff's office. Reaching the office, he pushed the door open and walked in.

"Close the door!" the man at the desk shouted. "You want to freeze us out?"

As cold as it was outside, it was oppressively hot inside. The pot-bellied stove was glowing. He quickly shucked the coat and tossed it on a chair. "You the deputy?"

"Acting sheriff. What can I do for you?"

"I'm Clay Barlow. I've got some questions about the bank robbery."

The man took a long look at Clay. "Why?"

"I have money in the bank, and the Grahams are my friends. I'd like to find out what happened."

The man thought for a moment and seemed to make up his mind. "All right. Shoot."

"Do you remember anything special about the robbery?"

"No. The sheriff had sent me over to Sabinal to deliver some papers. I got back the next day, only to find Sheriff Haskins dead."

"How long have you been deputy?"

"About a year. I heard tell about you. Sheriff mentioned you a time or two. You own a ranch up north of here, right?"

"Yes, I do. What's your name, Deputy?"

"It's Cooley, Mason Cooley. Sheriff hired me when I was out of work. He was a good man. Reckon I'm not much of a lawman, more of a cowpuncher. Jobs are hard to find now."

"Yes, they are." Clay stood and slipped his coat on. "I'll be hanging around until we find out what's going to happen with Mr. Graham. I'm over at the hotel."

Clay stepped back outside into the cold night. The sky had cleared, and the stars were twinkling, clear and bright. He walked to the hotel and got a room, then slogged back over to the doctor's office. Lights were on, so he stepped inside. The little bell on the door tinkled, bringing a flash of memory of a black-haired beauty with violet eyes. Then it was gone.

The doctor stepped into his front office. "No change. He's a fighter. I'm surprised he's hung on this long. I really don't expect him to last through the night. Although, I haven't expected him to last through any of the previous nights."

"I'll check on him in the morning," Clay said, turning back to the door. "See you tomorrow, Doc."

Clay thought about grabbing some supper, but he was exhausted. He had some jerky in his saddlebags, and some biscuits. That would have to do for tonight. He made his way to his room. After shedding his coat and guns, he pulled the jerky, a couple of biscuits, and a cleaning rag out of his saddlebags. He ate while cleaning his guns. His eyes kept drooping on him. Finally, with the guns clean, he tucked the rag back into the saddlebags, positioned the guns, and slipped himself into the waiting bed. He was asleep by the time his head hit the pillow.

CLAY AWOKE as dawn was breaking. He tossed back the cover and pulled out some clean clothes. He felt great after a good night's sleep. His youthful body rebounded quickly. He needed a bath, and, fortunately, the hotel had a bathhouse in back. Slipping pants, shirt and boots on, he shoved the pocket pistol in his waistband, grabbed his clean clothes, and went down to the front desk to tell the clerk to make sure there was hot water in the bathhouse.

After being assured there was plenty of hot water, he headed for the back.

Steam was rising from the cracks in the bathhouse. The cold nipped at him as he dashed across the short distance between the hotel and the out building. Stepping inside, he was greeted by a wave of escaping steam. Once the steam cleared, he was able to see there were three tubs and a big stove with a smaller tub of water sitting on it. The young man looked up as Clay walked in.

"Good morning, sir. Need a bath?"

Clay started shedding clothes and tossing them on a stand. "Darn right I do. Which tub?"

The boy pointed to a tub three-quarters filled with hot water.

"That'd be the one, sir. Just have a seat in it, and I'll pour the rest of this water over you."

"Perfect," Clay said. He stripped and settled into the tub, his knees almost under his chin.

The young man picked up the smaller tub filled with steaming water and poured it over Clay's head, drenching his upper body.

"Whoo-wee," Clay said. "That's hot, but it sure feels good. Thanks."

A stand between the two tubs had a big square of lye soap resting on it. Clay picked it up and went to work on his legs. It felt terrific to be taking a hot bath, getting the road dirt off. He had been on the trail for four days in the winter cold. It felt like the hot water had soaked the chill right out of his bones. When he'd finished, his upper body was lathered and so was his black hair. "Could I talk you out of some more water to rinse with?"

"Yes, sir," the young man said. He dipped a bucket of hot water from the tub on the stove, brought it over, and slowly poured it over Clay's head and shoulders. The boy handed him a towel and turned back to the stove.

Clay stood and worked the towel through his black hair, rubbing with vigor. Then he toweled off his body and slipped his clean clothes on. It felt good to be clean again. He wiggled his toes in his warm socks and slid his feet down into his stovepipe boots, grabbed the pulls, yanked and stomped, and his clean, warm feet slid into his boots.

"What do I owe you?"

"That'll be fifteen cents," the young man said.

Clay handed him two bits. "Keep the change. The bath was worth it."

The boy beamed. The hotel didn't pay him much, but the extra ten cents would really help. "Thank you, sir. Have a nice day."

Clay nodded and took off back to the hotel. He wanted to get something to eat, and then head over to the doctor's office and see how Mr. Graham was doing. He was not going to leave Uvalde until he knew whether the man was going to live or die. He found himself in a time crunch, because Blessing's trial was scheduled on November twenty-third. He needed to testify. If he wasn't there, the judge would probably release the old scoundrel. The man belonged in prison, not on the loose trying to put a hole in him or any of his family or friends.

The day was warming under the heat of the sun. Clay elected to forego the buffalo coat and stick with the frock coat he had been wearing beneath it. Armed and ready, he headed out of his room and down the stairs. He stopped at the front desk and paid his bill, then crossed the lobby to the restaurant. His order was prepared quickly, and he set about putting away five eggs, a pile of bacon, and a stack of hotcakes. His hunger comfortably satiated, he dropped four bits on the table, grabbed his gear, and headed for the front door.

As he reached for the doorknob, the clerk spoke up. "Mr. Barlow, I am sorry. A message came for you earlier."

Irritated, Clay went back to the front desk and took the white piece of paper from the man. He read it, then turned and dashed for the doctor's office.

He burst into the office, moving straight to the room Mr. Graham was in. The doctor stepped into the hall. "You got my note?"

"Yes."

"Good, I'm glad you're here. Mrs. Graham is also inside. Mr. Graham's fever broke early this morning. His color is good, and I feel sure he is going to make it. I don't know how. It certainly was out of my control."

Clay shook the doctor's hand. "Thanks, Doc. You had a lot to do with it. If you hadn't operated on him, he would never have made it."

"Well, be that as it may, come in."

Mrs. Graham was in the room with her husband, standing by his side, holding his hand. She looked up, eyes glistening, when Clay walked in. "He's just too stubborn to die. Thank goodness."

Mr. Graham turned his head toward Clay and shot him a weak grin. "Hi, Clay, boy. How are you doing?"

He smiled down on the older man. "A lot better now that you're doing better. How does it feel to be a real live hero?"

"Shaw, boy. I'm no hero. Anybody else would have done the same thing."

Clay shook his head. "No, sir. Nobody else would have done the same thing. You should have let them have the money, then you wouldn't be going through this. The town owes you a lot."

Mr. Graham started to give a feeble shake of his head.

"Listen to him, Graham," the doctor said. "Clay's telling it straight. You saved this town's bacon. You and your wife have helped a lot of people through this depression, and now you did this? Why, they ought to change the name of the town to Graham."

Mrs. Graham wiped her eyes. "That's so kind to say, Doctor Taylor. We love this town. It has helped us in the past. We're just returning the favor."

Mr. Graham raised his hand and Clay grasped the weak fingers in his own. "Thank you for coming, Clay. Mrs. Graham told me you planned on chasing those criminals. Please leave it to the sheriff or the rangers. You're a lawyer now. Don't risk your life over a few dollars."

Clay laughed. "You mean like you did?"

Graham cleared his throat and smiled. "Well, I take your point, but this is not your job. Let it be—although I am thrilled to see you. My sweet wife told me you rode all the way from Austin in a terrible norther to get here. Thank you, but please let it end here."

Clay looked down at the frail man. The doctor was right, his cheeks were almost rosy, not the pasty white they were yesterday.

He was healing. "Mr. Graham, I'm going to look into their location. I'll not make a point of trying to track them down, but I will give the information I have to the deputy and to the rangers. I ran into this bunch about three years ago. It's time they were stopped, but I'll leave the law to do it. Since you're on the mend, I'm going to head back to Austin."

The doctor leaned over the bed. "Graham, you need to rest." He turned to Clay. "It's time you leave. He's had enough excitement for one day. Looks like he's out of the woods, but he still needs to rest. If anything happens, I'll let you know."

"Goodbye, Clay," Mrs. Graham said. She came around the bed and gave him a tight hug. "You have no idea how much it means to us to have you come out to check on him, but please be careful."

Mr. Graham raised his hand again and waved. "Bye, Clay." He dropped it and closed his eyes.

Mrs. Graham turned and went back to her husband. She sat in the chair by his bed and took his hand. Clay watched for a moment, then followed the doctor into his office. He pulled a card from his pocket with the Barlow Law and Land logo on it and gave it to the doctor. "Doc, you can reach me here, or they'll know how to find me. Let me know of any changes."

The two men shook hands, and Clay stepped out on the porch and looked north toward his ranch. *I've got time before the trial. It's been almost three years since I've been there. I think I'll stop by the ranch and see how everything's going. No telling where those bandits are now.*

## 18

Clay stepped onto the street. The temperature was warming quickly. It was starting to feel like a spring day. He turned and headed toward the bank.

Entering, he stepped up to the teller's cage. "Morning, Mr. Simpson. I need to withdraw a little money." The teller slid a form across to Clay.

"Leaving town?"

"Yep. I've got to get back to Austin." He withdrew three hundred dollars, put fifty of it in his coat pocket, and, since the bank was empty with the exception of Mr. Simpson, he sat in a chair and stuffed the rest of it in his boot. Then he pushed his pantleg back down in the boot and stood.

Mr. Simpson chuckled. "I always said you were a smart hombre."

Clay laughed. "I figure the smell of my feet should keep any thieves away." He raised his hand. "Adios."

Stepping outside again, he headed for the livery. He breathed in the fresh air, a smell of cedar on the soft breeze from the north. His stride was that of a man with a purpose. He had a trial to get back to. That was certainly true, but he planned to make a couple of stops along the way. He wanted to see the Hewitts and find out how the ranches were doing. Then, maybe he'd mosey on up to the homeplace and spend a couple of days there. He had left the woodpile stacked tall, and supplies in the kitchen cabinets, in case some busted cowboy came along. Hopefully, there would still be sufficient supplies there. Never leaving anything to chance, he had picked up additional supplies from the Grahams' general store. He'd get that loaded, tack up the horses, and be on his way.

He just wished he knew which direction those outlaws took off in. Of course, that didn't mean a lot. If they were smart, they could have waited until they were out of sight of the town and turned in a different direction.

He walked into the barn to find old Mr. Johnson mucking out the stalls. The man looked up as he walked in. "You've got that travelin' look, Clay. I bet you need yore horses."

Clay walked over and picked up the saddle blanket and laid it across Blue's back, then turned and headed back for the saddle. "Yes, sir. I'm on my way." He nodded at the stall Johnson had been working in. "Can't find someone to help you do that?"

"Sure I can. Just can't find a body to do it as good as me. You want these blankets on that white nag?"

Clay laughed. "Careful, if the senator hears you say that about his horse, you might be in trouble."

"The old man rubbed Pearl on his back. "Humph. I knew yore grandpa when he was hardly big enough to stay on a horse. He best not give me no lip."

Clay laughed. "I'll remember that. Where'd you know him?"

"I knowed his pappy. That would make his pappy yore great-grandpap. It's been a smart while back. I was just a young feller then, not much older than yore grandpap. His pap hired me to break horses. Anyway, what you want me to do with these blankets?"

"I'll roll them up and tie them with the saddlebags."

"Boy, yore sure loading up Blue. I've got an old saddle back here that you can slap on this here white horse. Then you can tie a bunch of stuff on it, and if you needed to switch horses, why you wouldn't have to change saddles. How's that sound to you?"

"How much?"

"Did I say something about money? I'm loanin' it to you."

"Mr. Johnson, that's mighty kind of you, but I don't know when I'll be back this way."

"Son, I got several of these things laying back in the store-room. It ain't like I'm going to miss this one."

"Well, thank you. I'll get it back as soon as I can."

The old man turned for the storeroom. "Fine." He brought out the saddle. It was old and dusty. With a rag from a peg on the office wall, he started dusting off the saddle."

"Mr. Johnson, that saddle looks to be in good shape."

"Got my own formula. Every once in a while, when I ain't got anything to do, I'll pull one of them saddles out and clean her up. Keeps me busy."

"That's really a good idea, but why don't you let me pay you for it?"

The old man looked up in frustration. "Dad-blame it, boy. I said no."

He raised up from the saddle, put a hand to his back, and stretched for a second. Then his clear, sharp eyes focused on Clay. "What you did, when you sent that message to the Grahams, just before this here depression started, saved many a fine folk around here. This town owes you big. I figger I can help out on that debt a little bit. Now, let me do it, and quit pesterin' me."

Clay started to ask if he could help with the saddle but decided to keep his mouth shut. With both horses ready, and the heavy load removed from Blue, Clay swung up into the saddle.

He had a quick thought. "Mr. Johnson, you didn't happen to see which way those bank robbers left town, did you?"

The old man looked up at him with a small grin, and then he winked. "Well, ain't you the smart one. You know that good-for-nothing deputy ain't never asked me one question, and me standing here the whole time, watching them head out of town.

"With the first shot, I grabbed ole meat-in-the-pot and came hot-footing it outside. It's an 1860 .54-caliber Lorenz, with adjustable sights. I used to be able to break a turkey's neck at three hundred yards. Anyway, those fellers hung around long enough for me to get out here and take a shot. Can't believe I missed. I was aimin' for his head. But it looked like I hit him in the right shoulder. If they ain't got it out, he's carrying around my hunk of lead."

"Good for you, Mr. Johnson. Could you tell if any others were hit?"

"Far as I saw, they was all in good shape, exceptin' the one I blasted. He was squeezing the biscuit. I mean, he was hanging on to that saddle horn for dear life."

"So did you see which direction they took?"

"I did better than that. After they had took off, I mounted Rosy, back there." Johnson indicated the mule munching straw in the last stall. "We rode out after 'em. I ain't expected to catch those bandits. Don't know what I'd done with 'em had I caught 'em. They took off toward D'Hanis on Wolls Road. They was slick, though. After they crossed the Frio, they turned up north, following the river. They wuz headed into some rough country, up toward the Hewitts' and yore ranch."

If they kept going into the broken hill country, they would probably never be found. But there was an off chance that Hewitts' riders might have seen something. "You said nothing about this to the deputy?"

"Dumb as a rock, I tell you. He ain't never asked me, and me the only one what rode after them." The old man shook his head with disgust. "The only reason Sheriff Haskins hired him was to keep the jail clean, and he did a mighty poor job of that."

Clay leaned over and shook his hand. "You've been a big help, Mr. Johnson. I've got to be on my way, but I'll get your saddle back to you as soon as I can."

"Glad to help, and don't you worry none about that old saddle. You just watch out for yourself."

Clay touched his hat. "Adios, amigo."

With Pearl on a lead, Clay walked the horses out of town, taking the road he always used to go back and forth to the ranch. It was almost due north from Main Street and immediately led into the foothills. With this early start, he should be at the Hewitt ranch around three or four, close to suppertime. He rocked easy in the saddle as Blue made his way out of Uvalde. The horse could tell they were headed home.

They had been climbing for a while when they came out of a patch of trees. Clay pulled up and looked over the cedar, or ashe juniper, as Pa called it, and oak country. Pa always said that it was unfair to say this country had only ashe juniper and oak. There was willow, ash, cottonwood, and sycamore, just to name a few. There were also some wonderful grazing areas for stock. The land they owned, cut through by the Frio River, provided healthy grazing for their herd. Blue continued through the rough-cut country, riding past prickly pear patches taller than a man.

The sun was drifting toward the forested horizon when he topped the last hill overlooking the Hewitt ranch. If he continued riding north, that would put him home at a reasonable hour.

He wondered what Sarah would think, seeing him. It had been almost three years. Both his folks and Sarah's had figured on them getting married. He never had. She was a good friend, but that was all. True, he had kissed her one fall day when their families were on the Frio together, picking up pecans. But he always felt like she had caused the incident, not that he hadn't enjoyed it.

Sarah was the oldest of the Hewitts' children. When her ma died, her pa relied on her to take over the house, and she did it well. Clay had always thought she was a bit bossy. However, she took care of the family well, especially her younger brothers. She comforted them, after their mother's loss, and kept them focused on their schooling as they grew older.

Clay knew that Sarah had also planned on them getting hitched. He felt like she was really hurt when he announced he was going after his folks' killers. She had been cool to him when he returned from the manhunt. He had seen her several times before he left for New York, and it had never been the same. He admitted to himself that one day, he'd like to have a family. He just didn't think that Sarah would be part of it. Anyway, it wouldn't be now. He had things to do. He headed the horses downhill.

It was getting late, and lamps had been lit in the house. Not being dark yet, he rode boldly up to the hitching rail in front of the barn. He dismounted and led the horses to the trough that sat where the horses could drink either from inside or outside the corral. He heard the door of the house open and close. Turning, he saw Mr. Hewitt standing on the porch with a rifle. Alongside him were his sons, Toby and Tyler. Both boys were nearing their man years, and both were armed. Toby had to be seventeen, Tyler fifteen. The boys were slim waisted, with wide shoulders. Toby was building into quite a man. His shoulders and neck was getting thick like a rutting buck. Mr. Hewitt looked older, but still demonstrated the energy Clay remembered.

He heard footsteps from the barn. Glancing in that direction, he recognized Bo Nelson, one of Mr. Hewitt's cowhands. He'd been here as long as Clay could remember.

"You folks look like you're going to war," Clay said. Everyone recognized him at the same time, relaxed, and started toward him. Bo got there first.

"Boy, you're a sight for old eyes. We was just speculatin' about if you was still in New York City. It's mighty fine to see you. It shore is." He grabbed Clay's hand and gave it a hard shake.

"It's good to see you, Bo. You haven't changed a bit."

"Thanks, Clay. Reckon Sarah's good cookin' might have put a few extra pounds on me." He reached up and squeezed Clay's shoulder. "Ole Son, you've turned into a big bull."

Clay laughed and started to respond, but held off when the rest of the men gathered round. After hand-shaking and greetings, Mr. Hewitt said, "Your timing is just right. Take care of your horses and come on inside. You'll have a bite of supper with us and fill us in on what's been happening in your life."

"I'll help," Tyler Hewitt, the youngest of the family, sounded off.

Clay clapped Tyler on the shoulder and said, "Thanks, Tyler. You've grown so much, I don't think I'd recognize you if I met you somewhere off the ranch."

Tyler grinned, grabbing Blue's reins. He led the horse inside, followed by Clay and Toby. Mr. Hewitt and Bo headed toward the house.

They had finished with the horses and Tyler had gone back to the house. Clay was checking his gear before following him. The hay rustled behind him, and he figured Tyler had returned.

"Hello, Clay."

He turned to see Sarah standing there, her dark hair hanging loose over her shoulders, glistening in the last light of day. He stood and turned around to face her.

"Hi, Sarah. It's good to see you. How have you been?"

She looked smaller than he remembered. Of course, it had been almost three years. He hated how awkward it always felt around her now.

"Did you become a lawyer?"

"Yes. It's not what I expected."

"Are you going to set up your practice in Uvalde?"

"I don't know. I'll probably work with my grandpa for a while, until I make up my mind."

She grabbed onto his last comment. "Make up your mind about what?"

"Shouldn't we be going inside? It's getting dark out here."

"You've been outside in the dark before," she snapped. "Make up your mind about what?"

*Yep, that was the old Sarah. Sharp wit, sharp tongue. Well, give her what she wants, or we'll be out here till midnight.* "I'm still conflicted about the law and the rangers."

"Good gracious, Clay. Is there a choice? You practice law and help people that aren't shooting at you." She paused and said pointedly, "Or you shooting at them."

"Sarah, it's not that simple."

"It is that simple."

"After getting to know some of the lawyers I worked with in New York and Austin, if I was like them, I might stand a good chance of getting shot."

"Clay Barlow, don't turn this into a joke. You need to make the right decision."

She did it to him every time. He could feel himself getting angry. Not the cold anger he felt meeting a gunman, but the frustrated anger that came around when he felt he was wrong but didn't know why.

He took a deep breath. "It's really good to see you, Sarah. Why don't we go inside?"

She started to say something, thought better of it, and marched to the house. Clay had to stretch his long legs to keep up with her. He opened the door for her and she slid by him, no touch, no word. Everyone was finishing up eating when the two of them walked into the kitchen.

"Grab a chair, Clay," Mr. Hewitt said, indicating the chair next to Tyler. Sarah moved around and took her seat on her father's right, across the table from Toby.

Clay looked around the table. "Is Luke still here?"

Mr. Hewitt laughed. "He and Bo know more about this ranch than I do. I'd be hard pressed to let either one of them get away from me. Luke's out checking the condition of the cows up north on your property. We lost a few head from this norther. Fortunately, not many. Just the older, weaker ones.

"So, Clay, I bet you've got some stories from New York. Why don't you tell us some of them."

Clay forked some mashed potatoes onto his plate, followed by a big helping of pinto beans. He loved Sarah's pinto beans. He didn't know what all she put in them, but they were some kind of good. Toby passed the platter of venison.

Tyler said, "I killed this buck just over the south ridge. Hope you like it."

Clay swept two steaks onto his plate, cut off a piece, and took a bite. "Yes, sir, Tyler. That is mighty good. Tastes like you got yourself a good one."

The boy grinned with pleasure as he set the dish down. "So, come on, Clay. Tell us some stories."

He thought over what they might like to hear. "Well, would you believe I took up boxing?"

Toby leaned around Tyler so that he could see Clay. "You think you could teach me?"

"Sure I could, Toby. I'll teach you a couple of moves tomorrow, before I leave."

At the mention of his leaving, Sarah looked at him and then looked back down at her plate.

Tyler whipped around in his chair, facing Clay. "You don't have to leave so soon. You just got here."

"I'm really sorry, but I've got to be in court on the twenty-third, and the clock is ticking."

Tyler went back to his plate, his disappointment obvious.

Mr. Hewitt said, "Go ahead, Clay, tell us about your boxing experience."

"Well, I met a fella from New York, and after seeing me in a fight in Austin—"

"You were in a fight in Austin?" Tyler interrupted.

In a stern voice, Mr. Hewitt said, "Tyler, don't interrupt."

"Yes, sir."

"Go ahead, Clay."

"This fella made the comment that I was fortunate to have won the fight. He said that I obviously knew nothing about boxing.

"That got my ire up, and I asked him if he'd like to show me, fully expecting him to start backing up. But that didn't happen. He said yes, and I went with him to a rundown gym with a boxing ring in it. We climbed into this ring, and this little guy proceeded to read to me from the good book of boxing. I couldn't believe it. He could move and dodge my punches while landing blows on me I never saw coming. There's a lot more to it than just standing toe to toe and slugging it out."

Clay paused and scanned the table. Everyone was listening with rapt attention. Everyone except Sarah. When he started talking, she stood and moved over to the counter, where several pecan pies were sitting. She cut two of them in quarters and put them on the table. She took a smaller piece and walked from the room. Moments later, one of the rockers could be heard squeaking from the porch.

"Go ahead, Clay," Toby said. "What happened next?"

"You really want to hear?"

"I sure do! What happened?"

"All right," Clay said. "He was working me over pretty good, trying to maneuver me against the ropes. Finally, I couldn't keep him off anymore. He got me up against the ropes." Clay paused for effect.

Both boys, in unison, said, "What happened?"

"Well, for a small guy, he had a powerful right, and he hauled off and hit me right on the left temple."

Everyone was sitting on the edge of their chairs, anticipating what would happen next.

## 19

"And," Clay said, "he hit me so hard, he killed me." He took a big bite of his pie and then grinned at the boys. Their eyes were big with amazement. Bo and Mr. Hewitt sat chuckling as they cut into their pie. Finally realizing they'd been had, the boys stared at their plates. "That ain't funny, Clay," Toby said.

"Sure it is," Bo said. "Why, when I was younger, I remember getting killed several times." With that statement, he leaned back and roared.

"Jokes aside, boys. That fella I met taught me a great deal about boxing. In fact, he taught me enough to where I fought several fights and made a little money."

He had their attention again.

They sat around talking for a while, but were interrupted by the sound of a horse running down the hill into the yard. Everyone grabbed a gun and started for the front door.

"It's not a problem, Papa," Sarah called from the front porch. "It's Luke, but he does seem to be in a hurry."

The men got outside just as Luke jumped from his horse and

tied him to the rail. He quickly loosened the cinch. Turning to Clay, he said, "Howdy, Clay. It's good to see you." Then he turned to Mr. Hewitt. "Men in Clay's house. Four, by the count of horses in the corral. They've been there for a while. Got garbage just thrown out in the yard. A bunch of stained rags. I'm bettin' they was stained by blood. I was too far to tell for sure. Been watchin' the house most of the day. Never saw more than one or two come outside."

Hewitt turned to Bo. "Could be that rough bunch you saw a couple of weeks back."

"Yep, one of 'em was riding all bent over in the saddle. Like I mentioned, he was sick or hurt."

Mr. Hewitt said to Clay, "When we heard about the bank robbery, we figured those men were the robbers. That's why we've been on extra alert, this past week or so."

"Could be them," Clay said. He looked at Sarah and back to Mr. Hewitt when he continued. "I thank you for your hospitality. That was a mighty fine meal, but I've got to get going. If that's the scum that killed the sheriff and shot Mr. Graham, I can catch them in the house and stop this rampage."

He stepped off the porch and started for the barn. Sarah rose from the rocker and watched him.

"Sarah," Mr. Hewitt said, "would you make up some grub for us to take?"

"Are you going too?"

"Yes, we are. Normal travel, it's three or four hours to the Barlow place. Darkness will slow us, but we should be there before daylight."

She turned and hurried back into the house, her brow furrowed.

Clay heard Hewitt say to the men, "Grab your bedrolls. Figure on being out for two or three days."

"Us too, Pa?" Tyler said.

"Tyler, I want you to stay with the ranch. Don't plan on leaving here. Keep a rifle near you all the time. Protect your sister."

"Yes, Pa," was all he said, but Clay could hear the dejection in the youngest son's voice.

"Get your stuff, and let's move," Hewitt said.

Clay had Blue and Pearl saddled, loaded, and in the yard when the men came to the barn to grab their tack. They had their bedrolls and slickers. Luke had brought his horse to water, then into the barn, where he gave him a good rubdown and fed him.

Clay tied the two horses to the hitching post in front of the house just as Sarah came out with several bags, each containing food to last for a couple of days. Except for one, she dropped them on the porch. The one she carried over to Clay. "You're off again, aren't you? Just like the last time."

"Sarah, I've got it to do. These are bad men that need to be stopped."

"Why is it you that has to stop them?"

"Sarah, you've been a good friend, but you must understand that I have responsibilities."

"You're not a lawman, you're a lawyer. Lawyers don't go after people with guns!"

"Sheriff Haskins and Mr. Graham were good friends of our family, and me."

"I'm sure they both have other good friends in Uvalde. I don't see any of those friends chasing the robbers."

"I do it, because I can. I'm a good tracker. For some reason, even though I get afraid, it doesn't stop me, and I'm good with a gun. The most important thing of all, Sarah, is I'm willing."

He watched a look of resignation come over her.

"Yes, Clay. You are good with a gun. Sheriff Haskins was good with a gun, until he wasn't. Someday, someone will be better. I've waited for you these past years, but that's over. You have your road. I have mine." She handed him the bag, stood on tiptoes and brushed her lips lightly against his cheek. She stared, for only a moment, into his eyes, turned and walked over to the bags she had dropped on the porch.

Clay stood there, holding the bag. He felt like a major moment in his life had just taken place. He had never felt love for Sarah. At least, he didn't think so. They had played together when they were children. The two of them had grown up together, sharing secrets that only good friends had. He could always depend on her to listen to him when he had a problem, and quite often she would come up with a solution, and sometimes he did that for her. She was headstrong and could be bossy at times, but she never shirked when it came to work around the ranch or assuming many of the responsibilities left by the loss of her mother.

He had been there when her mother died, even holding her as she cried her heart out. He had never felt that he loved her, but what was love, if it wasn't sharing those types of intimacies? He watched her as she handed the bags to her father and brother, to Luke and Bo, and he saw her as the strong, caring woman she had become. He watched her and felt a great loss.

"You going with us, Clay?" Mr. Hewitt said.

He snapped out of his reverie, stuck the bag into his saddlebags, and swung up onto Pearl, with Blue's lead rope. "Yes, sir. I'm ready." He waved to Tyler. "It was good to see you again, Tyler. You take care of your sister."

"I will, Clay. Be careful."

Clay looked at Sarah, with the house lights outlining her trim figure. He could barely make out her features in the darkness. "Goodbye, Sarah."

"Goodbye, Clay."

*That sounds so final,* he thought.

Hewitt said goodbye to Sarah and Tyler, then the men

wheeled their horses in unison and trotted them out of the yard, taking the trail to the Barlow spread.

Clay glanced back as they topped the ridge north of the house. He could see Sarah outlined in the lights from the house, still standing on the porch watching. He waved, knowing she couldn't see him in the darkness. She raised her petite, but strong hand, and held it up for a moment, then turned and disappeared into the house. The men topped the hill and dropped down into the ravine, the first of many they would cross tonight before arriving at the ranch.

Clay brought up the rear. No one spoke, though they were several hours from the ranch. The only sounds from the riders was the steady clop of the horses and the squeak of leather.

They had ridden for several miles, when Mr. Hewitt turned and spoke in a low voice. "Clay, can you ride up here?"

Toby had been riding next to his dad. He dropped back and made room for Clay as he rode forward.

When Clay was riding next to him, Hewitt continued. "We're still a long way from the ranch, so I don't think talking will be a problem. This seemed like a good time to bring you up on your ranch. We're running about a thousand head on your property. It's well under grazed. I wanted to make sure that when you decided to come back, it would be in good shape for you."

"Thanks, Mr. Hewitt. I appreciate it."

"Having that extra land," Hewitt said, "has been a big help for us. You have around five hundred head that belong to you, that we work right alongside ours. We haven't had a drive in two years, because of the depression, but we do drive a few to San Antonio every year. We make a little bit off them but not much. But all in all, things are going pretty well, considering we're in the middle of a depression and have no idea when it's going to end."

"The industry is about to change, Mr. Hewitt. Now, this is just talk right now, in New York, but I've heard men making plans for setting up packing plants out West, butchering the cattle, and shipping the finished product to the East. They're also looking at buying better beef. From the sounds of it, Goodnight has just imported the shorthorn breed to his ranch in the panhandle, but they're already losing cattle from the fever.

"A new breed is being imported into the U.S. It's called the Hereford, and it's taking over up north. The Hereford has been here for a while. The animal makes a great beef producer. I had a steak from one, back in New York. It was so tender you could danged near cut it with a fork. That's a far cry from the longhorn."

Hewitt laughed. "That's for sure. I know of cowboys breaking a tooth on a longhorn steak. Course, I don't know if that was the meat or a rotten tooth."

Clay nodded in the dark. "What I was thinking, is that we pick up some breeders while the market is down and grow our herd. When it comes back, depending how long it takes, we could be ready."

"That's a good idea, Clay. I'll follow up on it. By the way, I haven't said anything, but thanks. We had a note at the bank when we received your letter. We were able to sell stock before the market crashed and pay off the note. If you hadn't sent us that message, we could have been in real trouble."

Clay watched Pearl maneuver around a big boulder that had fallen in the trail, then nodded. "Thanks, Mr. Hewitt. I was just fortunate to be at the right place to hear the forecast. Glad it helped."

The men continued into the dark night, with only a sliver of a moon to light their path. The ashe juniper and oak stood as silent sentinels to their passing. They moved constantly forward to a meeting that could mean death to any one or all of them. Wrapped in his own thoughts, each rode determined to stop the killers.

THEY TIED the horses off the road, out of sight. The moon had set, leaving them in almost pitch darkness. Clay looked at the stars. "We have less than an hour before daylight starts breaking. That'll give us time to get in position, but we have to do it carefully, as dark as it is. Any sound could alert them."

"I'd like Toby to stay with me," Hewitt said.

"Dad, I can take care of myself."

"I know you can, Son. But it would comfort me if you were close."

"That's actually a good idea, Mr. Hewitt. I'd like two people positioned behind the house, on the slope just north of the orchard. Whoever's there can cover the back of the breezeway and the north road. I'm moving down near the house, in case one of them comes out to relieve himself. I'll be on the east end of the porch. From there, I'll be able to cover the front and the south road. Luke, you and Bo cover the front and back of the barn. Everybody hold your fire until you hear me shoot. I'd like to keep the house as unventilated as possible."

Luke turned his head and spit. "We gonna hang 'em like they deserve? They killed the sheriff and shot poor old Mr. Graham."

"Everyone listen to me," Clay said. "There will be no lynching out here. This house has seen enough of that."

Luke scuffed the toe of his boot in the dirt. "You're right, Clay. I'd forgot about your pa. Sorry."

Clay nodded, though he was unsure if he could be seen in this darkness. He could barely make out the other four. "For one thing, we're not even positive it's them, but if it is them and they make a fight of it, shoot to kill. That's what they've done. Okay, let's go, as quietly as possible."

The men disappeared into the darkness. Clay started walking up the trail toward his house. He topped out at less than seventy-five yards from the front porch. When they were in bloom, his ma used to sit on the front porch, with her sewing, and admire the field of blue bonnets, interspersed with the bright orange of the Indian paintbrush. That was now years in the past.

He eased over the crest of the hill and moved toward the big oak standing just to the side of the house. Reaching the old tree, he cleaned some of the rocks from around the base of the tree. Once free of rocks, he sat down and leaned against the trunk, facing the house, not more than fifteen yards away. He had spent many an hour in that tree. The big limbs had made a great perch to sit on and look east down into the Frio Valley.

Time passed slowly. Though the weather had warmed, it was still cold at night, especially just before the warming sun of day struck the hillsides. He pulled his coat around him tighter, wishing for the warmth of the buffalo coat left on Blue's back.

Dawn was just beginning to break when heavier smoke started issuing from the brick chimney his pa had built. Clay stood and unfastened the buttons of his coat, letting it hang open. He slipped leather thongs from the hammer of both revolvers and checked them loose in their holsters. Drawing the Smith & Wesson Model 3 from his right holster, he slipped over to the east corner of the house, just behind the porch.

He had no sooner positioned himself than the door from the parlor opened and slammed closed. Boots clomped on the solid cypress flooring that his pa had hauled up from the Frio River. Clay removed his hat and peeked around the corner. A man had just walked to the edge of the porch. He was busy opening his pants to relieve himself.

Clay quietly stepped out from the side of the house. The man was concentrating on what he was doing, and never noticed. Clay waited. Nothing. Finally, in a soft, low tone, Clay went, "Psst."

The man slowly turned his head, his hangover-clouded eyes found Clay, and they grew as large as a silver dollar. Clay motioned with his six-gun, for the man to come to the east side of the porch. When the man got closer, Clay whispered, "You might want to put that thing up."

He did what he was told and fastened his pants. Clay motioned for him to step down from the porch. When he was close, Clay whispered, "Call out your boss."

The man shook his head. "He ain't here."

"What's your name?"

"Cooper. Hank Cooper."

"All right, Hank Cooper, I want you to lay facedown on the ground."

The man started to say something, and Clay shoved the cold muzzle of the forty-four up against his nose.

"I don't have time to argue."

Cooper dropped to the ground and rolled over on his belly.

"Put your hands behind your back."

As soon as the man was on his belly, he stuck his hands together, behind his back. Clay pulled out a piggin' string and whipped it around Cooper's hands, securing them. Once they were secure, he pulled out another one and tied his feet together.

Clay leaned over, placed the muzzle of the revolver against the back of Cooper's head, and said, "Now call one of your amigos out."

Cooper raised up, as best he could, and called, "Hey, Walt. Come out here."

Clay slipped quietly down to the breezeway. Looking around the corner, he could see all four doors. He watched until the front door to the parlor started to open, then jerked his head back. As Walt passed, Clay slammed the forty-four across the back of the man's head. Walt collapsed on the porch.

Clay waited. Sure enough, a third man came running out, with a gun in his hand. Clay stepped out from behind the front wall and snapped the Smith & Wesson up to shoulder height, aiming at the robber's head. "Drop it, or your hat will never fit again."

The man spent no time thinking. He threw the gun on the floor of the breezeway. "Don't shoot, Mister. I ain't armed."

Clay again motioned with the barrel of his gun, and this man walked toward him. "How many more inside?" Clay asked.

## 20

"Onliest one."

Clay gave him a hard look.

"Mister, I swear. There ain't but one inside, and that's poor old Shad. That feller has mighty poor luck. He's laid up inside with a gunshot wound in his right shoulder. He ain't no harm to nobody."

"Which room?"

"That there room what's behind the kitchen."

"Is he armed? Tell me the truth, because you're going in there ahead of me."

"Yes, sir. But he won't use it. He's hurtin' something fierce."

Clay stepped back off the porch where he could cover all three men. He called to Bo and Luke. "Come on in."

They walked over from around the barn.

"I seen it all," Bo said. "Wouldn't have believed it if I hadn't seen it. Why, Clay here never fired a shot, and he's caught three of these fellers." Luke went over and grabbed the one who was lying on the porch and dragged him to his feet. "Stand up, you varmint, and be mighty careful. This here Colt is worn like me. It has a mighty touchy trigger."

"Luke," Clay said, "would you go around back and get Mr. Hewitt and Toby?"

"Shore 'nuff," Luke replied, and headed around the house.

"So what's your name?" Clay said to the bandit he was holding.

"Earl Griffin."

"Well, Griffin, we're going into the house, you first. If your friend has a gun, guess who's getting shot?"

"He won't shoot. Like I said, he's hurtin' too bad."

They walked to the parlor door, with Griffin leading the way, Clay's gun in his back. Clay said, "Shad, this is Clay Barlow. We're coming in. If you have a gun, throw it aside. If there's a gun in your hand when I come through the door, I'll kill you."

There was no answer.

"Open the door," Clay said.

The two men stepped through the parlor door. Clay looked around in disgust at his homeplace. It was a mess. Dishes had been left unwashed. Empty cans and papers were scattered all over the room. He shoved Griffin around the end of the kitchen counter, to the left. The door into the adjoining bedroom was opened, and a man lay on the bed. He had both hands raised as high as he could get them above his head.

"Clay, are you in here?" came from outside.

"Back bedroom, Mr. Hewitt. Can you watch this one?"

"Sure," Hewitt said. He grabbed the man by one arm and spun him around. "Get outside!"

Clay looked down on the man in bed. "Shad, you're not looking too good."

"I been shot. I need doctorin'."

"I imagine you do. Do you remember me?"

"How could I forget you? You're the one that ruined me forever. I ain't been able to throw a loop since that day you broke my shoulder."

Clay nodded. "Yep. I'd call that the wages of sin."

Shad shook his head. "I made a big mistake listening to Cotton when he talked me into going after you. But I've made an even bigger mistake following him the past few years. He ain't gotten me anything but trouble."

"You're a big boy, Shad. You can make your own decisions. Where's your gun?"

The man motioned to the gun hanging on the bedstead.

Clay picked it up, shoving it behind his waistband. "This the only one?"

"My rifle is standing in the parlor."

Clay grabbed the rifle on his way outside, knowing there was no chance, nor inclination, for Shad to go anywhere. He stepped out in the breezeway and looked to the right. The leafless peach trees had grown. They probably bore a large crop of peaches this past season. He turned to his left and headed for the front porch. All the robbers were sitting on the edge of the porch with Hewitt's men covering them.

Mr. Hewitt walked up to Clay with Toby tagging along. "Bo was telling us what you did. That's pretty amazing. You captured all these men without firing a shot. No one was hurt. Your pa would be mighty proud of the man you've become."

"I reckon not Sarah," Clay said.

"Oh, she's proud of you, Clay. She talks about you all the time. She talks about how determined you are. Make up your mind, and obstacles might as well get out of your way. She was proud of you bringing those outlaws to justice, and proud of you going off, by yourself, to New York City and getting a law degree." Hewitt turned to his son. "Toby, why don't you go get the horses, bring them in, and make sure they get feed and water."

"Sure, Pa," Toby said, and started walking back for the horses.

"Toby," Clay called after him. "why don't you saddle one of these crooks' horses and ride him back to ours."

Toby grinned at Clay. "Thanks, Clay. Guess I wasn't thinking." He turned and headed to the barn.

Hewitt turned back to Clay. "Toby doesn't need to hear this. Now, Son, she's just sorry you haven't included her in your life. She has real feelings for you."

"I'm sorry, Mr. Hewitt. I do care for her, but not in the way she wants. She thinks she wants to be a part of my life, but she really doesn't. Look how she's taken over your household. She runs it, and, I think, enjoys the doing of it. But she wouldn't enjoy my life. I haven't stopped since I got back from New York, and I didn't stop there. As much as I like the thought of it, I just don't think I'm the settling down kind of man."

"Well, boy, I'll tell you, I agree with you. As much as it might hurt my daughter, I don't think she's the one for you. If she was, she wouldn't have tried to stop you from going after the killers of your parents, but she did. But this time, I was watching you two before we left. This time, I think she's finally figured out that you're not the man for her. I know you care for her, but it takes more than that. One of these days, you'll find the woman for you. You're too good a man not to, but it won't be Sarah. I want to thank you for never leading her on, and always treating her with respect.

"Now, enough of that. What do you want to do with these bandits?"

"First, I want to ask them some questions. When I'm done, I was wondering if you could see to their being taken back to the Uvalde jail. They killed the sheriff there, so I think they ought to face a jury there."

"I'll be glad to, Clay. What about the one that's shot?"

"He wouldn't have been shot if he hadn't tried to rob the bank. I'd say put him on his horse and let him ride to Uvalde. If he can't hold on, then tie him on."

Hewitt looked at Clay for a moment. "You can be a hard man."

"We're dealing with hard men, Mr. Hewitt. I just do what I can to deal with them."

Hewitt nodded. The two of them turned back to the bank robbers.

"Boys," Clay said, "I've got some questions for you. I expect all of you know who I am, by now, so you must know that I'm going to get the answer out of you, one way or the other." Clay turned where the outlaws couldn't see him, and winked at Hewitt.

He turned back to the three sitting on the porch. "My first question should be easy for you. Why'd you try to rob the Uvalde bank?"

Griffin gave the other two a hard look, and nothing was said.

"Come on, boys. I'm sure you heard of my dealings with Zeke Martin. I know he was a big talker. I heard he gave up coffee. Any of you boys like coffee?"

They all shook their heads. But still no answer.

"All right," Clay said in a soft voice. "Any of you fellers left-handed?"

No one said anything.

"Good, I won't have to think about which hand I'm going to maim. You, Earl, you're sitting on the end. Put your right hand flat on the porch." Clay pulled the Smith & Wesson Model 3 from his left holster. "I don't use this one much, so I'm not quite as accurate with my left hand. Sometimes I miss.

"Wait, Griffin, I don't want to mess up the porch." He stopped and looked around at all three men. "Did you boys know this is my ranch? All this mess you've made"—he swung the revolver, pointing at the piles of garbage in the front yard—"you've made in my house?" The last words came out in a flat, emotionless voice.

Nervous, the men looked at each other. It was a cool day, the breeze blowing through the oak leaves, but all three were sweating. "Come on over here, Griffin." Clay placed the man's right hand on the top timber of the corral. "Spread your fingers, I wouldn't want to shoot off more than one."

Mr. Hewitt spoke up. "Clay, are you sure about this?"

"Dead sure, Mr. Hewitt. These men have killed and gone on to do it again, and again, so please, don't interrupt me."

Clay walked ten paces from the fence, and dropped the revolver back in its holster. "Last chance, Griffin."

Clay's left hand flashed. The blast of the Model 3 reverberated through the yard, simultaneous with the yelp of pain from Griffin and the hurried calls from the two men still sitting on the porch.

"Mr. Barlow, Mr. Barlow."

Clay ignored them, while he opened the top-break Model 3, extracted the spent cartridge, and dropped in a fresh round, all done in mere seconds. He dropped the revolver into its empty holster, ignored Griffin, who was at the corral holding his hand, and walked over to the robbers still sitting on the porch.

Hewitt moved to take care of Griffin, while his crew stood aghast at what Clay had done.

"We'll talk," Hank Cooper said. "Ask us any question. We'll be glad to answer you."

Walt Nelson sat next to Cooper, nodding his head enthusiastically.

"I'm glad to hear that, boys. I just have a couple. Why did you rob the bank in Uvalde? Nelson, you can answer that one."

"Yes, sir," Nelson spoke up quickly, a quaver in his voice. "It was Cotton's idea. He said the sheriff was gettin' to be an old man, and the bank was owned by some old man and woman that couldn't stop a flea. He said that safe was packed with money."

Clay shook his head. "You boys are dumber than dirt. Don't you understand there's a depression going on? No small-town bank is 'packed with money.'"

He turned to Cooper. "Maybe you can tell me where Cotton Davis is?"

Cooper looked at Nelson, who was nodding his head. "He went to see his ma. He takes her most of his share of the money we get from robberies. He thinks a lot of his ma. She's had some hard times since that horse kilt his pa. You know his pa, Marshal Davis in Brackett."

Clay nodded as he looked at Nelson. "I thought I recognized you. You were the third one that jumped me in Brackett."

"I'm right sorry about that. Cotton talked us into it, him being the leader of our bunch. Said it would be easy, just one man and all." Nelson paused for a moment. "It weren't."

Mr. Hewitt brought Griffin over to the porch and sat him down. He was holding his bloody hand and moaning. The two other men on the porch tried to see if his hand had all of its fingers. Blood dripped from his hand, but the fingers were all there, including his thumb. Unfortunately, they were all full of splinters blown from the corral fence when the slug plowed into the wood.

Clay had not shot at the man's hand. He had aimed several inches from the tips of the fingers. He had been practicing for years with his left hand, even while in New York City. He was almost as fast with his left as his right hand, and he was deadly accurate. He had never intended to shoot between the man's fingers, but it was a good threat.

"Just a couple more questions, boys," Clay said. "Why did you hit the stage on the Austin road, a couple of years ago?"

Nelson spoke up. "It was Cotton's idea. He said there was a lot of money in the strong box. We believed him."

"Do you have any idea why he killed the man riding shotgun?"

Cooper answered this time. "I sure don't. After his pa died, Cotton got awfully bloody." The man looked up at Clay. "I think he likes killing, and he talks about you all the time. I reckon he hates you."

"Griffin," Clay said to the man with the bloody hand, "where can I find Davis?"

The man glared at him.

"We can go through the corral exercise again, if you like. I can see how much closer I can get and still leave you with a usable hand and fingers. It's up to you."

Griffin looked at his hand, then looked back at Clay. "He'll be in San Marcos. He went to see his ma, and take her his cut of the bank money. It weren't much, since that stupid old man wouldn't open the safe."

Clay felt the cold, steely anger rumbling deep inside after Griffin referred to Mr. Graham. He stepped toward Griffin.

"Clay," Mr. Hewitt said.

"It's all right, Mr. Hewitt," Clay said, never taking his eyes off Griffin. "If I was going to kill this animal, I would've done it when I caught him. I just want a good look at the kind of man that can refer to a conscientious citizen like Mr. Graham, using those words. I wouldn't hit him."

When Clay had moved forward, the arrogance in Griffin's eyes had turned to fear, but his confidence returned when Clay stopped and spoke to Hewitt. He turned his head and spit, then said, "He deserved it."

Clay's anger boiled over. He took one more step, putting himself in range. The pain of seeing the old man, so small, lying in the doctor's office on the edge of death, exploded.

"Oh, the heck I wouldn't." He slammed his big right fist into the side of Griffin's head, driving the man off the porch and into the dirt. Then he turned to the other two.

"Where does he stay when he goes to San Marcos?"

"Well, he might stay with his ma," Cooper said. "But most of the time, he'll stay with his lady friend over in Wimberley, used to be Cudes Mill. She's a schoolmarm. Don't that beat all? Here he's a bank robber and killer, and a fine woman like that would have anything to do with him. Why, back home, he was sparkin' a banker girl—"

"What's the teacher's name?" Clay cut in.

"That'd be Nina. I don't rightly remember her last name."

Cooper turned to Nelson. "You remember that schoolmarm's last name?"

"Yep. It's O'Keefe. Catherine O'Keefe. She's the one in Wimberley, but ain't there one in San Marcos, not far from his ma's house?"

Cooper scratched his head. "Maybe. I seem to remember something about a girl there, but he ain't a big talker where she's concerned."

"That's all I remember," Nelson said.

Clay turned back to Mr. Hewitt. "I think I've gotten everything I need from this bunch. It's starting to get up in the day. Do you want to start back?"

"Yes, we'll get started. I don't want Sarah and Tyler worrying about us." He turned to his men. "Get these men on their horses, and we'll head back. Don't forget the one inside. If he can't sit his horse, you might have to tie him on. Toby, why don't you get their horses saddled, son? We'll eat riding."

Bo and Luke walked over and yanked the men from their seats on the porch and shoved them toward the corral. Toby headed for the barn to get the tack.

Hewitt turned back to Clay. "I thought you were going to shoot that man's hand off."

Clay laughed. "I'd never do that, Mr. Hewitt. I just needed something to push those men over the edge. That popped into my mind. I've gotten pretty good with my left hand, but they didn't know that."

"Neither did I. You're fast with that hand, Clay. I can only imagine how fast you are with your right. I understand how you beat those other men we heard about. You'd make a good lawman, but I know you'll make an equally good attorney."

"Thanks, Mr. Hewitt, but I've been thinking about something else. Maybe at some point, we might consider a partnership. Whether we do or not, I know money's short. I learned a lot about investing in New York and made quite a bit. I really feel we would both benefit by switching to Hereford stock. If you're willing, I could buy some good bulls and cows."

Hewitt stared at Clay. "It's a good idea. But like you say, money is short now. I don't see how I could invest anything."

"That's the beauty of it, Mr. Hewitt. I have the money but can't work the ranch. I really think we can make this work. Let me buy the cattle. I'll have them shipped to you, and you do the work. I'll be satisfied with a twenty-five-percent share, if you're agreeable to it?"

"Clay, that's not enough. You should have more."

"No, sir. We both know how much work is involved. I'm just putting up the money. I wouldn't deserve more. Why don't you have the papers drawn up and send them to me in Austin? I'll get the cattle ordered, so that we can have them ready when this depression is over."

"You've got a deal."

The two men shook hands.

They were interrupted by Bo and Luke supporting Shad Ross, as they brought him out of the house.

"Wait," Ross said, as he passed Clay and Hewitt. The man was in obvious pain from the bullet wound as he turned to Clay. "I know I've gone down the wrong road. I sure ain't turned out to be what my ma hoped for. But all this time, I've had one regret. That was jumping you that night. I'd like to say, I'm shore sorry." The man went on. "I've got to tell you, Cotton is fast. I know you've got a reputation, but he is rattlesnake fast, and he likes to hurt people. You best watch out." He looked at Luke. "Now git me on that horse.

## 21

Clay continued with Hewitt. "Get the paperwork done when you're in Uvalde, and send it to me. I know some Eastern stockmen. I'll get the cattle ordered when I get back to Austin."

"I'll have it done when we take these bank robbers to Uvalde."

Clay and Hewitt walked over to the crew. Everyone was mounted except Toby. Clay took his arm. "Let's walk over to the oak."

They moved over beneath the big oak that carried so many memories, good and bad. "I know I told you I'd give you some points on boxing. I'm sorry we don't have the time we need, but let me give you some pointers."

The boy's face lit up with excitement. "Sure, Clay. Thanks."

"First, and this one my pa taught me, a man lives in his belly. Everyone goes for the face, and I'll talk about that in a second. But the belly is the target. You get enough hard blows in that bread basket, and you'll take anyone down. You might take some punishment doing it, but with a little protection, it'll work every time.

"Now, the face. You can do some psychological damage with

the face. Most people get upset when they see their own blood. Some get worried or scared, but there are a few that just get mad. You can't forecast the response unless you know the person. Even the biggest bully can get scared when he sees his own blood. So cut an eye, or lip, or even break a nose, and you've got a man's attention."

"Gee, thanks, Clay."

"I'm not finished. One more thing. Most people have a tendency to hit to a spot, whether it's someone's face or body, they aim to hit it. They stop their punch once they hit their target. Don't do that. You want to hit through it. If you punch a man's face, try to punch through his face. If you drew a line from where you're hitting to the back of his head, you'd want to be hitting that point on the back of his head through his face. Same with his belly. You want your fist going to his backbone. You understand?

"Yeah," Toby said. "I think I do."

"You take good care of yourself and your family, Toby. You're a good man. You did good today. I'd ride with you anywhere."

Clay took Toby's hand in a firm grip and threw his arm around the boy's shoulder. The two shook hands as they walked back to the men and horses.

"You've got a fine man, here, Mr. Hewitt," Clay said.

"Thanks, Clay, you're right," Hewitt said. He then looked around the yard, and toward the house. "Don't worry about cleaning your place up. We'll return in a couple of days and straighten up." He leaned from the saddle and took Clay's hand. "You take good care of yourself, Son. There's always someone faster. Remember Sheriff Haskins."

"Thanks, Mr. Hewitt. I'll keep that in mind."

Hewitt nodded, then raised back up in the saddle.

Bo said, "You take care, Clay. Come see us."

Luke nodded his agreement. "Yep. We'll be looking for you. So long."

Clay touched his hat, and they were gone. Four good men and

four desperadoes out of his life. He watched them top the hill to the south of the ranch, breathed a long sigh, and looked around the yard. *What a mess,* he thought. *I'll get this cleaned up, rest up today, get a good night's sleep and head out in the morning.* He immediately went to work cleaning.

He labored all day. Finally, in the late afternoon, he surveyed his efforts. The house was clean. He had opened all the doors and let out the unwashed stench. After burning the pile of trash in the front yard—it was helpful that there was no wind today, no worry of fire spreading, which was always a concern—he raked the remaining ashes into the flower bed, and then raked the front yard, the way his ma had liked it.

Once done, he sat down in the rocker on the front porch. Pa had made the rocker for Ma long before he came along. Blue and Pearl were watching him from the corral. "Rest up, boys. We'll head out early."

He checked his watch, then looked at the long shadows in the yard. It was getting late. He got out of the rocker and headed for the corral. He moved the horses into stalls in the barn and tossed some oats in the feed bins. "In the morning, boys." He closed the barn door and walked toward the house.

This was probably his last night, for a good while, in the house where he had spent most of his growing years. Even with the intrusion of the final horrible memories of his parents, he had many good memories of this home. He closed the parlor door behind him and lit a lamp, moved to the fire, pulled some lint from his coat pockets, and grabbed kindling from near the fireplace. Striking a match, he set the lint on fire and laid the kindling across it. The kindling caught, and he laid a few sticks across the kindling and then a couple of logs. It wasn't long before he had a fire blazing in the fireplace. No books and little furniture was left in the house. After his parents' death, his French grandparents from D'Hanis had driven two wagons up and cleaned out the house, leaving one straight-backed chair in the parlor. Someone, probably the bank robbers, had sawn off a stump to make another sitting place. After that, if you wanted to sit in the parlor, you sat on the floor.

His mind drifted to his French grandparents. They weren't very happy with him for not staying longer. They were from the old country, having moved to Texas when his ma was a young girl. Farming was in their blood. So upon arrival, they had purchased some land and started planting. Their farm was successful, and their next step was to open a general store in D'Hanis.

Clay was sorry the books were gone. He would have loved reading one. He opened his saddlebags and pulled out the sack Sarah had given him. Opening the sack, he dumped the contents onto the counter that separated the kitchen from the parlor. The fire was crackling and giving off plenty of warmth. It almost felt like home.

In the sack, he found several sausage and biscuit sandwiches. He tasted one and smiled. Sarah had remembered. He loved venison sausage. It had a distinct taste from pure pork sausage. He stood, leaning against the kitchen counter, savoring the sausage and biscuits. There were two small glass containers. One contained fresh-churned butter, and the other homemade plum jelly. He broke a biscuit in two, separating the top from the bottom, and, using his knife, slathered the thick butter across both halves. Next, he smeared the plum jelly across the bottom half and put the top back on. He had a plum and butter biscuit. It couldn't get much better.

With the biscuit in hand, he moved to the straight-backed chair and sat. Not the most comfortable, but it sure beat sitting around a fire on a rough, thick-barked log.

He doubted if he would be this way again for a long time. He thought about his grandfather's law business. *I really don't know if that's for me. Maybe I should move to Galveston or Fort Worth, or even El Paso, and start my own practice. Maybe that's the answer.* Clay sat in the chair, thinking about his future and considering the possibilities, until the fire in the fireplace burned down, leaving only glowing red coals.

He shook his head in frustration and walked back to the counter, closed up the jelly and butter, and with the remaining biscuits, put everything back in the sack. What was left would be tomorrow's breakfast.

He had spread his bedroll on the floor, in front of the fire, preferring the warmth. Often, as a boy, Ma would let him sleep by the sitting room fireplace.

Unfastening his guns, he laid them in the chair, handy in case he needed them, hung his hat on the back of the chair, and strained, finally getting his boots off. Sitting on his bedroll, he stretched his legs out and wiggled his toes. They felt good, free after being imprisoned inside his boots all day. He stood, slipped off his shirt and pants, and laid down in his bedroll, pulling the quilts up around his neck. It had been a long, hard day, but productive. He knew where to find Cotton Davis, and he still had time to take care of him before getting back to Austin for Blessing's trial. He was concerned about getting a conviction, after the way the jailer had talked, but hopefully, justice would prevail.

He yawned, slipped a revolver under the blanket with him, listening to the night sounds while his eyelids grew heavy, and was sound asleep.

~

Two days later found him riding into San Marcos on Blue, leading Pearl. He was tired. For some reason, he hadn't slept well last night. Maybe it had to do with that rock underneath his bedroll that seemed to follow him wherever he turned. He had moved three times with no luck. He'd even checked his bedroll without finding anything. He'd get a good sleep tonight. The bed in the hotel had been very comfortable when he'd stayed here before.

Past the livery, he pulled up at the sheriff's office, dismounted, tied the horses, and stepped inside. There were several men in the office, all trying to talk at once. When he stepped through the door, everyone turned to stare at him.

He closed the door. "The sheriff around?"

One well-dressed, pudgy man, who seemed to be the leader of the group, answered. "What's your business with him?"

"I'll take that up with the sheriff."

The man, trying to control the conversation, but finding it difficult while looking up at the tall, wide-shouldered, and armed young man, said, "Young man, the sheriff has been murdered."

Clay immediately thought of Cotton Davis. "Do you know who did it?"

Again, the man paused.

Another well-dressed businessman spoke up. "For heaven's sake, Claude, answer the man. It's not a state secret."

The pudgy man looked over at the speaker. "Jack, I'm the mayor, and I have no idea who this man might be. He could be another killer loose in our town."

Clay could see what was happening. A meeting of city fathers was obviously going nowhere, as they frantically tried to figure out what to do now that their sheriff was dead. "Mr. Mayor," Clay began, in a consoling tone, "I'm not a killer. My name is Clayton Joseph Barlow. I'm an attorney. My grandfather, Senator Joseph Stedham Barlow, is a retired senator and the owner of the Law and Land office in Austin. I am in his employ. I'm just trying to find as much information as possible on Sheriff Nelson's murder."

Clay's little speech calmed the mayor significantly. "Mr.

Barlow, I apologize for saying you might be a killer. It is very tense around here. My name is Mayor Devin, Claude Devin. Our sheriff was shot last night, shot in the back as he was making rounds. We are in a meeting to determine what to do about finding a new sheriff. He had no deputy, and unfortunately, Sheriff Nelson did not care for paperwork, therefore we have no written record of what or who he might have been investigating. However, he did speak with Dr. Magill." The mayor indicated the man who had spoken up a few moments before.

Dr. Magill stepped forward and offered his hand to Clay. "Mr. Barlow, I'm glad to meet you. The sheriff mentioned talking to a man a week ago, who came through town during the storm. He said that the man gave him information about a killer who might be in our midst, but he didn't give me his name."

Clay shook the doctor's hand. "Dr. Magill, I was probably that man. I was headed down to investigate the bank robbery in Uvalde. I don't understand why the sheriff kept this so close to his vest. The man in Uvalde that killed Sheriff Haskins, is Cotton Davis. He's a killer that has murdered several other men. I'm looking for him."

The mayor piped up. "Do you think it could have been him?"

"Yes," Clay said. "Unless you men know of someone else that might have had it in for the sheriff." He looked around at all the men in the office. Everyone was shaking their head no.

Clay continued. "I'm here to see Mrs. Davis. Cotton, unfortunately for her, is her son. Possibly, I can get information leading to his capture."

"Do you think he might still be here?" Mayor Devin said.

"I don't know, but I'll find out. Now, if someone can direct me to the home of Mrs. Davis, I'll be on my way."

"I can do that," Dr. Magill said, and started for the door.

"Oh, Mr. Barlow," the mayor said, "would you be interested in the sheriff position here in San Marcos? It is normally a quiet little town that has great promise."

Clay shook his head. "No, Mr. Mayor, I've got a job in Austin. But thanks for the offer." He turned and followed Dr. Magill from the sheriff's office.

Standing on the boardwalk, the doctor pointed to a street that paralleled the main street to the west. "Mrs. Davis lives with her sister Mrs. Wilma Norton. She's divorced. She ran off her alcoholic husband a few years back. He was a good businessman but loved the bottle. Can't say as I blame her. Anyway, they live in the stone house near the north end of the street. You can't miss it. She has all the trim painted yellow. Repaints it every few years. Guess she likes the color."

Clay mounted Blue and started to swing up the street toward Wilma Norton's house. "Thanks, Doc. You've been a big help."

"Don't mention it. Those are nice ladies. I feel bad for them both. Seems like the men in their life haven't worked out too well."

Clay touched his hat and bumped Blue. "Adios."

His mind wandered to his last meeting with Cotton Davis. He walked the horses along a cross street and turned right. The man had been a bully, but backed down at the last minute. Too bad. If he had killed him then, a lot of good people would still be alive.

As soon as he came out from behind a two-story corner building he could see the stone house with the yellow trim. If Davis wasn't here, the next stop would be Nina O'Keefe, the schoolteacher in Wimberley. Of course, he might get a lead from Mrs. Davis. He pulled up in front of the house and tied the horses. The home was kept neat. There were rosebushes along the front of the stone house, and he could see a fall garden growing in the back. The yellow trim looked freshly painted. Before he moved out from the horses, he removed the leather thongs holding his Model 3s in their respective holsters. Next he made sure each one was easy in its holster.

A cardinal sat in a big chinaberry tree in the front yard, singing away. It was a pretty day. After the norther, the weather had warmed to feel like a comfortable fall day. Though warm, he had left his coat on so that his shoulder holster remained covered. A light breeze from the southeast touched his cheek and brought the smell of meat frying. He checked the time, then slipped the watch back into his vest pocket. Almost noon, dinnertime.

After tying the horses at the hitching rail in front of the house, he stepped up onto the stone walk that led to Mrs. Norton's wide front porch. The house was a good size. Not small or large, just comfortable. Reaching the front door, he knocked on the door facing, twice. It opened slowly, and a lady of middle age stood facing him. She had a tired face with sad eyes. "Mrs. Davis?"

"Yes, may I help you?"

Clay removed his hat with his left hand. "Mrs. Davis, I'm Clay Barlow. I don't know if you know who I am."

"Yes, Mr. Barlow, I know. You're the young man who, three years ago, didn't kill my son."

"Yes, ma'am. That's been a while back. May I come in?"

She hesitated, then opened the door wider. "Please."

Inside, he wasted no time checking out the visible area. She had invited him into the parlor. He could see into the kitchen on his left, and across the room, an open door led to a hallway with three more doors, probably bedrooms. He heard someone in the kitchen.

"Please, sit down, Mr. Barlow."

She indicated the leather barrel back club chair, and she slowly lowered herself onto the red leather chesterfield. He looked around the room. Part of his education in New York had been learning to recognize quality furniture, and that was what he was seeing now. Either one or both of the two sisters must have had money at one time.

"How can I help you?"

Clay crossed his long legs and looked directly at Mrs. Davis. "First, let me say I am sorry about Marshal Davis. He was a good man."

"Thank you, and why are you here?"

"I'm looking for your son, ma'am."

## 22

A small frown crossed her face. "I feared that would be the case."

A taller lady, of similar age, walked in from the kitchen. "I'm Wilma Norton, Mr. Barlow. May I get you something?"

Clay stood when she walked into the room.

"Please remain seated, Mr. Barlow. I could be coming and going, and you'll tire yourself jumping up every time I come into the room."

Clay smiled at her. "Thanks, Mrs. Norton. I was telling Mrs. Davis that I'm looking for her son. Would you know where he is?"

She returned his smile and said, "I am afraid I do not. He comes and goes at will, although I do believe he is seeing the young widow who lives up the street."

Mrs. Davis stared at her sister, her face stern.

Mrs. Norton returned the look, and said, "Well, dear, he is." She then returned to the kitchen, where pans started rattling.

"Mrs. Davis," Clay said, "can you tell me where he is now?"

She gave a long sigh. "James, that's his name, you know. I

never liked that ignorant name of Cotton. He should be back before long."

"Mrs. Davis, I know no other way to tell you than just straight out."

"That's the only way, Mr. Barlow."

"Fine. Your son is a thief and a killer. There are eyewitnesses willing to testify that he's robbed banks and stagecoaches. I'm not sure of what else. But it's time he was stopped. He has killed at least two men and shot another good man, a banker. If I can bring him in, I can at least offer him a chance. If the rangers come after him, they'll kill him on sight."

"Mr. Barlow, my son travels as a consultant. Occasionally, he brings me money. With what he brings us, and the sewing and laundry that we do, we get by quite well. When he comes home, he fixes things around the house and works in the garden. He even helps me with the laundry when we're very busy. Those are things I really appreciate, his willingness to help out with chores. I can't believe that is the man you speak of. He has killed people? I think not."

"Ma'am, I'm not lying to you."

"I refuse to believe you. Now, will you leave our home?"

Clay stood. "I'm going, Mrs. Davis, but I promise you, you don't want the rangers coming after him."

"Nor do I want you after him, Mr. Barlow."

Clay pulled the door open, stepped onto the porch, and paused, turning back to the lady. "Mrs. Davis, I'm glad your son is good to you, but he isn't to others. He's downright cruel."

She slammed the door in his face.

He walked out to the horses and contemplated his next step. He'd look around town to see if he could locate Davis, maybe take a couple of days. His time was getting short. There wasn't enough time, before the trial, to head out to Wimberley and check on Cotton's other girlfriend. He took the reins in his hand, grasped the saddle horn, and started to swing up into the saddle, when he

212 DONALD L. ROBERTSON

saw him. Davis was walking down the street toward him. He seemed to be unaware of him.

Clay watched for a moment. If there was any way to get behind him, he might get the drop on him and take him alive. He looked from building to building. He was in the open. There was no chance that Davis wouldn't see him. Clay could hear him whistling. He looped the reins back around the hitching post and moved out into the street, waiting.

With Clay's first step into the street, the whistling stopped. Davis continued on his path but slowed his walk. He moved closer, recognizing Clay at last.

"Barlow, you been talking to my ma?"

"Sure have. Told her about the killer she's raised. She's not inclined to believe it, I'm sorry to say."

Davis angled so that he gradually moved into the center of the street, stopping about forty feet away. "You had no call to talk to her. She needn't know my doings."

"Of course I have the right. She should know what you've turned into. You're the one that's brought her pain. It all lies with you."

"Barlow, I haven't liked you since I first met you. Now I can do something about it."

Clay shook his head. "Drop your guns, Cotton. I don't want to have to kill you, but I promise you, I will if need be."

Cotton Davis laughed. "I've been practicing. I've gotten really good while you've been in New York City, living easy. No, I'm not dropping my guns. I'm going to gut shoot you and watch you squirm in the dirt."

"You talk like that for your ma to hear? You're just not much of a man, are you Cotton?"

Clay could hear his pa's words in his head. *Watch their eyes. Eyes are a dead giveaway of when they're going to make their move.* He watched Davis closely.

"You ready to die, Barlow?"

Clay could feel the calmness come over him. He felt cool, relaxed, with just a light tingling in his fingertips. "Not today, Cotton."

He could see Cotton's eyes draw tight, his eyebrows moving only a little. Cotton Davis made his move. He had lived to a ripe old age of twenty-two and had killed five innocent men.

Clay felt his right arm moving. The synapses were firing. The thousands of hours of training, the exquisite coordination given only to a few, guided the muzzle of his Smith & Wesson to its perfect position. As the revolver was coming out of the holster, Clay's thumb was pulling back on the hammer, bringing it into the locked position, waiting for the precise moment his hand, working as a team with his depth perception to judge distance and angle, sent the signal to his trigger finger. Recognizing that moment, Clay's finger softly caressed the trigger once, hammer back, twice, hammer back, three times. Sending sizzling hot lead toward Cotton's chest.

The first bullet plowed into Cotton before he could pull the trigger. It hit him three inches above his heart, slightly off target. But the blow of the bullet swung Cotton to the left, pulling his arm and hand along with the body. He fired when he was lined up with Clay's chest, but unfortunately for him, his Colt Peacemaker also followed his body, and kept moving up and to the left. The bullet only came close. Close enough to burn the right shoulder of Clay's frock coat in passing before it plowed into the cornice of a house across the street.

The second of Clay's bullets arrived on scene immediately after the first, striking almost the same place, still above his aim point. With this hit, Cotton physically took a step backward, firing again. No one could figure where that bullet went.

Before Clay's second bullet was hardly out of the barrel, the third

was on the way, driving into Cotton's mutilated flesh, pushing him back farther. He struggled to bring his Colt on target.

Clay remembered another lesson his pa taught him. Never stop shooting until the man is down and unable to shoot back. Cotton was moving sideways, causing Clay to again miss the heart. But not miss Cotton, for his bullet drove into the man's chest several inches to the left of his heart, and the fifth bullet slammed into the sheriff killer's left arm.

Cotton had also been busy but seemed unable to hit any part of Clay's body. The outlaw was rapidly losing blood, and, without the life-giving liquid, his legs had lost the strength to hold him up. He dropped, but only to his knees. He had emptied his weapon, so he dropped it in the dirt and went for the Colt in his belt.

Clay had also emptied his Smith & Wesson Model 3. He dropped it back into the holster, while simultaneously bringing the left into action. He had put in dedicated effort to train his left hand, and now that training was paying off. He saw Cotton pulling the Colt .45 from behind his waistband, and this time fired at the man's hand. The bullet went through the wrist, shattering the bones, and continued into his belly, doing fatal damage. The Colt dropped to the ground. Clay walked up to the man kneeling in the dirt on both knees.

Davis tried to pick up the Colt, but neither arm worked. His strength fading, he slowly brought his head up to look at Clay, towering above him, and in a low, venomous tone, said, "I hate you."

Clay said nothing, the Smith & Wesson still in his hand, waiting. He heard a door slam and reacted, spinning to his left, bringing the revolver to bear, starting to apply pressure to the light trigger.

"Clay, no!" Dr. Magill yelled.

Clay recognized Mrs. Davis racing down the steps and across the yard to her dying son, and immediately lowered the weapon, a shudder coursing through his body as he realized he had come so close to shooting the mother of the man he had just killed.

She reached Cotton and dropped to her knees. Cradling the bloody boy in her arms, tears coursed down her wrinkled cheeks.

Cotton tried to talk, coughed, foamy blood spraying across the cream-colored blouse his mother wore, waited a moment, and tried again. "I'm sorry, Ma. You shouldn't have seen this." He started coughing again, the pain working its way through the shock, contracting his face in an awful grimace. A guttural groan came from the man's mouth. He summoned the strength to look up at his ma. He attempted a smile, but the result was just a grotesque display of bloody teeth. She put her arm around his head and pulled him to her breasts.

The three people in the street were surrounded by gawkers who had poured from the buildings after the gunfight was over. Everyone was talking. Several times Clay heard, "the Del Rio Kid." Would he never get away from that name?

Dr. Magill stepped out of the crowd and moved up to Cotton and Mrs. Davis. He knelt down, felt the man's neck, and announced what everyone could see. "He's dead."

He lifted Mrs. Davis from her son's body. "You go home," he said. "We'll take care of Cotton. You can see him at the funeral."

She looked into the eyes of Dr. Magill. "My boy's name is James." Her sister had come to her, and now wrapped her arm around the grieving mother and led her back to their house.

Clay had reloaded both guns, and they now sat secure in their respective holsters. He turned back to his horses and started switching the tack. He'd ride Pearl into Austin.

Dr. Magill stood nearby, watching him work. "We don't have a sheriff. I'm the coroner. I guess I should take a statement."

"Here's my statement. He drew first. I beat him. He's dead."

The doctor nodded. "That'll do. You want his gear?"

"No, give it to his mother, or sell it and give her the money. I think there's a reward out for him. She won't like it, but make her take it. Tell her he'd want her to have it." Clay had finished switching the saddles and gear. He swung up on Pearl, felt him tense, then decide to do nothing. Clay turned to the doctor. Taking two twenty-dollar gold pieces from his left vest pocket, he said, "This'll pay for the funeral. She shouldn't have to do that." Then he looked across the hill country, heard the cardinal start up again, and the dog that was still barking. "I did find out one thing," he said, looking down at the doctor. "He loved his mother."

For a moment longer, he stared at the doctor. The memory of that slamming door, the rushing footsteps, and the doctor's yell coursed through his mind. "Thanks, Doc."

The doctor's nod and a look of understanding were his only reply.

Clay turned Pearl, and leading Blue, he rode past Cotton's body and through the thinning crowd, north to Austin.

He had killed another man. Was this his destiny? How many lives had he taken in his short life? True, these were men who had committed themselves to living in crime and harming innocent people, but they were still human beings. Maybe he'd be better off in a law office, like Sarah had said, away from guns and violence.

But he faced the fact that he was good at it. Unlike many people, he was able to face deadly killers and remain calm. When Pa was training him to use a gun, did he know that he would have this skill? To stand face-to-face with another man and take his life? But maybe it was needed. This certainly wasn't New York, where there was a policeman on every corner, ready to come to the aid of any citizen. Most of this country was overrun with thieves and killers, thin on lawmen.

But he had almost made a horrible mistake today. Would he have shot Mrs. Davis if the doctor hadn't yelled? He'd never know. Would the thought of this possibility slow him down? He'd have to be more careful. The last thing he wanted to do was kill an innocent person. For now, it was behind him.

As he plodded on toward Austin, his thoughts raced ahead.

What about his grandfather and the Law and Land office? As an attorney, his grandfather had made a successful life. Now times were tough for everyone, even the old man, and getting shot didn't make things any easier. Many of his clients had been ruined with the depression. Even with all of the work the old man had done trying to save them, many still went under.

With the loss of so much business, it had been necessary for him to trim the size of his office. Clay knew that for him to stay on, working for the senator, it would be necessary to again trim the staff size. Others, dedicated employees who had managed to hang on during this depression, would be out of work. It was time for him to move on.

HOURS PASSED QUICKLY, as his mind continued to work through the quandary that he had been in for years. Would it be practicing the law in court, or exercising it in the field? When Austin came into view, he had made a decision. Either way he went, he would leave Austin.

Shadows had lengthened when he pulled up at Platt's livery. Climbing down from the saddle, he checked both horses. They, too, were ready to call it a day. It had been a hard trip.

"Made it back, I see," Platt said, walking from the interior of the barn. "Looks like you worked a couple of pounds off these two nags."

Clay patted Blue on the neck. "Best be careful calling them that. They might become resentful."

Platt took Pearl's reins, and Clay led Blue, taking them to the water trough. While the two horses drank, gear was stripped from them and taken into the tack room.

"You can just leave those long guns in the tack room, if you want. They'll be fine there."

"Thanks," Clay said, "Good idea. I've got enough to carry back to the apartment. Anything happening in Austin?"

"Not so you could tell it. It's been almighty quiet around here. How about you?"

Clay paused for a moment before responding, "I've been a little busy."

The horses had stopped drinking, and the men led them into their respective stalls, and started brushing them down.

"When you pulled out in that storm, I halfway expected you to end up as a block of ice on the side of the trail."

"Yep," Clay said, "that day was a little chilly. Weather's feeling better now."

Clay finished and put the brush on a shelf. He put on the buffalo coat, leaving it open, and picked up the Roper, saddle-bags, and bedroll. "Thanks for your help, Mr. Platt. If you'd feed them and include some oats, I'd appreciate it. Adios." Clay headed out the door and up the street to his grandfather's apartment. He couldn't wait to get there, to see how the older Barlow was doing.

The sun had disappeared behind the Texas hill country, as Clay turned the corner, nearing his destination. He had glanced down to watch his feet for a second as he stepped up onto the boardwalk.

"Whoa, Cowboy, don't run over an old pard."

Clay looked up to see Jake Coleman standing in front of him. He dropped his bedroll and saddlebags, and transferred the Roper to his left hand. "Howdy, Jake. Guess I ought to look out for other people. It's been a while. How are you doing?"

Clay looked Jake over. Still the same old Jake, a little more age, a little more gray. Still erect and confident.

"I'm right as rain. How about you? How's the lawyering business?"

"I'm doing good. How long are you in town for?"

"Not for long," Jake said. "I'll be pulling out for Fort Griffin in a few days. Got a little trouble with buffalo hunters hoorahing the town. But enough about that, I'm about to grab some supper over at Daisy's. Care to come along?"

Clay considered the offer for a few moments. He really wanted to see his grandpa and talk to him, and he was beat from these past days of travel, but talking to Jake was enticing, and he was sure hungry. "Yep. That's a fine idea. Lead the way."

"Well, then, ole hoss, why don't you let me help you with that gear." Jake took the saddlebags from Clay, and the two men crossed the street toward Daisy's Diner.

Stopping at the front door, Clay, using his hat, beat as much of the trail dust off as he could, and followed Jake into the eating house. The smell of fresh-cooked food attacked him as he entered, and the big man's stomach started growling.

"Reckon they can hear your stomach all the way up to the state house," Jake said, dropping the saddlebags into one of the empty chairs at the corner table. He moved the table so that they both would be able to keep an eye on the door and then sat. Clay dropped the bedroll in the same chair, pulled off the heavy coat and laid it on the bedroll, then leaned the Roper against the coat.

A trim, middle-aged woman, wearing a full-length apron and carrying two cups and a coffee pot that looked almost as big as she, marched up to the table.

"No coffee for me, ma'am," Clay said, as she dropped the cups to the table.

She looked Clay over and turned to Jake. "Jake, how many times do I have to tell you, don't drag your rangers into this establishment until they've had a chance to clean up?"

Clay immediately stood. "Sorry, ma'am, I just got in off the trail. Haven't had a chance even to clean up."

"No need to get huffy. Take yourself back into the kitchen and wash the grime off your face. I'll be glad to serve you."

Clay looked at Jake. Jake's raised eyebrows and nod indicated for him to do just that. He walked into the back, looking around.

The cook, a big, burly man standing over the cook stove, his face covered in sweat, looked up at him.

"Myrtle must have jumped you for being dirty. You'd think she'd run business off, but folks keep coming back. There's a wash tub and a towel over there in the corner. Help yourself."

"Thanks," Clay said. He looked at the water and decided he wasn't going to stick any part of his body in there. The color was almost black, and it was impossible to see the bottom of the tub, not to mention the towel was covered in dirt and grime. "This water's filthy. I wouldn't wash my horse in it."

"Good idea," the cook said. "Why don't you grab that tub and dump it outside. The pump's just outside the door."

Clay looked at the cook, shook his head, and grabbed the heavy washtub. He took it out back and dumped it, and then filled it from the pump, after rinsing it several times. Grabbing the wire handles, he lifted it, managed to work the door open with the fingers of one hand, and carried the now fresh water back into the kitchen, setting the tub on the stand.

"Got you a clean towel. That's Myrtle's rule, whoever empties the washtub gets a clean towel."

"Thanks." Clay grabbed a bar of soap that was resting next to the washtub and scrubbed his hands and face, dried off, and brushed his hair back.

Myrtle came through the kitchen as he was about to head back to his table. "You clean up pretty good, Cowboy. Get in there and have a seat, and I'll get you something that'll stick to your ribs."

"Ma'am," Clay said as he walked back to his table. The restaurant was crowded, but he picked up on three men sitting at a table across the room. It appeared he was being watched.

## 23

Jake was chuckling when Clay returned to the table. "Myrtle can be a bit picky, but folks don't seem to mind. She stays busy all the time. Why, I seen her grab a cowboy by his ear and drag him out back to wash up, and if a fella says anything about the water being dirty, he gets to dump it and refill it."

Clay grinned as he sat down, forgetting about the men at the other table. "She sure likes her customers clean." He looked around at the other people eating. "Doesn't she have a menu?"

"Nope. You get what she's fixing. But I haven't been disappointed yet."

"Well, I'll tell you," Clay said, "if I have to look at another piece of beef, you'll see a disappointed man."

Myrtle walked up. "Wouldn't want anyone to be disappointed." She set big plates of fried chicken, biscuits, and gravy in front of Clay and Jake.

"No, ma'am. I don't think I'm going to be disappointed tonight." Clay picked up a big, fluffy biscuit and dipped it in the gravy before taking a bite. He chewed, swallowed, and sighed. "Now that's about the best biscuit I've ever tasted."

With both hands on her hips, Myrtle said, "That's what I like to hear. Now tell me, would a big glass of milk suit you?"

"That would fit perfect, thank you," Clay said, picking up a crisp chicken leg.

"Myrtle," Jake said, "this here fella is Clay Barlow. He's Senator Barlow's grandson."

"Hello, Clay," Myrtle said, pushing a lock of thick brown hair back under the red-and-white scarf she wore around her head. "I've seen you around town. Heard about you too." She looked up as a man and woman walked in. "Gotta go. If you boys need anything else, let me know." Myrtle spun around and hurried over to her new customers.

"I don't know how she does it," Jake said. "Every time I come in here, this place is humming. Myrtle is a ball of energy."

Clay nodded, his mouth full. The fried chicken was delicious, and he was hungry. He stayed busy with the food until his plate was clean. The milk Myrtle had brought was fresh and cool. It fit perfectly with the meal. He leaned back in the chair. "Now that was good food."

"Well, try this," Myrtle said as she appeared out of nowhere with two big pieces of pecan pie. She placed a piece in front of each of them. "Nate cooks most of the food, but I insist on doing the baking. I think you boys will like this. Just leave your money on the table when you leave."

Clay was enjoying the sweet taste of the pecan pie when Jake leaned across the table. "You know those three boys at the table across the room?"

Clay turned and looked directly at the men. They were staring at him and talking among themselves. "Can't say as I do. I noticed them when I came out of the kitchen. I thought then they might be watching me but shrugged it off."

"Always listen to your gut, Clay. Let's finish up and head out. Keep your gun hand limber."

Clay checked both of the Model 3s, flipping the leather thong back from the hammer on each. "How much does Myrtle charge for dinner?"

"Thirty-five cents. A little on the pricey side, but she provides good food and plenty of it."

Clay dug out four bits from his vest pocket and dropped it on the table, stood, moved the Roper, put on the coat, then picked up the bedroll and shotgun in his left hand. He noticed Jake was also keeping his right hand free. They headed for the door.

"Come see me again," Myrtle called as they were leaving. They both nodded, keeping their eyes on the three men. As they neared the door, the men stood. The biggest one, though it was hard to say who was the biggest, held his hand out to stop them, and said, "You Clay Barlow?"

Clay stopped and looked pointedly at the man's hand in front of him, and then at the man, saying nothing. The big man slowly dropped his hand, obviously not intimidated. "I said, are you Clay Barlow?"

Looking the man directly in his eyes, Clay could see the fella was as tall as he was. Clay said, "And you are?"

"The name's Seth Blessing. These here be my brothers Silas and Simon. Mister I don't make a habit of resayin' my words. I'm askin' for the last time, are you Clay Barlow?"

"Yes, Mr. Blessing. How can I help you?"

"Why, ain't that nice? I'm glad you asked. You can help me by staying away from the courthouse tomorrow. Our pa's being tried tomorrow, and we'd see it as right neighborly if you found yourself busy somewheres else."

"Boys," Myrtle called from the kitchen entrance, "I'd appreciate you not blocking my door. There are people that would like to get in."

"Sorry, Myrtle," Jake said. Then he stepped up to Seth."If you boys want to talk, then take it outside. Otherwise, step out of the way."

Seth looked down at Jake, a sneer on his face. "And who are you, little man?"

A gun suddenly appeared in Jake's right hand. "I'm the man that's going to put a couple ounces of lead in your belly if you don't get out of the way. If you want to talk, take it outside, now."

Seth looked down at the barrel of the Colt .45 Peacemaker that was jammed into his side. He looked at Jake, no fear in his eyes, and said to his brothers, "Pay for the meal and let's go."

The men left money on the table and walked out into the night, ahead of Jake and Clay.

"Now, speak your piece, and make it quick," Jake said. When the trio made no threatening move, Jake slid the Peacemaker back into its holster.

"I done did," Seth said. "You, Mister Barlow, had best stay away from Pa's trial."

"Now, why would I do that?" Clay asked, his voice even, but tired.

"Mister," Seth said, "we don't hanker to having our pa in no jail. Without you, they ain't got a thing against him. You git my meaning?"

"I understand completely, Mr. Blessing, and I assure you, under no circumstances will I miss the trial. It is my goal to ensure your murdering old man spends as much of his remaining life in Huntsville as possible."

In unison, the brothers moved toward Clay.

"You boys don't want to forget about me," Jake said, the Colt again appearing in his hand.

The men stopped and glared at Jake.

The ranger smiled. "Hopefully, you remember that little ditty, 'God created men, and Sam Colt made them equal.' This here fine handgun I'm holding just happens to be a Colt forty-five-caliber Peacemaker. In my estimation, the finest handgun made. Of course, Clay here might argue with me. Inside this cylinder,

I've got five two-hundred-fifty-grain pills that will surely mess up that fine dinner you just ate." He turned to Clay. "You want me to arrest them? It would surely make my day."

The three Blessings stood frozen in their boots. The Colt and the word arrest had brought them to a standstill.

"No," Clay said. "Let them go."

"All right," Jake said. "Boys, it's time for you to jingle your spurs."

The men stood still for a moment too long.

"Now!"

The metallic sound of a Colt hammer cocking carried through the Austin night. The three big men turned slowly and started walking away. Seth turned his head to Clay and said, "Don't forget what I told you." He continued walking with his brothers.

"Whew, boy. You got you some hardcases there. Blessing. Are they sons to the old fella you brought in a while back? The one that took a shot at you?"

"Must be. I heard him ask the jailer if he could get a message to Arkansas, but they must be wrong. His case isn't due until the twenty-third. That's next week."

"No, it could be true. If it's Judge Moore's court, he's leaving town next week, so he's set all of his cases for this week."

"That's a surprise, but since I made it back in time, it won't be a problem." Clay picked up his gear. "I best be heading over to my grandpa's place. That's where I'm staying. It's good to see you, Jake. Maybe I'll see you before you leave."

"Maybe so. I'll walk with you to the senator's place, just to be safe."

Clay started to decline, and then thought better of it. Another set of eyes and ears were always welcome. They walked in silence to the bottom of the steps.

"Why don't you come up and meet the senator and Ray?"

A smile crossed Jake's lips. "Not necessary. Seems like I've known them most of my life. Adios."

Jake walked across the street. Clay watched Jake for a moment before he turned and headed up the stairs. He had taken only three or four steps when he heard a rush of feet. Turning, he made out at least two men charging up the stairs. He aimed to kick one in the crotch, when the man dove to tackle him. The toe of his boot caught him in the throat, and he rolled to the ground, holding his neck and gasping for air. In the light from the buildings, he could make out Seth reaching for him, with one of the brothers pushing to get around him and grab Clay.

With the first noise, Clay had dropped everything except the Roper. He drove the muzzle of the shotgun into Seth's belly. The attacker stepped back, losing his footing on the steps, and fell, rolling down the stairs, holding his belly, and giving Clay the room he needed. Grasping the forearm of the shotgun in his left hand and the small of the grip in his right, he slapped the other brother on the side of his head with the butt stock. The man staggered back, lost his balance, sat down hard in the street, and flopped on his back, out cold.

By this time, Jake had returned, hearing the ruckus, and Ray was standing on the steps, above Clay, holding a sawed-off double-barrel shotgun. The senator was standing on the landing, holding his revolver.

The brother who had caught Clay's boot toe in his throat—turned out to be Silas—was finally able to draw air through his ravaged throat. He was wheezing, still holding his throat, but no longer gasping. Seth was lying in the street moaning. His shirt was bloody around his hands. Simon had been the unlucky one who collected the butt stock of the Roper on the side of his head. He was still out, not moving.

"Pardner," Jake said, looking at Clay, who stood calmly on the steps, looking huge in the buffalo coat, "remind me never to make you mad."

By this time a crowd had gathered. Stepping out of the crowd was Deputy Biles. He looked up at Clay and said, "Drop the shotgun."

"Sure, Deputy." Clay set the Roper against the wall.

"I'm gonna have to take you in. We can't have brawling in the streets of Austin."

Jake stepped up to Biles. "You're not taking Clay Barlow anywhere."

Someone in the crowd yelled, "Arrest them hillbillies on the ground. They're the ones that started it."

About that time Senator Barlow spoke up. "Deputy Biles. You know who I am. I give you my word. My grandson was jumped by these three men. Otherwise, he would have never engaged in this action."

The deputy looked around the hostile crowd and turned back to Clay. "I'll need a statement. Be at the courthouse tomorrow."

"I'll be there. Their pa is being tried for attempted murder, and I'm the witness. If you're around, I'll see you then. I'd also suggest you check the big one's belly. I jammed the muzzle of my shotgun into it pretty hard. For now, you need to lock these men up for assault."

Someone else yelled from the crowd. "Looks like they're the ones that got assaulted." The crowd roared.

Jake turned to Clay. "You go get some rest. I'll help the deputy here get these hillbillies to jail."

"Thanks, Jake. I'm much obliged."

Jake grinned up at him. "I sure best keep an eye on you. You're forever getting into trouble."

"Thank you, Jake," the senator called.

Jake raised his hand to his hat, in salute, then kicked one of the brothers in the leg. "Get up!"

The three brothers got on their feet and staggered toward the jail, followed by Jake and the deputy. Jake hadn't even bothered to draw his gun.

Ray picked up the bedroll, and Clay grabbed his saddlebags, following Ray up the stairs. He pushed the door closed, looked at Ray and his grandpa, and smiled. "Grandpa, you're looking a lot better than you did when I left. You're up and moving around."

"Can't keep him in bed," Ray said. "Let's put these things in your room."

With Ray leading the way, Clay followed him to the room he'd been using. He dropped the bedroll, and Ray set the saddlebags down beside the bedroll. Clay lay the Roper across the bed, muzzle facing the wall. "It's good to be back."

"We'd like to hear all about it. Can I get you something to eat?"

"No, thanks, Ray. Jake and I just finished eating at Myrtle's."

"Myrtle fixes some good meals," Ray allowed. "But she sure doesn't want folks in her establishment that are dirty."

Clay laughed. "Yep, I found that out." He slipped out of the buffalo coat, thankful for the warmth it had provided, but glad to be out from under the weight.

The two men were laughing when they walked back into the parlor. The senator was sitting in his favorite chair. He patted the arm of the sofa next too him. "Come sit, Clay. Tell us all about your adventure."

"How about I fix some hot chocolate?"

Clay looked at Ray. "Ray, I'd never turn down a cup of your hot chocolate. All my time in New York, I never tasted any hot chocolate as good as yours."

Ray nodded. "You're a smart young man. Keep the compliments coming, and I'll keep the hot chocolate flowing." He walked back to the kitchen.

Clay turned back to his grandpa. "Now, let me tell you what happened."

～

Several hours later, everyone was whipped. Hot chocolate had flowed like water. Clay could hardly keep his eyes open, but he had one more thing to do. After these past years, his mind was finally made up.

"Grandpa, I need to talk you about something serious."

"That's my cue," Ray said. "Senator, can you make it to bed by yourself?"

"Of course I can, Raymond. I'll see you in the morning."

"Thanks for the hot chocolate, Ray."

Ray nodded and left for his room. When he had gone, Clay turned back to his grandfather.

"Grandpa, I've come to a decision."

The senator nodded. "Let me see if I can guess what it is." He thought for a moment, feigning deep concentration. "You're going to join the rangers."

Clay was astonished. "How did you know?"

"Son, I knew before you went to New York. It's like I told you. My main goal was to get you educated. Then your life was your business. So when are you signing up?"

"I see no reason to wait. I'll be at the courthouse tomorrow for the trial. I might as well do it then."

"Good. If you don't mind me tagging along, I'll go with you. Now, let an old man go to bed."

The senator stood and started down the hallway, stopped, and turned back to Clay. "Bringing those outlaws in was no small feat, and killing Davis was hard but unavoidable. You did a good job." He continued on to bed. Clay heard the senator's door close.

*Grandpa knew all along. I feel like I have a weight off my shoulders. I'd never have been happy making a living in an office.*

He walked down the hall to his room and pulled the door shut. It was dark in the room, with only the lights of Austin providing illumination. He undressed and lay down on the bed. His guns were in reach on the chair. Clay considered the courtroom, tomorrow. It would be his word against Blessing's. It would depend on the jury.

## 24

T he morning dawned bright and cold. Clay, along with Raymond, arrived at the courthouse early to check the schedule. Posted outside the clerk's office, it showed the case would be heard in Judge Willard Moore's courtroom at 11:00 a.m.

"I best be getting back to let the senator know," Raymond said. "See you at court."

"You're bringing him in the buggy, aren't you?"

"Yeah. Don't reckon he's strong enough yet to make it down here from the apartment. He might fuss a bit, but he'll ride."

"Good. Thanks, Ray."

Clay walked through the hall to the courtroom. He opened the door and stepped in, looking around. The courtroom was empty, and a chill penetrated throughout the room. Someone had started the two stoves, but they had a great deal of empty space to heat.

The judge's bench was on a raised platform at the front of the room with the witness stand to his left. Farther left was the jury box, containing two long, high-backed benches, slightly raised, but not as high as the judge's. Two plain tables, with three chairs each, sat in front of and facing the bench. There were six rows of benches across the entrance of the courtroom, split by an aisle in the middle of the room. Clay moved down the aisle and sat in the front row in the right bank of hard benches, near the jury box.

The courtroom looked similar to every courtroom he'd seen, even the moot court at Columbia. The difference was that today, he would be sitting in the witness box answering questions, not standing in front of it asking them. He stood and exited the court, headed for the Law and Land office.

Once there, he pulled out two blank sheets of paper with the Law and Land logo on both. He started writing. When finished, he folded them and walked to the telegraph office, at the train station. He climbed the steps, walked inside, and stepped over to the telegrapher's cage. The young man was leaned back in his chair, feet propped on the desk. When Clay walked up, he dropped his feet, leaned forward, and adjusted his green visor. The morning sun, through the east windows, was at just the right angle to strike his visor and reflect a green glow across his thin, sparse mustache and mouth.

"Howdy, Mr. Barlow."

"Hi, Bill. Can you send some messages for me?"

"Glad to."

Clay handed the two messages to the thin man, who took them from him and started reading.

"Buying some cattle?"

"Yep. How much will those messages be?"

"You're sending this other one to the home office?"

Clay pulled out a card that had been given him by the executives of the H&TC railroad and handed it to Bill.

"Yes, sir, no charge for the one to the home office. You want them to arrange shipment by rail for twenty-six head of Hereford cattle, including six bulls, from Philadelphia, Pennsylvania, to San Antonio, Texas?

"That's right, Bill, and please include my billing address."

"What kind of cow is that, Mr. Barlow? Will it withstand Texas heat and cold?"

"Bill, it will certainly handle the cold. We'll have to see how it takes to the heat."

"Yes, sir." He handed the card back to Clay, and he slipped it into his wallet. "That'll be one dollar and twenty-five cents."

Clay paid the telegrapher. "If I'm not here, for any reason, please have the messages sent to Senator Barlow. He will be familiar with the arrangement. Have a good day."

"You too, Mr. Barlow."

Clay exited the station and headed back to the courthouse. He reached the steps just as Ray pulled up with the senator. The older man stepped slowly from the buggy and started up the steps.

"Need a hand, Grandpa?"

"No, Clay, I can make it."

Clay held the door for his grandfather and entered behind him.

"Do you have a moment before we go in?" Clay asked.

The senator stopped and turned to him. "Certainly."

Clay explained his venture with Adam Hewitt in detail. "The money for all expenses is in my account, which you have access to. If I should need to leave, I would appreciate you handling any necessary expenses, and keep Mr. Hewitt apprised so that he can have hands meet the train in San Antonio when it gets in with the cattle."

"I'll be glad to, although you're taking a big risk bringing a new breed into this country. You could lose every dime."

Clay grinned. "It's only money, Grandpa. You and Pa taught me that if you made it once, you can make again."

The senator laughed. "Indeed I did. Don't worry, if you're not here, I'll take care of it."

Ray came walking up.

"Let's go to the courtroom," the senator said. "We're early, but I need to put these old bones down somewhere."

The three men moved into the courtroom and sat in the front row behind the prosecution's table. Several people Clay didn't know were sitting on the left side of the aisle, chatting about things of importance to them. A few more minutes passed and the attorneys came in. They opened their cases and placed documents on the tables in front of them.

Clay let the prosecutor get organized, before he stood and said to the man's back, "Good morning."

The attorney turned around, a questioning look on his broad face, and replied, "Morning."

"I'm Clay Barlow."

"Ah, yes, Mr. Barlow. My name is Sam Pettibone. I understand you're the man Mr. Blessing took a shot at. If I understand correctly, when he rode up to finish you off, he was talking to himself, and he mentioned he had killed a man in Arkansas. Is that what you'll be testifying?"

"That's the truth, Mr. Pettibone. The old man was talking as if he knew I was dead and talking to me. I have a pretty good memory, and I can come close to quoting exactly what he said."

Pettibone nodded to Clay's answer and turned toward the senator. "Good morning, Senator Barlow It is good to see you."

After shaking the senator's hand, he said, "Senator, I assume this man is a member of your family?"

Senator Barlow placed his hand on Clay's shoulder. "Why, yes, Sam, he is my grandson, and as soon as we finish here, he's going to the rangers office to sign up."

Pettibone leaned in to Clay. "Mr. Barlow, you're joining the rangers today?"

"Yes, right after the trial."

"If it were possible for you to be a ranger when you take the stand, that would carry weight with Judge Moore. Do you think you could go around the building to their office right now and sign up?"

Clay nodded. "Sure, now or later makes no difference to me. I'll be right back."

"Son," his grandpa said, "reckon I'm gonna miss it. I'm pretty beat from the buggy ride here, but I'll be thinking of you."

"Nothing to be concerned about, Grandpa. I'll be right back."

Clay walked from the courtroom, his long legs carrying him quickly around the building to the Rangers' office. He walked through the door to see Jake sitting behind the front desk.

"Jake, there's not much time. Mr. Pettibone wants me to sign up before I testify in court. Can you do that?"

Jake grinned at him. "I can, but I imagine Major Jones would like to do it, since he's here."

"Indeed I would," Major Jones said, stepping out of his office. "Come on back here, Clay. Sounds like you're in a hurry, so I'll make this quick." Major Jones picked up the Bible from his desk and held it in front of him.

"Place your left hand on the Bible and raise your right hand."

Clay felt a current, like when you slide across a room on a dry, winter morning, passing through his body. He had dreamed of this day for years. Even while training to be an attorney, he felt sure this was his true destiny. Now it was happening. His left hand on the Bible, he raised his right hand.

Major Jones continued. "Do you, Clayton Joseph Barlow, solemnly swear that you will bear true allegiance to the State of Texas, and that you will serve her honestly and faithfully against all her enemies or opposers whatsoever, and observe and obey the orders of the Governor of the State, and the orders of the officers appointed over you according to an Act of the Legislature for raising a Battalion for frontier protection approved April 10, 1874?"

"I do."

"Good," Major Jones said. "You are now a duly sworn Texas Ranger. Congratulations."

"Thank you, sir."

Jake took Clay's hand and shook it vigorously. "Your pa would be proud. Welcome."

Major Jones wrote out a document and stamped it with his seal. Once finished, he laid down his pen and reached into the side drawer of his desk and pulled out a badge. "Wear this with pride, Clay. You represent a fine organization. Who's the judge in Blessing's trial?"

"It is Judge Moore."

"Good. When you go back into the courtroom, I want you to wear this badge on your vest, underneath your coat. At the appropriate time, pull your coat back, exposing the badge. That just might help, since from what I heard, it's his word against yours." He handed Clay the paper he had filled out. "This is your commission, should the judge ask to see it. Now get out of here. Judge Moore does not like people late in his court."

"Thank you, Major. Thanks, Jake. I'll be back as soon as court is over." He left the office and hurried back to the courtroom. The senator had saved a space for him at the end of the row. On the other side of Ray sat the owners of the Bar 3 horse ranch, Jethro and Mrs. Bates.

Clay sat down, and almost immediately, the bailiff called, "All rise for the Honorable Judge Willard Moore."

The judge walked in wearing his black robe. He was a rather forgettable-looking man, thinning gray hair, a large red nose, vivid veins coursing through the end of it, and big ears mostly covered by his longish, graying hair. The striking elements about the judge were his eyes, hard and black as the darkest obsidian. The wrinkles along his eyes and mouth all turned down.

*This is a hard man*, Clay thought.

"Bring in the defendant," the judge ordered.

Washington Jefferson Blessing was led in by two policemen,

one on each side. Clay was shocked at the change. The man's hair had been cut, and his beard, once long and brown with tobacco juice, was now neatly trimmed. His boots were shined brown, to match his pants and frock coat. A brown bow tie accented the white shirt, with a cream-colored vest looking quite professional. His frock coat was a deep coffee. His attorney had been busy. Blessing walked erect, with his head up, and seated himself at the defense table. He looked like any reputable businessman.

Clay leaned over to his grandfather and whispered, "That doesn't look like the man who took a shot at me. He cleans up way too well."

The senator said, "His attorney, James Dial, is one of the best in Austin. He knows how to handle a defendant, but unfortunate for him, he's tried cases before in Judge Moore's court. The judge is onto his tricks."

The judge looked at the two attorneys and said, "You fellas ready to choose a jury?"

Pettibone nodded. "Yes, Your Honor."

Dial, the defense attorney, said, "Your Honor, Mister Blessing and I have discussed the importance of a jury trial, but he has insisted on waiving the jury. He says that truth can be recognized by an honest man, and he feels that man is you."

"Don't try flattery on me, Mr. Dial. You'll find it ineffective. However, consider the jury waived.

"Mr. Pettibone, make your opening statement."

Pettibone rose, while remaining behind the prosecution table, and addressed the judge. "Your Honor, the state will prove that the defendant"—he pointed at Blessing—"attempted to murder Clayton Barlow, and during the subsequent conversation admitted to shooting Senator Joseph Barlow, and a peddler in Arkansas." Pettibone sat down.

The judge looked at Blessing's attorney. "Mr. Dial?"

Dial rose, straightened his coat, cleared his throat, and walked out from behind the defense table. "Your Honor. Unfortunately, this case is about a man and an accident. It is only an accident. A grave accident to be sure, but only an accident. Mr. Blessing, while deer hunting, saw movement across the narrow canyon, and, thinking it was a deer, fired at Mr. Barlow. As far as the allegations of the prosecution's attorney that somehow Mr. Blessing admitted to the heinous shooting of our fine Senator Barlow and the peddler in Arkansas, that can only be deemed as hearsay, and begs to be thrown out.

"Mr. Blessing, my esteemed client, is a God-fearing family man, who, due to an accident, which he admits to freely, has been accused of this crime, and will be found innocent from this act. Unfortunately, the district attorney's office has decided to place this poor, innocent man"—Dial dramatically swung his arm around, his hand open and pointing toward Blessing—"in jail, and hold him on the word of a gunfighter." Now disgust filled his words and face, as he pointed an accusing finger at Clay. "A killer, known to the world as the Del Rio Kid. Thank you, Your Honor." Dial moved back to his seat, seating himself with a big sigh while shaking his head.

"Mr. Dial," the judge said, "we have no jury, therefore your performance goes wanting. Understand, your theatrics in my courtroom will not aid your client and could very well find you in contempt of this court."

Dial politely bowed his head, then looked at the judge, a hurt expression on his face. "Yes, Your Honor. I meant no disrespe—"

The judge cut Dial off. Looking at the prosecutor, he said, "Call your first witness, Mr. Pettibone."

Pettibone responded, "Your Honor, I would like to call Mr. Jethro Bates, respected owner of the well-known horse ranch, the Bar 3."

Jethro rose, passed his hat to his wife, and walked to the witness stand. The bailiff swore him in, and he took his seat.

Pettibone stayed standing behind his desk. "Good Morning, Mr. Bates."

"Howdy."

"Could you tell the court," he began, indicating Judge Moore, "what happened on the evening of October twentieth?"

"I sure can," Jethro said. Turning to the judge, he told of Clay's arrival, the shot that was fired, and the hoofprint they found.

"Now, you're saying," Pettibone asked, "that the hoofprint of the shooter's horse, the left front hoof, had a deep injury to the right of the frog. Is that correct?"

"I reckon so."

"And the boot prints were round toed and low-healed? Boots that could be construed as belonging to a farmer?"

"I ain't knowing the meaning of construed, but yes to the rest."

Light laughter sounded throughout the courtroom.

"Objection," Dial said, standing. "It would be unknown as to the type of employment the wearer of such boots would be engaged in, Your Honor."

"Sustained."

"Thank you, Mr. Bates." Pettibone looked up at the judge and said, "No more questions, Your Honor."

Jethro started to get up. Judge Moore looked over to him. "Jethro, we're not through yet. Keep your seat."

Jethro sat back down and looked at the judge. "Why, shore, Will. I thought I was done."

"It's Judge in the courtroom, Jethro."

"Right," Jethro said, with a grin working at the corners of his mouth. "Judge."

The judge turned to Dial. "Your witness."

Dial walked with purpose to a position directly in front of the witness stand. "Jethro. May I call you Jethro?"

Jethro looked at the attorney for a long moment. "My friends call me Jethro. I don't know you. So, I reckon you can call me Mr. Bates."

Scattered laughter drifted across the courtroom. The judge looked up and frowned. The laughter quieted.

Dial cleared his throat and emphasized Jethro's name. "Mr. Bates. Did you see my client when the shot was fired?"

Jethro was starting to enjoy being a witness. "Dial, I already said it was dark. Not only that, I was hiding myself and every soul of my family inside the house so we wouldn't get shot. Now, how the blazes could I see that old bushwhacker?" While making his statement, Jethro pointed at Blessing.

Dial turned to the judge in frustration. "Your Honor, would you direct the witness to answer the question without editorials, please?"

Judge Moore looked down at the witness. "Jethro, answer the man's question without your homespun humor."

"You bet, Wi—Judge."

Dial turned back to his chair. "I have no more questions."

Jethro looked up at the judge.

Judge Moore nodded. "You may step down, Jethro. Thank you."

As Jethro was passing, Pettibone stood and said, "Your Honor, I now call Texas Ranger Clayton Barlow."

Dial and Blessing jerked around and stared at Clay as he stood and walked to the witness stand. He was sworn in, and, before the prosecutor could begin his questioning, the judge held up his hand and turned to Clay.

"Mr. Barlow, you are a ranger?"

"Yes, Your Honor."

"When were you sworn in?"

Clay pulled out his watch, checked the time, and turned to the judge. "Judge Moore, I took the oath exactly forty-three minutes ago."

A murmur went through the courtroom, which the judge silenced with a look, and then turned back to Clay. "Congratulations, Mr. Barlow. I want you to know that I had the honor of serving many years ago. The rangers always need good men."

Dial sprang to his feet. "Your Honor, I object."

"To what, Mr. Dial?"

Dial looked at Clay and then the judge. "Your Honor, the previous statement of the court to the witness could be thought to be favoritism."

"Mr. Dial, I choose not to take affront to that statement. Sit down." He turned to Pettibone. "Begin your questioning, Mr. Pettibone."

The prosecutor began. "Mr. Barlow, are you known as the Del Rio Kid?"

Clay looked up at the judge. "Unfortunately, that name has been going around. I did not start it, nor do I like it. The name my folks gave me is Clayton Barlow. I prefer to be known by that."

Next the prosecutor asked him to explain how he came to be known by the name. Clay explained while the courtroom listened with rapt attention.

Dial shot to his feet. "I object, Your Honor."

"You opened this door, Mr. Dial, with your opening statement. Now, sit down, and don't interrupt Ranger Barlow."

When Clay finished, Pettibone took him step by step through the shootings. He continued by asking Clay to explain what Blessing had said about shooting the peddler and the senator.

Dial again jumped up. "Your Honor, this is hearsay. I object to it being allowed in the courtroom."

"Sit down, Dial. There's no jury. I'll decide whether or not to believe the evidence."

"Judge," Clay continued, "Mr. Blessing talks, a lot. When he rode up, he was certain he had killed me. In fact, he said so. This was no mistake. He said that he never misses with his Winchester '73. While he was talking, he bemoaned the fact that he had shot the senator twice without killing him. He stated that he had shot him in hopes it would bring me home from New York. He didn't know that I was already on the way. He blames me for killing his son in a train robbery."

Dial jumped to his feet with the intention of objecting, but before he could utter a word, the judge waved him down.

Clay continued his testimony. "Blessing also stated that he had taken the Winchester '73 from 'a drummer,' I believe those were his words, that he had killed."

"I have no more questions, Your Honor," Pettibone said.

The judge turned to Dial. "Your witness."

Dial stood quickly, and again marched to a point in front of the witness stand to begin his questioning. He questioned Clay relentlessly but could not intimidate or confuse him. Clay calmly answered each question, turning many back on the defendant.

Finally, Dial sat back down. "No more questions for this witness."

"I'm done, Your Honor," Pettibone said.

The judge again turned to Dial. He stood, looked at his client for a moment, then turned back to the judge. "No witnesses, Your Honor. The defense rests."

Judge Moore leaned back in his leather chair and addressed the prosecution and defense. "Often, in trials like this, it is necessary for me to adjourn to my office and consider the opposing testimony. Since there is none, I shall make my ruling now. Mr. Blessing please stand."

Blessing and his attorney, James Dial, stood.

"Mr. Blessing. You have chosen to come to the state of Texas to seek revenge on the man who killed your son, while your son was in the commission of a train robbery. Thinking you could draw the young man back to Austin by killing his grandfather, you shot him twice—in the back. I have heard that your other sons are currently guests of the city for attempting to injure or kill Mr. Barlow, but it is my understanding, they came out on the short end of the stick.

"So, having said that, it is obvious that your sons have closely

followed your example. Therefore, since you have been unsuc-
cessful in killing anyone, through no fault of your own, I find you
guilty of one count of attempted murder. I sentence you to fifteen
years in the state penitentiary at Huntsville."

The judge banged his gavel. "Court's adjourned."

Blessing, normally talkative, went quietly from the courtroom, handcuffed and in leg irons, between the two policemen
who had brought him in. The people in the courtroom stood as
the judge exited.

Handshaking was taking place all around. Clay turned to the
senator. "Grandpa, I'll see you at the apartment. Major Jones
wanted to see me as soon as the case was finished."

"Congratulations, Clay," the senator said. "You would have
made an excellent attorney, but I wish you good fortune as a
ranger. They are lucky to have you. See you at the apartment."

Clay thanked everyone for being there and left the courtroom. Walking into the Rangers' office, he found it bustling with
activity.

"Glad you're back, Clay," Major Jones said. "How soon can
you be ready?"

"Major, all I need to do is to throw some things in my saddlebags and make up my bedroll, and I'm ready."

"Good, you'll be riding out with Captain Coleman. Sounds
like Fort Griffin is about to bust wide open. The army's requested
we send rangers to control it. I figure you and Jake should be
enough."

Jake reached up and clapped Clay's broad back. "I'll fill you in
on the way.

"Let's ride, Ranger!"

# AUTHOR'S NOTE

Thanks for reading *Law and Justice,* the second book in the Justice Series. I hope you enjoyed reading it as much as I enjoyed writing it.

I strive for historical accuracy in my novels. If there are errors they are mine alone. You'll find missing, in all of my novels, crude language and overt sexual situations. There will be an occasional damn or hell, but even those will not be prolific.

No book is a product of one person. I am extremely grateful to my wonderful wife, Paula Robertson. She inspires and supports me, besides providing critical suggestions and ideas. I am truly a fortunate man. I love her for more than what she does, but for who she is.

I want to thank the editors of this book, Melissa Gray and Beverley Scherberger. They did a super job.

Huge thanks go to my graphic designer, Elizabeth Mackey. The cover is the first thing readers see, and it must be compelling. Her's are.

I love to hear from my readers. My email address is: Don@DonaldLRobertson.com or fill in the contact form at:

www.DonaldLRobertson.com.

**Lonesome Justice**, the third book in the Clay Barlow, Justice Series, is now available on Amazon. Don't miss the opportunity to follow Clay as he continues to mature while chasing Texas bandits.

**Logan Family Series**

*LOGAN'S WORD*

*THE SAVAGE VALLEY*

*CALLUM'S MISSION*

*FORGOTTEN SEASON*

*SOUL OF A MOUNTAIN MAN*

**Clay Barlow - Texas Ranger Justice Series**

*FORTY-FOUR CALIBER JUSTICE*

*LAW AND JUSTICE*

*LONESOME JUSTICE*

**NOVELLAS AND SHORT STORIES**

*RUSTLERS IN THE SAGE*

*BECAUSE OF A DOG*

*THE OLD RANGER*

Made in the USA
Coppell, TX
20 July 2020

31329054R00146